James Meeker Ludlow

A King of Tyre

A Tale of the Times of Ezra and Nehemiah

James Meeker Ludlow

A King of Tyre
A Tale of the Times of Ezra and Nehemiah

ISBN/EAN: 9783337022785

Printed in Europe, USA, Canada, Australia, Japan

Cover: Foto ©Andreas Hilbeck / pixelio.de

More available books at **www.hansebooks.com**

A KING OF TYRE

A Tale of the Times of

EZRA AND NEHEMIAH

BY

JAMES M. LUDLOW

AUTHOR OF "THE CAPTAIN OF THE JANIZARIES" ETC.

NEW YORK

HARPER & BROTHERS, FRANKLIN SQUARE

1891

A KING OF TYRE.

CHAPTER I.

THE island city of Tyre lay close to the Syrian coast. It seemed to float among the waves that fretted themselves into foam as they rolled in between the jagged rocks, and spread over the flats, retiring again to rest in the deep bosom of the Mediterranean. The wall that encircled the island rose in places a hundred cubits, and seemed from a distance to be an enormous monolith. It was therefore called Tsur, or Tyre, which means The Rock. At the time of our narrative, about the middle of the fifth century B.C., the sea-girt city contained a dense mass of inhabitants, who lived in tall wooden houses of many stories; for the ground space within the walls could not lodge the multitude who pursued the various arts and commerce for which the Tyrians were, of all the world, the most noted. The streets were narrow, often entirely closed to the sky by projecting balconies and arcades—mere veins and arteries for the circulation of the city's throbbing life.

I

For recreation from their dyeing-vats, looms, and foundries, the artisan people climbed to the broad spaces on the top of the walls, where they could breathe the sweet sea air, except when the easterly wind was hot and gritty with dust from the mainland, a few bow-shots distant. The men of commerce thronged the quay of the Sidonian harbor at the north end of the island, or that of the Egyptian harbor on the south side—two artificial basins which were at all times crowded with ships; for the Tyrian merchantmen scoured all the coast of the Great Sea, even venturing through the straits of Gades, and northward to the coasts of Britain, and southward along the African shore; giving in barter for the crude commodities they found, not only the products of their own workshops, but the freight of their caravans that climbed the Lebanons and wearily tracked across the deserts to Arabia and Babylon. The people of fashion paraded their pride on the Great Square, in the heart of the city — called by the Greeks the Eurychorus — where they displayed their rich garments in competition with the flowers that grew, almost as artificially, in gay parterres amid the marble blocks of the pavement.

But one day a single topic absorbed the conversation of all classes alike, in the Great Square, on the walls, and along the quays. Councillors of state and moneyed merchants debated it with bowed heads and wrinkled brows. Moulders talked of it as they cooled themselves at the doorways

of their foundries. Weavers, in the excitement of
their wrangling over it, forgot to throw the shuttle.
Seamen, lounging on the heaps of cordage, gave
the subject all the light they could strike from
oaths in the names of all the gods of all the lands
they had ever sailed to. Even the women, as they
stood in the open doorways, piloting their words
between the cries of the children who bestrode
their shoulders or clung to their feet, pronounced
their judgment upon the all-absorbing topic.

A bulletin had appeared on the Great Square
proclaiming, in the name of the High Council of
Tyre, a stupendous religious celebration. Vast
sums of money had been appropriated from the
city treasury, and more was demanded from the
people. A multitude of animals was to be sacrificed, and even the blood of human victims should
enrich the altar, that thus might be purchased the
favor of Almighty Baal.

To understand this proclamation, we must know
the circumstances that led to it.

The Phœnician prestige among the nations had
for many years been steadily waning. The political dominance of Persia, with her capital far over
the deserts at Susa, was less humiliating to this
proud people than was the growing commercial
importance of the Greeks across the sea. For not
only had the Greeks whipped the Phœnicians in
naval battles, as at Salamis and Eurymedon, but
they were displacing Phœnician wares in foreign
markets, and teaching the Greek language, customs,

and religion to all the world. Yet the Greeks were
thought by the Tyrians to be but an upstart people.
They had not so many generations, as the Phœnicians had ages, of glorious history.

How could Phœnicia regain the supremacy?
This was the all-absorbing question which appealed
to the patriotism, and still more to the purses, of
the Tyrians, and of their neighbors along the coast.

Many were the wiseacres who readily solved this
problem to their own satisfaction. Thus, for example, the priests of Melkarth — the name they gave
to Baal in his special office as guardian of the city
— had a theory of their own. It was to the effect
that the gods were offended at the growing laxity
of worship, and especially at the falling-off of the
temple revenues, which were in great measure the
sumptuous perquisites of the priests themselves.
They were especially disaffected towards their young
king, Hiram, whom they regarded as an obstacle to
any reforms on this line. Hiram had spent his
early training years with the fleet, and was conver-
sant with the faiths and customs of many countries.
Thus he was educated to a cosmopolitan, not to
say sceptical, habit of mind, and was led to doubt
whether any movement that originated in the ambition of a horde of unscrupulous and superstitious
priests could win the favor of the gods, even admitting that such supernal beings existed, of which
the king was reported to have expressed a doubt.

King Hiram had been but a few months on the
throne, to which he had succeeded on the death of

his father, when he opened the meeting of the
Great Council which issued the proclamation regarding the sacrifice.

His Majesty sat upon the bronze throne. Above
him shone a canopy of beaten gold. At his back
hung a curtain of richest Tyrian purple, in the centre of which gleamed a silver dove with outspread
wings, the symbol of Tyre from those ancient days
when its commerce and renown began to fly abroad
over the world.

Hiram's face was typically Phœnician, and betokened the clear tide of his racial blood. His
forehead was broad, and prominent at the brows.
His eyes were gleaming black. His nose started as
if with the purpose of being Jewish, but terminated
in the expanded nostril that suggested the Egyptian.
His hair was black, with the slightest touch of red,
which, however, only strong light would reveal.
He wore the conical cap of the sailor, for his pride
of naval command had never become secondary to
even his sense of royal dignity; and many a time
had he declared that a true Phœnician king was
chiefly king of the sea. The royal cap was distinguished from that of common sailors by the urœus,
or winged serpent's crest, which was wrought in
golden needlework upon the front. The king's
throat and chest were bare, except for a purple
mantle which hung from his left shoulder, and
crossed his body diagonally; and for a broad collar of silk embroidered with silver threads, which
shone in contrast with his weather-bronzed skin.

His arms were clasped above the elbows with heavy spirals of gold. He wore a loose white chiton, or undergarment, which terminated above the knees, and revealed as knotty a pair of legs as ever balanced so graceful a figure. But one thing marred his appearance—a deep scar on his chin, the memorial of a hand-to-hand fight with Egyptian pirates off the mouth of the Nile.

The king leaned upon one of the lion-heads that made the arms of his throne. One foot rested upon a footstool of bronze; the other in the spotted fur of a leopard, spread upon the dais.

Sitting thus, he spoke of the subject before the council. At first he scarcely changed his easy attitude. He traced the rise of the Greek power with voluble accuracy, for he had studied the problems it presented in another school than that of Phœnician prejudices. As he proceeded he warmed with the kindling of his own thoughts, and, straightening himself on the throne, gesticulated forcibly, making the huge arm of the chair tremble under the stroke of his fist, as if the moulded bronze were the obdurate heads of his listeners. At length, fully heated with the excitement of his speech, and by the antagonism too plainly revealed in the faces of some of his courtiers, he rose from his throne, and stood upon the leopard skin as he concluded with these words :

" Let me speak plainly, O leaders of Phœnicia, as a king of men should speak to kingly men ! Why does the Greek outstrip us? Because he is stronger. Why is he stronger? Because he is

wiser. Why is he wiser? Because he learns from
all the world; and we, though we trade with all the
tribes of men, learn from none. Our guide-marks
are our own footprints, which we follow in endless
circles. We boast, O Phœnicians, that we have
taught the world its alphabet, but we ourselves
have no books beyond the tablets on which we
keep the accounts of our ships, our caravans, and
our shambles. It is our shame, O men of Tyre!
We have instructed the sailors of the Great Sea to
guide their ships by the stars, but in all our customs of government and religion we dare not leave
the coast-line of our ancient notions. We go up
and down the channels of our prejudice; ay, we
ground ourselves in our ignorance.

"And hear, O ye priests! Our religion as practised is our disgrace. If Baal be the intelligence
that shines in the sun, he despises us for our
stupidity. Nay, scowl if ye will! But look at the
statues of our gods! A Greek boy could carve as
finely with the dough he eats. Look at our temples! The Great Hiram built a finer one than we
possess five centuries ago, there in Jerusalem, for
the miserable Jews to worship their Jehovah in.
Ye say that Baal is angry with us. And well he
may be! For we open not our minds to the brightness of his beams: we hide in the shadows of
things that are old and decayed, even as the lizards crawl in the shadow of the ruins that everywhere mark our plains.

"Ye say, O priests, that we must sacrifice more

to Baal. Truly! But it is not the sacrifice of death, rather the real offering of life, of our wiser thoughts, our braver enterprise, that Baal would have.

" This, this is the end of all my speaking, O men of Tyre ! Heap up your treasures, and burn them if ye will ! Slaughter your beasts ! Toss your babes into the fire of Moloch ! But know ye that your king gives you no such commandment ; nor will he have more of such counsel."

So saying, King Hiram strode down from the dais, and left the council chamber. As he passed out, the members rose and made deep obeisance ; but their bowed forms did not conceal from him their scowling faces.

The councillors, left alone, gathered close together, evidently not for debate, but to confirm one another in some predetermined purpose. Their words were bitter. Old Egbalus, the high priest of Baal-Melkarth for the year, thanked his god that the throne of Tyre had lost its power, since one so utterly blasphemous, so traitorous, had come to occupy it.

" That travelling Greek, Herodotus, who is even now his guest, has bewitched the king with his talk," sneered one.

" Or with his Greek gold," timidly ventured another.

The last speaker was a young man, in princely attire, with marked resemblance to King Hiram ; but such resemblance as is often noticed between

an ugly and a beautiful face; certain features
attesting kinship, while, at the same time, they pro-
claim the utmost difference of character. This
person was Prince Rubaal, cousin to Hiram, and,
in the event of the death of the latter without
issue, the heir to the crown. His naturally selfish
disposition had brewed nothing but gall since Hiram's accession. From polite disparagement he
lapsed into the habit of open contempt for the person, and bitter antagonism to the interests of his
royal relative. That the king was hostile to the
pretensions of the priestly guild was sufficient to
make Rubaal their slavish adherent.

The sneer with which he attributed a mercenary
motive to the king brought him a look of blandest
encouragement from the high priest, Egbalus.

This latter dignitary, however, instantly cast a less
complacent and more inquisitive glance into the
face of another councillor, Ahimelek. How much
was meant by that look can be understood only
by recalling the character and career of this man.

Ahimelek was small in stature, of low, broad
brow, thin lips, restless gray eyes, which seemed to
focus upon nothing, as if afraid of revealing the
thought back of them; as a partridge, when disturbed, flits in all directions except over its own nest.
He was the richest merchant in Tyre, the largest
ship-owner in all Phœnicia. His fleets were passing, like shuttles on the loom of his prosperity, between Tyre and Cyprus, Carthage and Gades.
His caravans, too, were well known on every route

from Damascus to Memphis. He inherited the wealth of several generations of merchants, and also their ancestral shrewdness. His waking dream was to surpass them all by allying his financial power with the political prestige of the royal house of Tyre. To this end he had spared neither money nor sycophancy in order to gain the favor of the late king.

It was therefore with genuine elation that the merchant had noted the growing intimacy between Hiram and his daughter, the fair Zillah.

From childhood Prince Hiram and Zillah had been much together, the old king having been, in the chronic depletion of his treasury, as little averse to a family alliance with the money-bags of Ahimelek as that aristocrat was to guarding his bags with the royal seal. Indeed, on more than one occasion the king had discovered an authority in Ahimelek's darics that was lacking in his own mandates. It was rumored that the recognition of Hiram's sovereignty by the court at Susa had been deferred until the appointment of Ahimelek as his chamberlain gave promise of substantial benefit to the politicians who surrounded the Great King, Artaxerxes.

It is true, however, that the personal attractions of Zillah, without such reasons of state, had captivated young Prince Hiram. She was the goddess who inspired his dreams during his voyages, and into her ear, on his return, he narrated his adventures, and confessed his most secret projects and

ambitious hopes. On the very day of his coronation, a year before our story begins, he left the
great hall of ceremony, not to return to his palace,
but to visit the mansion of Ahimelek, and then and
there placed his crown upon the head of Zillah,
claiming her oft-repeated promise to be his queen.
That very night, too, the delighted merchant had
given the hand of his daughter into that of her
royal suitor, accepting from him a splendid gift as
the marriage purchase, and presenting to him in return the dowry contract, which in this case was the
bonding of his estate to pay in cash a thousand
minas of gold, and half the revenues of his trade in
perpetuity.

But later events had disturbed the equanimity of
Ahimelek. The growing disaffection of the priestly guild towards King Hiram was too ominous to
be disregarded. Their power over the people had
never been challenged with impunity. Could the
king maintain himself against them?

One act of Zillah herself had seemed to endanger
her royal prospects. It was a sacred custom for
the wife of a Phœnician king to become also a
priestess of the goddess Astarte, thus consolidating
the sacerdotal and royal authorities. Into this
sacred office Zillah had refused to enter; in which
determination she was doubtless influenced by the
prejudices of her royal lover.

To Ahimelek's fears, therefore, the crown of Tyre
seemed suspended by a slender thread over an
abyss from which he could not rescue it if it should

fall. He therefore had, on various pretexts, postponed the marriage. But his scheming mind discerned a refuge for his ambition in the fact that Rubaal was a jealous rival for the heart of Zillah. Indeed, much of that young man's hostility to his cousin was due to his wounded affections. It therefore seemed clear to Ahimelek that, in the event of the overthrow of King Hiram, there would be an equal opportunity for his own aggrandizement in transferring his daughter's hand to that of the new king. Such were the thoughts that disturbed Ahimelek as he sat at the council table.

The high priest, Egbalus, had already fathomed the perplexity of the merchant's mind when he gave him that questioning glance.

Ahimelek's eyes fluttered more than ever as they met the inquisitorial gaze of the priest. What would he not give to know the future? On which side should he cast his vote?

Egbalus was too subtle a politician to press the query to a definite answer in the council hall. He knew his man, and knew that if Ahimelek did not dare go with the priests, neither would he dare to oppose them.

Other members of the council were more readily subservient. Indeed, the predominating influence of Egbalus in public affairs had already made itself felt in the selection of the persons who were nominally the king's advisers. He knew, indeed he owned, them all.

The decree ordaining the splendid sacrifice was

therefore issued. The proclamation was quickly posted on the temple gate, the door of the council chamber, and in the Great Square.

Would the king oppose it? If so, it would bring on the conflict the priests desired, and had long been preparing for.

CHAPTER II.

WHEN King Hiram left the council hall, pages swung aside the heavy curtains which screened the doorways; lackeys bore before him, so far as the exit, the ancient sceptre of Tyre, laid upon a gemmed cushion; palanquin-bearers took their places around the royal vehicle; while the outrunners, with trim legs and short fluted white skirts, balanced in their hands the long rods of their office, and ran to clear the way. The chief attendant was distinguished from the others by his crimson skirt, which hung from a silver belt tightening his loins, and by the long ribbons of purple that, encircling his brow, hung as streamers almost to the ground. With that superb grace which only accomplished athletes acquire, he bowed to the earth as the king descended the marble steps leading from the hall.

"Whither, O king?"

"The hour?" inquired Hiram.

"It begins the seventh, by the grace of Baal!" replied the attendant.

"To the Sidonian Harbor, then."

The runners flew. The crowds in the narrow

streets backed close against the houses on either side.

"Long live King Hiram !" murmured from hundreds of lips , but the king noted that it was shouted by none. If there were loyalty, it was without enthusiasm. The priests scowled, or, pretending to be preoccupied with pious meditation, allowed the royal palanquin to pass without salute.

Reaching the quay, the king stepped quickly from his carriage, and returning with equal courtesy the low salâm of an elderly man, embraced him cordially. Even if this person's garb had not revealed his nationality, his straight nose on a line with his forehead would have proclaimed him a Greek. His face was weather-beaten and bronzed by exposure to many climes. His firm lips and strong chin would have suggested to an observer that he was a man of resoluteness, perhaps one engaged in daring adventures; were it not that a certain quiet depth in his eyes, a passive introspective sort of look, such as they acquire who are accustomed to think more than they see, betrayed the philosopher.

"I feared, noble Herodotus. that my detention at the council had prevented my wishing you farewell," said the king.

"My thanks, your majesty ! But, without this final and unlooked-for courtesy, my voyage across the seas would have been gladdened by the memory of your many kindnesses. I shall bear to my nation the knowledge I have acquired of the past greatness of your people, and the prediction that, under the liberal rule of King Hiram, a new era of progress is to follow."

"The new era will come, sire, when the Phœnicians learn from the Greeks what I have learned from you. The benefactors of nations are not their kings, but their wise men."

"Blessed is the nation whose wisest man is their king," replied Herodotus, with almost reverential courtesy.

To which Hiram responded: "The throne of Tyre would not lack a wise king, if he could detain the sage of Halicarnassus as the man of his right hand. Do me the pleasure to accept the vessel you sail in as a reminder of your visit. Her deck planks are larch from the isles that lie to the north; her masts are of cedar from Lebanon, whose snow-peaks whiten the sky yonder; her oars are oak cut in Bashan beyond the Jews' river, her side-planks are from the slope of Hermon; her sails of linen were woven on the looms of Egypt; her purple awning is tinted with the dye of insects found on your own coast. If my orders have been obeyed, you will find on board wines that our caravans have brought from Damascus."

"No. Not a word of thanks," added the king, interrupting the exclamation of grateful surprise from his guest.

"Farewell, then," replied the Greek, kissing the hand of the young man, and stepping upon the deck of the craft. "But tell me, O king, to which of the gods shall a Greek traveller in a Phœnician bireme commend his journey? to Neptune, or to your Cabeiri?"

"To the One who is the None or the All, of whom we have so often spoken," replied Hiram.

The helmsman waved his hand to the rowers. A double score of blades dipped at the instant. A pearly sheaf of spray rose beneath the high prow of the *Dido*. The graceful craft glided out of the Sidonian Harbor, and, rounding the quay-head to the north, caught the swell of the Great Sea.

As the king watched the well-timed stroke of the oars, unvaried by the irregular heaving of the billows through which they propelled the bireme, a hand touched his arm.

"Ah, Captain Hanno! The man of all the world I want just at this moment. Is the *Dolphin* manned? Ten darics to one, you cannot catch the *Dido* within sight of land! Besides, I want to skim over the water, and get some cobwebs washed out of my brain. Cobwebs hold spiders, and spiders bite. So do some of my thoughts. Come, Hanno, give me a spurt."

Hanno put an acorn-shaped whistle of bronze to his lips. The shrill notes were answered in exact pitch, like an echo, from a splendid bireme anchored near the mouth of the harbor. In a moment more the *Dolphin* touched the end of the quay; but not before the king and his friend had leaped upon the deck.

Captain Hanno's favorite bireme was not one of

2

the largest of her class in length of keel, but seemed to be the very behemoth of the Tyrian pleasure-fleet by reason of her high prow and stern, both of which projected far beyond the water-line. Her unusual breadth of beam gave play for the long oar-handles, and immense leverage for each of the sixty oarsmen, who were arranged in four rows, two rows on either side, one placed above another. They worked their tough oaken propellers through upper and lower oar-holes in the side of the galley.

At the word of Hanno, "Away!" the chief of the rowers clapped his hands, timing the strokes which raised the vessel half out of the water, and sent it plunging and bounding like a veritable dolphin through the sea.

As the bireme struck the high waves King Hiram advanced to the prow. Throwing off his cap and toga, he indulged in a bath of wind and spray, that dashed against his bare head and breast.

"Oh, to be a sea-king indeed, with no councillors but you, Hanno! What a life!"

"I would counsel you to follow your own free mind," replied the captain.

"That is the reason I like you," said Hiram.

"Why have any adviser, then?"

"For the pleasure of being confirmed in my obstinacy."

"But I might thwart you some day."

"That would be impossible, for I should turn and follow your counsel. Will you be my prime-minister, Hanno?"

" No."

" Why not ?"

" Because I want to remain your friend."

" Why not be both ?"

" It might not be possible. The interest of the state of Tyre may be one thing; the interest of Hiram another."

" That's treason, Hanno."

" Hang me to the masthead, then," replied Hanno ; " for I am going to stick to Hiram, whatever becomes of the king."

" You think of me as a crab that may shed the shell of royalty some day," replied Hiram, laughing. " Well, I confess that if it were not for the claws of power, which I rather like the pleasure of using, I would let my shell go to-morrow. But I must pinch off the heads of some of the priests first. Thus—"

As he spoke the king took from a shelf just beneath the prow a half-dozen little clay images, uncouth figures representing the Cabeiri, the gods which were supposed to preside over the arts and navigation. He broke off their heads, and threw them into the sea.

" One day, Hanno, we shall throw overboard all such trumpery from the state of Tyre. That's what I told the council to-day."

" Told the council ? That was a bold speech," replied the captain, his face flushing and paling with sudden emotion.

" And an unwise one, I know from your look," said Hiram.

"Ay, and dangerous! May I take the liberty of cautioning you, my king?"

"Liberty? It's your duty, Hanno. Haven't I appointed you for life to be my other self? I have never had a secret from you since we were boys, and sent to sea under old Dagon."

The king took the arm of Hanno.

"Do you remember, old comrade, how once I even lied for you, and you lied for me; but the old water-dog believed neither of us, and flogged us both, though your father owned the craft, and mine was king of Tyre? I expect to see Dagon's ugly head rise from the waves some day, for the Cabeiri cannot keep such a restless ghost long down there with them."

"I remember, too, that it was just such a day as this," replied Captain Hanno, "that we ran away, and, in an open boat, went to Sidon to see the Sidonians fight with the Persians. I came near going after old Dagon when the boat capsized. I felt the gates of Sheol snapping at me like a shark's jaws, but you held me on the keel until we drifted into the shallows. Since then my life has been yours. I am only watching my time to save you. I had a notion of telling Mago, there at the helm, to drive the *Dolphin* on the reef as we came out of port, just to get a chance of pulling you out of the wreck. But if you go on wasping the priests you will give me my chance before long. Every one of those hypocritical butchers, from Egbalus to the dirtiest offal-carrier, thinks of you when he feels the point of his sacrificial knife. You need a thicker shell about your ribs than that of your kingship."

" Oh, the priests to Beelzebub, the god of all such venomous flies !" cried the king, in petulant rage.

" Have you, then, as the priests say, lost all faith in the gods ?" asked Hanno.

" Yes, in such as ours."

" But the Greeks, whom you praise so much, believe in them."

" Not in such as ours, Hanno. They make theirs beautiful. They deify the nobler sentiments. They have no hideous Moloch, no beastly Astarte. They leave their philosophy about unseen things unexpressed, until they can express it artistically. You remember the temple to the god Theseus which we saw in Athens. Herodotus explained its meaning to me. The religious idea enshrined there surpasses ours as much as the graceful proportions of the building are finer than anything we have built. Theseus was a hero-god ; that is, a man to whom they gave divine honors because of his heroism. His great exploit was slaying the Minotaur of Crete, which the people believed was a monster, half bull and half man, that fed upon the bodies of human beings. The people of Athens sent yearly a number of young men and maidens to appease the appetite of the monster and the greed of King Minos, its owner. According to the story, Theseus sailed to Crete, and slew the Minotaur in his labyrinth. Now, this Minotaur was nothing but our Moloch, whom we represent by a bull-headed image, and whom we pretend to appease by human sacrifice. We Phœnicians carried this monstrous worship to Crete, and thence it drifted across to Greece. But Theseus, who was a wise king, forbade such cruel offerings, demolished the images of Moloch, and saved his people from the horrors which our priests would perpetuate in our land. So they say he slew the Minotaur. And, by all the gods of Greece! I will slay our Minotaur. If I were El, or Bel, or Baal, I would wring the necks of Egbalus and his swarm of priests when they annoy me with their cries, 'O Baal, hear us!' just as I crush these flies that buzz in my face."

"Your words are safe with me, my king," replied Hanno, "but I beg you to have a care; for the priests are all-powerful in Tyre. Their hold on the people is tightening. They are plotting deeper than you and I know to-day; but we may know to-morrow. The old image of Baal-Moloch on the mainland is to be repaired, and I am told that the market at Aphaca has more maidens enrolled this year to disgrace themselves to Astarte than for a generation past. Your cousin Rubaal's sister, the Princess Elisa, has been announced as a candidate for the shambles."

"It is monstrous!" cried Hiram. "I would risk my crown to wipe out our shame; for the crown will not be worth keeping if I am to be king of a horde of devils and strumpets."

"And I pledge my wealth and life to help you," replied Hanno. "Except your own wealth, and that of Ahimelek—which the gods grant may come safely to your house!—my resources are, perhaps, the greatest in Tyre. But we must be cautious."

"No, no, Hanno! King Hiram will never take a skekel of his friend's riches to gild his own glory."

"But I am prime-minister, you know, and may do what I please," replied his friend, laughing. "But this is not resting you. Shall we give these steersmen a lesson?"

Two long oars rigged one on either side of the keel-line at the stern served as rudders. They were joined by a brace at the handles, by which they could be connected or disconnected, and thus be worked by one person in quiet water, but needed the strength of two in heavy seas, or in putting the bireme through rapid manœuvres. Two brawny fellows were manning them, as the wind was rising. The brace of helmsmen, doffing their caps, gave place to the king and his companion.

"Quicker!" shouted Hiram to the master of the oarsmen, whose hands beat out the gradually accelerating time, until the sixty blades cut the water as the wings of a kingfisher cut the air. The wind still freshening, they set the great square sail. Soon·they tacked far to the north, and, rounding to the west, crossed the bows of the bireme of Herodotus.

"The king! the king!" shouted the sailors on the *Dido*, as they recognized the well-known forms at the helm.

And "Hanno! Hanno! Hanno!" was given with equal enthusiasm.

All the oar-blades of the *Dido* were lifted from the water as the *Dolphin* dashed past. On the high stern stood the venerable Herodotus, his head uncovered, and his noble brow white and shining like an aureole, in contrast with his bronzed lower face and dark beard. He held aloft a goblet of wine, and shouted, as the *Dolphin* flew by :

"To Hiram! To Tyre!"

The *Dolphin* careened far over as she turned, her great square sail throwing a shadow on the deck of the *Dido* as it intercepted the western sun. It was a dangerous manœuvre for any but helmsmen of utmost skill to have attempted.

"It was never done better since your father, Captain Hanno, ran the gantlet of a score of Greek ships at Salamis," said one of the helmsmen, as they took again the steering oars.

"There's no praise we like so well as that of our sailors," replied Hanno.

Turning to Hiram, as they moved out of hearing of the men, Captain Hanno said: "So I would work with you, my king. The two oars, though disconnected, worked as one in our hands. I followed with my whole might every movement you made."

"No," said Hiram, "I waited until I caught your purpose, for you are the better helmsman. Had I not done so, we surely had gone over."

"It is strange! I thought I followed you, and you thought you followed me. I suspect that we both followed our common sailor's instinct. We will take it, then, as an omen. So we will work together for the throne of Tyre. Events may occur in which it will be wise for me to appear to take no part in the affairs of the court. But, believe me, I shall pull with you, as on the steering oar. I think I know your heart, O king! And I put my heart within yours. I believe as little in the gods as you do. I have but one object of devotion on earth, but one vow, and that I give to my king."

Hiram gazed into his friend's face. The tears started to his eyes. But, though the heartiness of this avowal was grateful to him, he could not repress his surprise at it. He knew Hanno's loyalty; but why should the noble fellow make so much of telling it? It was very unlike him. He was generally either reticent, or extremely laconic, in speaking of his purposes. He acted quickly—like lightning, that lets the report come afterwards. Hiram again searched his friend's face for some explanation, but saw nothing unusual, except a closer knitting of the brows as if from perplexity and pain; a silent prophecy of evil that the noble fellow would avert, though with the sacrifice of his own life.

CHAPTER III

THE two friends parted at the quay. The king entered the palanquin which had awaited his return.

"To Trypho, the dyer's!"

An unusual commotion was made in the streets, or rather the alleys, through which the king's litter passed; for seldom until Hiram's accession had royalty cast its aristocratic lustre among the shadows of the common artisan's life. But Hiram was well known in these places. As a lad he had spent many hours in the factories, amusing himself with tools, and questioning the workmen about the details of their various arts.

The palanquin stopped at a low door, from which a cloud of steam was emitted. In the midst of this, like the statue of some god in a halo of incense, stood a man, naked to the waist, his arms and parts of his bare breast red, as if with blood.

As the king alighted, the man made an awkward salâm, knocking his head against the low lintel in resuming the perpendicular. Without losing any of his courtliness of manner, Hiram put the fellow at ease by his genial familiarity.

"Ah, Trypho! You are like the god Tammuz,

killed by the wild boar, but coming to life with the blood-marks on him."

" Like a king, rather," said Trypho, " for the red will be purple when it dries."

" No, like a queen," retorted Hiram, pleased with the man's banter, " for I swear by Astarte that the dye on your arms is the same that is going into the robe of the future queen of Tyre."

" Such is the honor your patronage has brought me," replied Trypho, making another salâm, that ended by nearly tripping the king into a dyeing vat.

" But how goes the cloth?" asked Hiram, laughing.

" It is nearly completed," said the workman, leading the way to an inner room. " Come in, and judge for yourself. I need not keep the secret of my art from one who knows it already."

At a leaden sink a half-grown boy was drawing the snail-like murex from its shell. Cutting off its head, he dexterously detached from its body the long sac of yellow liquid, which, on exposure, changed first to green, and, passing through the intermediate shades, to a bright purple. At a bench near by a workman crushed with a wooden hammer the smaller shell of the insect since called buccinum, which, together with the body of the animal, was thrown into a vat, mixed with salt, the whole mass heated, and reduced to a liquid state by an injection of steam. The gritty substance from the shell was then carefully skimmed from the surface, leaving a lighter purplish liquid than that obtained from the murex.

"They tell me, Trypho, that you can mix these two dyes at sight, so as to produce the rare tint for which your cloths are so famous. Have you no written formula, and do you never measure out the proportions?"

"No, sire," replied the man, "I never learned the proportions by weight or by measure. If I knew them myself I might tell somebody; then my secret would be gone. So I never told myself how I do it. I think of a tint, and pour the dyes together, and they always come out the tint I think of. How do I do it? Just as my old legs carry me where I think of going, without counting my steps, or watching which way my toes turn."

The fellow was garrulous, and, seeing that he had the king's attention, went on :—

"I got this secret where I got my blood—from my father; and he from his, and he from his. For, you see, we have been in this trade for thousands of years. You know that story the priests tell about the discovery of the art of dyeing? Well, it is true, because it was to one of my grandfathers that the great god Melkarth came when his dog ate off the head of a shell-fish, and colored his jaws with such beautiful tints that the nymph Tyrus refused to marry the god until he gave her a gown of the same color. It was my ancestor, the first Trypho, who helped the great Melkarth get his bride; and to no one else than to Trypho, the last, should the noble King Hiram come for a gown for his beautiful queen : whom may Tyrus bless ! Come now, and see if the cloth I have prepared for your lady be not as lovely as was that of Tyrus herself. No woman could refuse a lover who wooed with such a garment in his hands as I have made."

Trypho led the way to another room, where cloths were hung before a window, by manipulating the screens of which the artisan adjusted the light that gave the required tone to the color.

"Truly a divine art !" cried Trypho, in his enthusiastic appreciation of his own work. "For see, I must use the beams of Baal, the sun-god, to bring it to perfection. It must be a divine art that uses Divinity."

"Does Baal let you use his beams at your will ?" asked the king. "Then you must be the god, and Baal your servant. Baal could not make that splendid tint without you."

The man stared at the king as if stricken dumb by the blasphemy he had heard. His look of perplexity tempted Hiram to banter him further.

"And indeed, Trypho, I think you are more divine in your naked muscle, daubed with this insect's blood, which you can transform into beauty, than the brass image of Moloch is when dyed with children's blood. No beautiful thing was ever taken out of the blood vat at his feet. How say you, Trypho ?" tapping the man's bare shoulders.

The workman made no reply, but moved a pace

or two away from the king, looking at him in a
sort of stupid terror. Recovering his senses, he
pointed to a hanging of finest texture, whose exquisite tint brought an exclamation of delight from
his visitor. It only needed to be washed in a de-
coction made from a certain sea-weed, found on
the coast of Crete, to fix its color.

"This is for the robe of the queen of Tyre,"
said Trypho, bowing low, in as much obeisance
to his own pride in his work as to the royal dignity
of his visitor.

"You, Trypho, shall have a skin of finest wine
from the marriage feast," said the king, grasping
the hand of the workman, and leaving in it a gold
daric.

Hiram and his attendants threaded their way
through a low arcaded street, which was lined on
either side with bazaars or cells of tradesmen, and
debouched into a small court surrounded by the
foundries of the bronze-workers. The open space
was covered with scraps of metal, heaps of charred
wood, broken moulding-boxes, piles of clay and
sand. Leaving the palanquin at the entrance to
the court, Hiram walked across it, followed by
the eyes of scores who gazed after him from their
various doorways. He entered the foundry of one
of the most noted artisans. The owner greeted
him with dignified cordiality.

"The Cabeiri have sent you at the right moment,
your majesty. Finer work than I have just completed was never done by the Greek Vulcan. You

admire the Greeks, as all artists must. But I shall prove to your own eyes that Tyre is keeping her ancient renown. See this bronze dish! But first listen to its musical ring," striking it with his centre finger. "It sounds longer than a diver can hold his breath. The gods have taught us the secret, which I whisper to you, sire: One part tin; nine parts copper. And never did embosser do better work with hammer and graving tool. Look at the muscles in the forearm of that figure on the rim."

"Finely wrought, indeed!" said the king. "But will they all be done in time? It wants but three moons to the wedding. And the number of pieces?"

"Yes, your majesty; five great dishes of gold, two-score of silver, a half-score of vases in bronze, and— But here is the order, which I shall have ready—"

"That is enough. I am pleased with your skill and promptness, and shall reward them," said the king, presenting his hand, which the artisan reverently touched with his lips.

King Hiram emerged from the network of streets and by-ways upon the Eurychorus Square, crossing which the royal palanquin disappeared beneath the portal of his palace. This was the residence of the ancient kings of Tyre. It was a large building, constructed of great blocks of stone, which were joined without mortar on smooth-fitting surfaces. About each stone was a depressed border, or bevel, which clearly marked the size of the blocks, making the whole more impressive to the eye, and at the same time revealing the antiquity of its construction. The edifice was windowless on the exterior. The only entrance was guarded by an enormous gate of oaken planks, which were banded together with thick and broad bars of burnished bronze. Pegs and sockets of the same metal made the hinges. It required the full strength of two burly porters to open these doors, for their great weight and the generations during which they had done service had worn the sockets into irregular shapes. As old Goliab, the porter, closed his half of the folding pair, and watched his comrade struggle with the other, he remarked :

"The hinges squeak like a howling priest. If they had not been used since the days of the Great Hiram, our king would order them to be taken off, and the new-fashioned ones put on."

"Hist, now!" replied his comrade. "They say that the king is going to stop the priests' howling first. The priests stick in the old ways they have worn for themselves, which, Baal save me! are not the ways the gods made when they lived in Tyre ; and may be they lived in this same palace, for they do say that the first king was a god."

"Have a care!" rejoined Goliab. "I have seen many a priest watching this gate of late. Who knows but they will take it for a temple, and move in themselves?"

"Then I move out. I serve none less than the king. But have you read the proclamation, Goliab ?

I thank Astarte for never sending me any children
to be burned to Moloch."

"That is not for such as we to talk about," replied Goliab.

"Why not?"

"Because," lowering his voice to a whisper,
"there's a priest outside this moment. I can see
his shadow through the crack under the gate."

The palanquin-bearers set down their royal burden in the court around which the palace was
built. Hiram alighted by the fountain that rose
in the centre and flung its spray over the beds of
flowers which tastefully decorated the borders of its
marble basin. He lingered a moment under an
orange tree, whose silver blossoms and golden
fruit, in simultaneous fulness, made him think of a
proverb that was common everywhere in those
lands famous for their orange groves: "A timely
word is like golden fruit in a basket of silver."
And then he thought of Hanno's words on the
bireme. "Were they timely? Does Hanno know
of dangers that I am ignorant of?"

He sought his private chamber, a room whose
high walls were lined with alabaster, great pieces
of which were cut into noble panels, and carved
with delicate tracery. The room was lighted chiefly through windows set near the ceiling, covered
with curiously shaped bits of glass, which flung
variegated colors, as in a floral shower, upon the
white walls and floors. Servants loosed his sandals, washed his feet, brought perfumed water for

3

his hands and face. His hair-dresser was ready with his ointment; his wardrobe-keeper with the special chiton and tunic which he knew his master liked. Others came bearing a repast.

When he had eaten and taken a double cup of wine—for the mental excitement of the council, together with the physical exhilaration of the run upon the sea, prompted that unusual indulgence—the king threw himself upon the divan to think. He first scanned with knit brows and curling lip a copy of the proclamation of the council, which he found upon his table. The parchment, however, soon fell from his hand, for he was tired even of his own wrath. The lines of writing changed into thick webs which, it seemed to him, gigantic spiders had spun about the room. He looked closely at one of these monsters. Its head was surely that of Egbalus. There was a smaller spider with the leering look of Rubaal. Ahimelek, too, with sleek, smooth face of hypocritical amiability, and a score of legs with anchors on them for sandals, was timidly crawling out of a corner. Then Hanno appeared, and walked straight through the tangled webs; and the spiders darted into holes from which, with little red eyes, they watched the intruder. Then, with unrustling robes, Zillah came. In the light which her presence dispensed the webs disappeared, as those on the dewy grass vanish under the sun's beams in the morning. The king dreamed—dreamed of such things as will never happen until Astarte abdicates her direction of woman's life, and love-sick Adonis takes her place.

CHAPTER IV.

THE Temple of Melkarth, the impersonation of Baal as that god was supposed to preside over the interests of Tyre, stood near the centre of the city. It was imposing, not so much because of its architectural lines, as for the enormous stones which made its foundation, each one of which was believed to have been laid in human blood some time in remote ages past. The space in front of the temple was a miniature paradise. Tiny rills, supplied artificially from the great aqueduct on the mainland, trickled over bright pebbles, and through the green grass. Fountains splashed in their basins of porphyry, marble, and bronze. Gay-plumed birds from distant countries, wing-clipped, that they might not fly far away, perched in delusive freedom upon the trees, and, with their various songs, replied to the challenge of lyre and flute that floated from the recesses of the temple court.

But on the afternoon of the day whose events we have been narrating, a vast multitude of people filled the little park, and drowned these sweeter sounds in the clatter of their voices. The streets leading to the temple were crowded with those who

had leisure from labor to indulge their curiosity.
An unusual number of people thronged through
the great gates of the temple to make offerings
upon the altars. The simple heralding of religious
revival is often the surest provocative of its coming. Thus it happened that the order of the council, respecting some stupendous rite that should be
performed, awakened a popular impulse for pietistic devotion.

The full coterie of temple officials was in attend-
ance. There were barbers who shaved the beards
and clipped the long forelocks of the worshippers,
by offering which to the god they signalled their
entrance upon the virile state of manhood. There
were venders of victims for sacrifice, and votive
objects of every variety; custodians of veils and
sacred furniture ; priests to slay the animals, and
others to supply the sacred coals to any who would
burn incense.

The devotees jostled one another in their eagerness to read and take down upon their little tablets
the exact tariff fixed by the temple code for the
services of priests, and prices of objects acceptable to the god, as these were placarded upon the
walls. Some were busy admiring the memorial
slabs or statuettes which had been presented by
wealthy Tyrians, and were often likenesses of the
donors, erected in reverent attempt to keep the
divinity and their fellow-citizens perpetually reminded of their pious munificence. A gaping
group gazed at the two columns, one of gold, the

other of emerald, which gave a mysterious light at
night, and which stood, one at the end of each of
the two aisles of the temple flanking the central
nave. These had been procured at vast expense
at some time of great deliverance, and were in-
scribed : " To the Lord Melkarth, Master of Tyre :
The offering of thy servants, because he has listened
to their voice. May he still bless us !"

Beyond these a crowd surveyed the altar of
bronze, beaten by skilful hands into delicate flower-
work, from the centre of which rose the perpetual
flame in commemoration of the adventure of the
goddess Astarte, who once caught a shooting-star,
and enshrined it among her favorite Tyrians ; or,
as some of the priests said, to express the faith of
the people in the divinity of fire, which was the
materialized brightness of the face of Baal, the sun-
god. A group stood near the great gateway, watching an opportunity to steal a glance between the
swaying curtains, which screened the inner court
from common eyes.

The most sacred precinct of the temple was an
artificial lake. From the midst of the water rose a
single stone, perhaps ten cubits high, on the top of
which was the Maabed, or ark, enclosing a statue
of the god, together with some objects sacred in
the history of Tyre, and believed, therefore, to be
the special delight of its divine protector.

The platform around the little lake was paved
with variegated marbles, white, yellow, red, brown,
and rose-colored, which were wrought into grace-

ful patterns of mosaic work. A roof, blazing with tiles of gold, sheltered the platform from rain and sun, and made it the rendezvous of the priests.

Just as the sun was going down a group of priests gathered about Egbalus in close consultation. They were dressed in white chitons, which clung close to their forms, except for the fine fluting of the skirts. Scarfs of violet ran over their shoulders and across their bodies diagonally. Their feet were bare; their heads shaved, and protected by close-fitting skull-caps, in some cases of gorgeous color, in others of knitted hair-work, which mingled confusedly with the black beards of the younger, and contrasted finely with the white beards of the more venerable.

Egbalus was speaking. "The council has but begun the reform which is to restore Tyre to its pre-eminence. It has decreed the sacrifice. It has prescribed that the offerings shall be worthy and notable. But what sacrifices shall be offered is not for the council to determine. This, only we who are admitted to the secret council of the gods themselves—we, the sacred order of priests—can declare. And woe to him who, in this day of honor to Baal, shall thwart the will of his priests!"

"Woe! Woe unto him!" echoed around the circle.

The high priest continued his harangue: "In the ancient days of Tyrian glory, when there was no power on land or sea to dispute our sway or rival our commerce; when ships returning from their voyages hung anchors of solid silver from their prows, having room only for more precious merchandise within—then Tyre gave great abundance to Baal-Melkarth, and offered its most distinguished citizens upon the altar. But how long, O Baal of Tyre! since thou hast had a princely offering? What are gems and beasts to the god who is offended with men? What are the babes which poverty gives because it cannot feed them, when kings have insulted the majesty of Heaven? And what—"

The old priest had either wrought himself up to a divine frenzy, or superbly acted the part of one who was supposed to be "filled with the god." His countenance became livid and white by turns. The great blue veins were swollen at his temples. His face seemed to expand. His neck thickened. His eyes fixedly glared towards a patch of sunlight that gleamed on the top of the wall. His form was rigid, except for a convulsive twitching of the fingers.

The attendant priests crowded close to their leader, and stared into his eyes, as if to catch the gleam of some coming revelation. The old priest's lips moved, but at first without articulation. He raised his hand, and, with unbent arm, pointed to the glint of sunlight, which seemed to hold him by some fatal fascination. At length his words became audible, very slowly uttered, and with oracular hoarseness:

"Baal permits me to know his will. Yonder light is no more surely from the sun-god than is a light that burns within me."

A slight zephyr at this moment ruffled the surface of the sacred water.

"It is the breath of Baal!" said one.

"See! See! The Maabed itself shook! It is the sign of the god! A miracle! A miracle!"

"A miracle!" they murmured, and prostrated themselves, crying, "O Baal, hear us! O Baal, guide us!"

Egbalus had remained standing, in unchanged attitude, watching the sunlight. He now whispered, impressing into his tones the simulation of awe:

"I see a mighty altar. On it lies one enrobed as a king. By it stands, august and venerable, a kingly priest, and—slays the victim. But hark! a voice! It is that of Melkarth himself, who bids me remember how, in our sacred traditions, it is recorded that the mighty god El, when a dire calamity had come upon his favorite city of Gebal, took his own son, adorned him in the robes of royalty, carried him to the altar, slew him, and so brought blessings for ages upon his people. Hear, O ye priests of Baal!"

He lowered his voice, either through sense of the awful solemnity of what he was about to utter, or fear of being overheard by others than those whom he owned, body and soul, as he did his infatuated band of priests. His followers arose from their prostrate positions, and drew close to him. This they heard: "Tyre must offer to Baal its king!"

A deep hush followed. Egbalus glanced nervously from one to another. Had he mistaken his men ?

" The king ?" said one, in a tone that might have been regarded as either assent or surprised interrogation.

"We have another king," was Egbalus's quick and altogether unghostly response.

" Baal save us !" cried one.

" The will of Baal be done !" was the sharp rejoinder of another—Mattan, a man of ferocious severity of countenance, whose body showed more scars from self-inflicted wounds than could be counted in half the circle besides.

Egbalus suddenly dropped all his mysteriousness of manner, with keen eyes searched their faces, by his very look challenging each one to dare resistance. He was now less high priest than he was politician and leader; seemingly forgetting his spiritual, he asserted his secular, power. Satisfied with what he saw in the half-cowed superstition or the crafty ambition of his followers, he boldly declared :

" It must be. Woe to the priest who, at this crisis of our order, dares to betray it !"

He drew his long knife, such as was used in sacrificing—" This for the heart of the first faithless priest !"

" And this !"

" And this !"

Half a score of gleaming blades were raised.

Egbalus continued : " King Hiram believes not

in the gods; would destroy them, and us with them. Rubaal must be king. 'It is the will of Baal, and it is the wisdom of men."

He allowed a silence to follow, that his suggestion might work. He did not for an instant, however, cease his search for any dissenting look upon a single face. He was correct in his judgment of them, and now knew that when the critical moment came there was not a man but would assault the king in any way that he commanded. Indeed, he had, during the few months he had held the high priest's office, gathered about himself, in the inner circle of priests who shared his counsels, only those who were desperate in their religious bigotry, or who were known to have some secret hatred towards the king.

"Let the god answer through our breasts!" at length he said, resuming his pietistic tone.

The priests bowed their heads until they touched the pavement. They then resumed a sitting posture, each with his eyes fixed upon his breast, as if listening to his own heart-beats for the articulation of the will of the god who possessed him.

"Baal speaks!" muttered one.

"He speaks!"

"He speaks!" was echoed from the circle.

"Baal has spoken through the lips of his high priest," said Mattan, rising.

One by one the others rose, and repeated, "Baal has spoken through the lips of his high priest. So let it be! and dies the man who says not so!"

The sun-glint had left the temple wall. Dark shadows dropped upon the corridors about the sacred lake, and in the gathering night the cabal of priests broke up.

CHAPTER V.

WAS it the night darkness that, by its contrast with his bright dream of Zillah, awoke Hiram? However that may have been, he aroused himself with the purpose of making his vision as near as possible a waking reality. He would go to her. Her hand upon his brow always exorcised his evil spirits, and he knew a pillow for a restless head softer than that of his divan. He struck with his finger a disk of bronze that hung by the couch. A deep, but exceedingly soft and sweet, note floated through the apartment, and was instantly answered by the keeper of the royal wardrobe. This honest fellow's loyalty was limited by the conviction that the king should be the handsomest man in his realm, and he spared no pains to make him such. Though he was not officially barber to his majesty, he yet wrought upon the short curls on his master's head with the exquisite care that a jeweller's etcher might have bestowed upon the locks of a goddess he was transferring from his imagination to a golden plate or goblet. The king was, ordinarily, far from fastidious regarding his raiment, and had often flung off the royal gewgaws in

which his attendants arrayed him for state display. The same indifference to appearance at
times led him to the opposite extreme; as, on the
day we are narrating, he had worn the dress with
which he had presided at the council, also on the
ship and amid the dirt of the foundries and workshops. But upon certain occasions he was not
averse to the consideration of a goodly appearance, especially when he made his visits to Zillah.
The male bird will display his plumage to the utmost, and pipe his sweetest notes, in the presence
of the female. We may leave the explanation of
this to the naturalist and the novelist; we here
only record the fact that Hiram made no objec-
tion when his attendant brought from the ward-
robe a close-fitting tunic of Sindonese silk, the
raw material of which, brought from far-away In-
dia, had been woven without a flaw on the Tyrian
looms, and embroidered by skilful and patient fingers with scarabs, lotus-blossoms, winged globes,
and royal uræi, in a combination of lines and colors that fascinated the eye with its general effect
as much as it bewildered by its details. About his
neck he suffered three collars to be placed; the
upper one closely fitting his throat, while the lower
one hung far down upon his breast; all sparkling
with tiny gems. He girded his loins with a scarf
of radiant colors, in the knot of which shone a
huge diamond, like a star in the belt of Orion. His
sandals were fastened with ribbons made of threads
of gold, and wound in cross-lines above his ankles,

thus setting off as fine a calf as ever kept time to the music of the dance. Could Hiram have seen himself in the glass with his own eyes, instead of through the imagined eyes of his mistress, he would have blushed for his effeminate bravery, and preferred to don the tight leathern uniform of a common soldier. But, to make his victorious entrance into a maiden's heart, he really thought himself arrayed in heroic style.

The house of Ahimelek was near the eastern wall, in the highest part of the city. From the east side it looked directly down upon the two harbors, and across the narrow strait that divided the island from the mainland. From its western balconies the view lay over the city, and far out over the Great Sea. The proud old merchant delighted especially in this prospect, which on every hand reminded him of the sources of his wealth. Far away towards Cyprus he could sight the incoming vessels, and towards Lebanon detect the slow-moving specks that were his caravans.

The house was of cedar. Its beam-heads and cornices were carved with objects beautiful or grotesque, as pleased the fancy of the architect; for Ahimelek had no standard by which to estimate its excellence beyond its expense. Its projecting windows were closely screened, one with a lattice-work of bronze, another of porphyry, another of alabaster, and one with strips of agate closely cemented. The interior apartments were panelled in richest woods, and floored with elaborate mosaics, upon which were skins of lions, wolves, and leopards. Objects of curiosity which his captains had brought from all the known countries of the world—enormous tusks of elephants, nuggets of precious minerals, diamonds with their incrustation of stone, plumage of strange birds, vases of malachite and lapis-lazuli, the weapons of savages, and bejewelled swords once worn by kings : these filled tables and niches, and stood in the corners.

Ahimelek met the king as the latter alighted from his litter in the central court. It needed no previous suspicion on the part of Hiram to detect something inhospitable in the merchant's welcome. As they passed the entrance together Ahimelek stopped. He seemed to be on the point of speaking, yet no words came. Awkwardly he made way for the young man to precede him ; and, as the lover sought the apartment of Zillah, her father stood looking after him with troubled countenance.

His formal and acknowledged betrothal to Zillah, according to Phœnician custom, gave to Hiram every privilege a husband has in his wife, except that of living with her. From the moment he had put the ring upon her finger, and had given to her father the legal document conveying certain property pledges, he became her virtual possessor and guardian.

At the entrance to the apartment of his betrothed, Hiram was met by Layah, Zillah's maid, a woman whose matronly manner contradicted the story of her youthful face. Layah had once been the handmaiden of Hiram's mother, and, but a little beyond him in years, had grown up as a sort of official playmate in the nursery. Upon his mother's death he had sent her as a gift to Zillah, who needed such a companion, since she had scarcely known a mother's protection, and, without brothers or sisters, was alone in the care of her father's house.

Layah's pride, when she ushered Hiram into the presence of her mistress, was warranted, for she truly thought there was no more beautiful woman in Tyre than the daughter of Ahimelek. And, indeed, Zillah's radiance this night was refracted in additional lustre through the toilet her maid had given her. A simple band of ribbon, with a single pearl studding it, bound her jet-black hair, but did not confine it. Her locks overflowed in clustering ringlets upon her forehead and temples, and fell in waves upon her white neck. Her features were small, but so clear-cut as to seem larger than in reality, and so animated were they with health and joy that the long, pendent ear-rings of crystal, which rested upon her shoulders, seemed to borrow from her face the light that flashed in them. Her upper garment came close to the throat, and was gathered into a sinus beneath the breast, by a girdle which was knotted in front. Her exposed arms were of such graceful shape that one scarcely noticed the wristlets and armlets with which her maid had insisted on decorating them. Her full-flowing skirt of silk was so artfully looped at the bottom as to reveal a foot and ankle, about which a serpent of silver coiled in loving embrace.

Zillah's first welcome of Hiram was followed by a playful frown. She held him at arm's-length, and curiously inspected his raiment.

"For shame, my Lord Hiram! I believe you have borrowed your cousin Rubaal's clothes—the same he came to woo me in the day before you and I were betrothed. You are more goodly-appearing with your sailor's cap and coarse chiton than in these fashions of Tyre. See! I have discarded my cap of pearls, and would not put on half the jewels Layah wanted me to, because I thought you would like me better as I am."

She dexterously loosed his triple collar, and flung it upon a divan; then plucked the great diamond from his scarf.

"Hold!" cried Hiram. "Do not throw that away. It may buy back our throne, if Egbalus steals it. Let me put it here, where Artaxerxes himself would not dare to pluck it."

He inserted the glowing jewel in the folds of the sinus of her dress.

"But why do you talk so much of Egbalus, dear Hiram?" she asked, as she drew him to her side upon the divan. Egbalus is only a priest, not even a prince. And you have often said you did not believe in the priests. Why care for what you do not believe in?"

"I do believe in the priests," said he, "just as I

4

believe in scorpions and other pests, because they
are disagreeable facts. I suppose I ought to be
above letting them annoy me, as the people in the
country build booths on the roofs of their houses,
and go to sleep there, knowing that the scorpions
cannot crawl so high. But I cannot sleep if I so
much as hear these priestly vermin scratch.

Do you remember, Zillah, the stories we used to
invent as children with Layah's help? They were
generally about a king who was driven from his
throne, and went wandering over the world, and
lost his queen somewhere, and could not find her.
You used to call yourself the queen, and imagine all
sorts of things you did without—without me; for I
was always the king, was I not?"

"And I always found you, too ; and now I am
going to keep you, and not let you go wandering
even in my dreams," replied the fair girl, throwing
her arm fondly about the shoulder of Hiram, with
her cheek against his. "Even Astarte does not
have so good a hold on Tammuz, or, as the Greeks
call him, Adonis, when she has found him come to
life again, as I have on my Adonai—my lord."

Her lustrous eyes, as she gazed into his, seemed
to drink love from his heart.

"Ah, but Astarte has to lose her Adonis first,
and her maidens go mourning for him. So you
might lose me. The Persian king has but to say a
word, and I must leave my throne. The satrap of
Syria—only a satrap—has more power than I, a
king, and could depose me. These priests could

poison the mind of Artaxerxes; or they could poison me. Do you not regret having promised to be my queen?"

The girl rose from the divan. She straightened her form to its full height. Her pose was majesty itself. Her black eyes flashed with indignant pride:

"Not even a king shall question either my love or my courage!"

Hiram, though startled, was not offended at this sudden transformation. He had been frequently treated to novel exhibitions of her character; but each one increased his admiration for her. She was to him a garden of graces. At every turn in their intimacy some new beauty was revealed, or some new sweetness exhaled from her life to gladden his. He did not, however, expect to find in his garden a stately palm-tree—a character so lofty and ruggedly strong. He now felt that she was more royal than he, and he could have thrown himself at her feet as a slave. But through all Zillah's severity of countenance there played a softer sentiment, that overtempted him to a different expression of loyalty, and he caught her to his arms, with the rapt exclamation: "A queen, indeed! My queen!"

She pushed him gently from her, and looked deeply into his eyes as if she would dry up the very fountain of his soul, as the sun-god dries the springs in summer, should he dare to question again the supremacy of her love. She then took his face between her hands, as she said:

"I shall be Hiram's queen if he reigns only in a

round boat, a pauper pirate of the sea, or carries
his crown on a camel flying across the deserts.
But "—her voice trembled, steadied only when his
hot kiss had acted as a tonic—" I would rather be
simply Hiram's wife. Wife means more than
queen, does it not?"

The superb woman again became a girl; the
palm-tree became a spray of delicate vine that
twined itself through and through Hiram's heart.

The long and silent embrace that followed was
disturbed by loud talking in the apartment of
Ahimelek, which was across the recess entering
from the court, a sort of hallway that divided
the business offices of the merchant from the
portion of the house that was devoted to domestic
use.

"Ah! I know that screech," said Hiram. "It
belongs to the night-hawk Egbalus. He is always
flitting about in the dark. Listen! What nest is
he putting his beak into now?"

The priest was evidently threatening and en-
treating by turns. Ahimelek was as clearly on
guard, like some fencer who knows the superior
prowess of his antagonist. His tones of voice
showed that he was now objecting, and now yielding point after point, only protecting his retreat.
Whole sentences were at length caught by the listeners, as the excitement of the priest betrayed his
caution :

" But, sire, you cannot prevent it. I have obtained the consent of every other member of the

council but yourself. No man can withstand the will of Baal."

"Ah!" whispered Hiram to Zillah. "Your father, then, did not vote for the sacrifice. I half thought as much. He has always assented to my view that we are making too much of religion. If they would only leave me to select the victims, I would order the sacrifice myself, and roast a score or two of priests' spawn. I would make such a feast that Moloch would be sick from surfeit for a hundred years. But listen!"

Egbalus was now fairly hissing his words: "You dare not refuse. It is ruin to you and to your house. Hark you, Ahimelek! Your dealing with the Egyptian is known. You accepted a bribe of ten thousand darics to abandon the commerce of Cyprus and Memphis to the sailors of the Nile. This is death by the laws of Tyre. And think not that having a son for king will save a traitor. The evidence of it is written out. It is on this parchment. A horseman stands ready to carry the news to the Great King at Susa. It was treason against Persia. You know the end. Sign this order of the priests of Baal, and I will tear up this damning document. If not—"

The two listeners looked at each other with consternation. They knew that the priests had spun some web about the merchant. True or false, their accusation would ruin him. Hiram's first impulse was to enter the room, and slay the priest as he stood. A second thought showed the unwisdom of such a course. The plot must have other meshes, though Egbalus held the chief string. A rash deed on the king's part would precipitate an issue between the throne and the temple, with the advantage in favor of the latter, since their plotting had been of long continuance, and their purposes were well ripened.

"I shall advise your father to yield the point," said Hiram, rising. "A few miserable babies more or less for a sacrifice, what does it signify?"

He strode across the open space, and, unannounced, stood before the men. His sudden appearance transformed the debate into a tableau. Egbalus was standing rigidly erect, his hand clenched, and raised above his head; his whole soul seemingly condensed into one act of will, dominating the soul of Ahimelek; and that will was blazing from the priest's half-demoniacal eyes. Had he uttered no words, the very pantomime would have been enough to crush a weaker man's resolution. Ahimelek sat limp and pale with terror before the priest.

Without awaiting an explanation, Hiram determined to rescue the merchant from the straits into which his loyalty had apparently put him, and said:

"Enough of this quarrel! Ahimelek, you have your king's permission to assent. Let the priests have what sacrifice they will."

"Your majesty! Your majesty is mad!" jerked out Ahimelek, holding up his hands in agonizing remonstrance.

"It is enough! I have said it," responded the king.

Egbalus was surprised, and stared as one confounded. But only for a moment did he lose his self-possession. He was a consummate actor. He could direct his most fiery passion by cold discretion, as the moulder leads the molten metal into his patterns of sand. A look of holy serenity suddenly diffused his countenance:

"Baal, I thank thee! Thou hast owned thy servant! Said I not so — that the heart of the king would be so led by Baal that he himself would consent? Most noble king! Servant of the gods! Let me kiss the feet of him whom Baal receives as his son!"

He threw himself upon the floor before the king, who could scarcely restrain an impulse to trample the hypocritical wretch with his heels. It cost Hiram a mighty effort to obey his quick, intuitive discretion. He did not even glance at the prostrate priest, but, with a look of scorn and pity upon Ahimelek, he withdrew.

"Oh, for the power of a king!" he exclaimed, as he re-entered Zillah's apartment. "I swear by all the gods that for the last time have I yielded to the cruelty of these priests. To Sheol with the whole brood of them!"

Hiram sank upon the divan by the side of Zillah, exhausted by the sharp conflict of emotions through which he had passed. He rebuked himself for the display of passion.

"But for your sake, my fair one, and the sake of your father, I would have died rather than have done it. But my time will come, if there be any power of justice back of these villainous gods who demand such things."

"I see," said Zillah, putting her hand upon his brow, as if to exorcise some demon there—"I see that you, too, could be cruel, dear Hiram."

"Yes, cruel as any other human beast, until I can abolish cruelty. And I will abolish it—abolish it by the sword."

He sat a long time in silent thought, then rose suddenly, exclaiming:

"But these are no scenes for you, my darling."

"Why not for me, if for you?" rejoined Zillah. "I am not a butterfly, that must needs flit only in the sunshine. I would rather be like our heroic Queen Dido, for all her troubles, than be a mere statue come to life, like that which her brother, our King Pygmalion, made. Your cares shall be mine, or I am not worthy to sit under the purple canopy of your throne."

"Right royally spoken!" cried Hiram, in an outburst of admiration. "But, for all that, I shall save you from such scenes and such priests, for I shall decree that there shall be no gods—except that every man shall have his own Astarte, and she shall be worshipped thus—" He laid his ardent offering upon her lips.

CHAPTER VI

A N unusual throng filled the streets and the Great Square when the king returned from the house of Ahimelek to his own palace. Priests were everywhere. It seemed as if the ecclesiastical hives of half the cities of Phœnicia had swarmed along the coast, and lit again on the rock of Tyre. Some of these priests, with unkempt hair and mad eyes, were haranguing the crowd ; others were engaged in excited debate among themselves. The palanquin of the king moved among the people as if it were the ark of some strange religion ; for, while a few glanced at it with respect, many regarded it with rage, and scarcely restrained the impulse to lay violent hands upon it. Egbalus and his devotees had evidently done effective work, not only in disseminating their own venomous spirit, but in organizing their various guilds for action in emergency. The royal attendants noticed that a band of priests moved just ahead of them, and that another band came behind, as if the king's person were either honorably escorted or dangerously menaced. Still another company of priests moved hastily, yet in order, away from the palace gate as the king approached it.

Hiram was himself too much engrossed with his own thoughts fully to take in what was transpiring beyond the closely drawn curtains of his carriage. But, having passed within his own gate, he suddenly awoke to a sense of some unusual environment that was being spun about him. Entering his private apartment, he was possessed by that mysterious power of clairvoyance through which one is made conscious of a presence that is neither seen nor heard. He was impressed with the fact that the room already contained an occupant. The instinct of danger, reinforced by an acquired habit of vigilance, led him to place his back against the wall, and his hand upon his dagger hilt. Uncertain of the loyalty of even the private servants of his chamber, he determined to face the unknown menace alone. He dismissed all his attendants, and closed the door behind them as they made their exit. Prepared to strike at any living thing that had dared to invade his privacy, he stood a moment listening, and searching with his eyes every object which the thick screen of the hanging lamp left in the shadows.

"Who goes here?" was his challenge.

A whisper came from beyond the curtains that shielded one end of the divan:

"It is I, King Hiram."

"Why, Hanno! what means this? Are you mad?" Is everybody mad?"

The low tones of his friend's voice bespoke continued caution. Hanno laid his hand upon the king's arm as he said, "Let us first make sure that we are alone. If I could steal admission here, others might."

He raised the shade from the flaming wick that floated in the oil. With drawn weapons the two men searched every nook where there was possibility of concealment. They were alone.

"You are in danger, my king. I anticipated no harm to you in the open streets, for the priests are interested in protecting you there; but I feared lest some of the devils might give you foul play here : so I crept in, no matter how. You know the plot? No? It was further along than I suspected when we parted this afternoon. You, Hiram! Oh, the treachery of it! the cowardice of it! You, my king!"

Hanno's voice was choked with uncontrollable rage. "You—you are to be the sacrifice to Baal!"

Hiram stood gazing stupidly into his friend's face. He heard his words. He understood them, and yet he could not take them in. The power of thought seemed paralyzed. Then, gradually, he came to realize the meaning of what he had heard. At first he thought only of the indignity offered his throne. Then, brave as he was, there came a tremor of dread, as the horrid rites of the sacrifice filled his imagination. That cruelty which he had refused to sanction, where the victim was the humblest babe among his people, was to come upon himself! He saw himself a bound and helpless victim. He felt the flames, but they chilled him to

the heart's core. For the first time in his life he
was afraid.

The two men sat down together upon the edge
of the divan. For a long time neither spoke. Nor
was it necessary. Rapidly the king put together
in his memory many recent occurrences. His keen
judgment saw their significance, and that they focused in the terrible fact which Hanno had announced.

"Blind! blind! blind I have been; but I see
it now," groaned the stricken man. Then, starting from his horrible reverie, he strode across the
apartment. Pausing under the full glare of the
lamp, he held aloft his dagger:

"I swear before Baal that if he demands the
sacrifice of the King of Tyre, the King of Tyre
shall be both priest and victim! My own hand
shall strike the blow; not theirs. And the altar
shall be the dead body of Egbalus. He first shall
fall. I shall seek him."

He moved towards the door. His friend stayed
him.

"You cannot go out. The house is closely guarded," said Hanno. "Egbalus has filled the city
with bands of Galli. They have been coming into
Tyre from the country around for days."

"I will cut my way through a thousand of them
to the dock, and take to the sea," cried the king,
in the valor of his despair.

"It is too late," replied Hanno. "When I heard
the decision of the priests this afternoon I tried to

arrange for that; but your biremes have all been scuttled, and mine is stolen away. The very captains in the harbor have been bedevilled by the priests. Brave fellows though they are, like all sailors, they are superstitious, and believe that Baal has put a curse on every wave for any one who would attempt your rescue."

"Then, my dear Hanno, you too must go, and leave me to my fate. I will not have my life if it endangers yours. Go! Appear as my enemy! Save yourself! I will know that your heart is true, even if your hand should tie the cords and cast me into the flames. Go!"

"Never!" cried Hanno. "Did not you and I see the flames when forty thousand Sidonians burned their houses over their heads and perished together, rather than fall into the hands of the Persians?"

"Then let it be so, Hanno! And right here will we emulate them. See, this flame to this curtain, and this couch shall be our altar!"

As the king spoke, he reached the lamp from its hanging, and brought it close to the heavy draperies.

"Hold!" cried Hanno. "This is no time for madness, but for cool heads. The sacrifice cannot be for some days yet. Time breeds opportunities. Let us watch!"

"For what?" cried the king, burying his head in his hands.

Nearly an hour passed in silence, broken at length by Hanno:

"Egbalus has made a prediction that, so powerful is the will of Baal, the god will send the spirit
of holy zeal into every heart in Tyre; that the very
rays of the sun-god to-morrow will inspire all they
fall upon with such acquiescence that every one
would gladly take the place of the sacrifice. As I
came in here, only a moment before you, a herald
was running across the square, crying, 'The king
consents! The king consents! Praised be Baal!'
The lying devil of a priest has already perjured his
soul with that counterfeit of the royal word."

"Ay, I did consent."

Hiram then related to Hanno the scene at the
house of Ahimelek, where, under misapprehension
of its full import, he had approved the sacrificial
celebration.

"It is well, then," said Hanno. "Why not seem
to verify the high priest's interpretation of your
assent? Apparently yield. It will divert suspicion
from any plan we might adopt."

The young men talked through the entire night,
and in the early dawn Captain Hanno, disguised
as a market vender, was let out the great gate with
a good volley of curses from old Goliab, the porter.

CHAPTER VII

THE ensuing day was one of intense excitement in Tyre. At every open space, on the walls, in the Great Square, at street corners, and especially in the court of the temple, were priests haranguing the people. Bands of Galli, the priests of Astarte, having set an image of the goddess upon an ass, swarmed about it as it was drawn through the streets, beating drums, blowing horns, cutting themselves with knives, tearing out handfuls of their hair, and chanting—or rather howling—the sentences of their wildest liturgy. Caught by the strange infection, many private citizens openly renounced their secular vocations, and joined the priesthood of Astarte.

Initiation into this order, according to an ancient custom, was signalled by the candidate's breaking into a neighbor's house, where he penetrated to the women's apartment, demanded a suit of female apparel, and arrayed his nether members in this, leaving the shoulders bare. In this mongrel attire the neophyte joined some roving band of Galli. The dress was presumed to symbol a cruel rite by which the enthusiast had made his priesthood more acceptable to the goddess.

Among the young men who appeared to have been especially filled with the spirit of Astarte was Captain Hanno. He had stopped to listen to an excited exhorter. Some invisible spell drew him closer and closer to the speaker. His eyes became riveted upon the countenance of the priest, the contortions of whose facial muscles he imitated. The orator changed from speaking naturally to a singing rhythm, timing the variation of his tones by a swinging motion of his body. In this he was closely followed by the circle of priests about him. Captain Hanno wedged himself among them. Shoulder to shoulder they stood, swaying now sideways, now forward, now backward. With every motion the spell deepened. Louder and louder they shouted, until shouts became shrieks. One after another fell swooning to the ground. A priest grasped wildly at the blade of a sword his comrade was waving, half severing his hand; but he did not heed the pain. At a moment when physical exhaustion had produced a temporary lull in the confusion, the priests recognized Hanno as a new-comer among them. Instantly they cried:

" The stigma! Make the sacred stigma!"

They held towards him their knives. Hanno seized one of them, and dashed the point through the fleshy part of his shoulder. The screeching grew wilder as the priests saw this evidence of the power of their goddess. Surely Egbalus's prediction was being verified, since the man who, of all Tyre, next to the king, was noted for coolness and indifference to religion, had become a convert! Suddenly breaking through the throng, Hanno ran from street to street, followed by the priestly rabble. He shook the gates of several houses which would not open to him. Up the steep lanes he went, as if impelled by some fury. He dashed through the gate of the house of Ahimelek, which flew open at his touch. In a few moments he emerged. A woman's skirt, of richest texture, hung from his waist and covered the upper portion of his legs, which protruded bare and bleeding beneath. The blood still trickled from his shoulder and smeared the garment. The Galli gathered about him. He broke out into impassioned praise of Astarte, of Melkarth, of Moloch. In his ecstasy he shouted every phrase that described divinity in the street speech of Tyre. His celestial rage seemed inspired by the beams of Baal, which were changed to molten fire, and poured through his veins. His eloquence was prodigious. He clamored for more haste with the sacrifice. He declared himself willing to be the victim. Then, abandoning the wildness of gesticulation, he suddenly became rigid as a statue of porphyry, and his face as red with the blood-flush of excitement. He swayed an instant, then fell. The Galli caught him in their arms. They bore his stiffened form on their shoulders to the temple.

Even Egbalus was astounded at such a tribute to his priestly astuteness and power, and fairly croaked with delight as Hanno, returning to con-

5

sciousness, prostrated himself at the high priest's feet. The addition to the priesthood of one who stood foremost among the Tyrians for social rank and for naval prowess was an event to be appreciated within the Temple of Baal.

CHAPTER VIII

WHILE these scenes were being witnessed in the streets of the city, King Hiram, left alone by the departure of his friend Hanno, enacted within his own soul a tragedy scarcely less terrible than that he feared. From his impending fate he saw no way of escape. Die he must. He queried with himself, what would it signify if he resented, even fought against, this monstrous cruelty? What if he died by his own hand, or by the blows of his captors? This would only throw over his memory a damning disgrace in the estimate of the superstitious people. His name would be hissed with imprecations, and become a by-word for impiety towards the gods, and for selfish, cowardly indifference to the welfare of his country. Though he were right in his views of religion, he would not be understood. Posterity, except in remote ages, perhaps, would attribute to him, and to his shrinking from the altar, all the misfortunes that might come upon Tyre. Should he risk this? Did consistency require it of him? Should he not submit to the inevitable with outward grace, if not with the grace of a submissive spirit?

Then he thought of Egbalus. He seemed to

see the sharp, triumphing eyes of the high priest, gloating over this fulfilment of his prediction that the god would draw the king to voluntary obedience. He saw the hands of this plotter binding the people more slavishly to his will through his victory over the only man who had ever yet dared to dispute the priestly rule in Tyre.

"No! Let me die by my own hand first! Thou, hated priest, shalt never conquer through me!"

He felt the point of his dagger.

Then a gentler emotion swayed him; perhaps it was the natural reaction from the strain of excitement. He thought, "And may there not be gods in spite of my doubts? I am but one man against a multitude. God cannot be Moloch, for such a god is less noble than man. But surely there is some One who is the mystery of existence; and does He not demand sacrifices? The Jews have no idols, but have altars. The Greeks, even Herodotus, who has taught me to doubt, worshipped his gods with sacrifice. If the god is good, then surely we have offended him. If the god is not good, then he is capricious, passionate, vindictive, and we had best humor him. O Baal! or Jove! or Jehovah! accept my life, which I offer to thee! I fling it forth into the great darkness. If there be light anywhere, may I enter it! If there be no light, let the darkness blot me out of existence. I give myself to god, or to oblivion."

He buried his head in the cushions of the divan. The sleepless night and the unintermitting intensity of his mental struggle overcame even his marvellous powers of physical endurance. He fainted or fell into a dreamless sleep; he knew not which.

When he came to himself, he recognized by the nearly emptied globe of the water-clock that it was late in the afternoon. He was surprised that no one had called him. His servants had prepared no meals. How did they know that he did not need them? He glanced into the mirror of polished brass. How changed his features! He was pale and haggard as one of the Galli.

Startled by his own apparition, he passed from his sleeping-apartment into its anteroom. It seemed to be filled with the statues of men. Was he demented? They moved towards him. One by one they fell to the floor. Then the statue nearest to him raised its head and pronounced, in tones of deepest awe,

"O holy sacrifice! Seven times blessed! Chosen of men! Accepted of our Lord Baal!"

Then this one's head dropped to the floor. Each head was raised in turn, and repeated the same words.

All the statues then rose. One of them was clothed in a long black robe— Could he mistake that figure? It was Egbalus. Bowing low, the high priest spoke:

"The holy spell has been upon thee, O royal son of Tyre, son of Baal! As thou wast lying on thy couch I saw a wondrous thing. All the souls of the ancient kings of Tyre came again from their abodes in the world of the dead. Each was like a shooting-star. They came from the dark bosom of the night. They flashed across my vision and entered thy body. One by one these starry kings came, until the last, thine own father. In thee, O blessed Hiram! is all the royalty of Tyre. I saw, too, the great spirit of Baal, like a globe of light, brighter than the sun himself. Baal came and enclosed thee. The divine light penetrated thee, purified thee, until thy body was light itself; bright even as the brightness of Baal. This was thy consecration for the sacrifice. The flames cannot harm thee, since thou art become light itself. But one duty awaits thee. Come thou, O divine king, and consecrate with thy presence the temple, the holy place of Melkarth. Then shalt thou enter the life of which Baal is the fulness. Come!"

Hiram knew not whether this were a dream or a mocking reality. But it mattered little which, since he had determined to outwardly obey and, with Hanno, to watch.

"As thou wilt, O servant of our Lord Baal!" he replied : and, preceded by Egbalus and followed by the attendant priests, he passed from his palace.

The royal palanquin awaited him in the court. It had been covered with a white cloth canopy and curtains which completely enveloped it, and concealed his person from all eyes. The priests became his bearers. A line of them marched ahead, playing lugubrious notes on pipes of reed, above which rose the words of a chant. As the proces-

sion wound its way across the Great Square the
multitudes prostrated themselves on either hand,
murmuring prayers and benedictions upon the
royal deliverer of Tyre. At the temple gate the
·popular reverence and awe were evinced by intense
silence. Not a form swayed, not a foot was lifted,
not a word was spoken. Only the slow-timed
tramp of the bearers of the royal victim broke the
stillness as the cortége passed between the massive
gates, which slowly swung upon their hinges and
closed again.

For three days King Hiram remained alone in
the chief chamber, that which opened upon the
corridor of the sacred lake. Priests incessantly
patrolled back and forth, saying nothing except
their prayers. They brought him food in golden
dishes, and left it, removing the remnants in the
same reverential manner in which they would have
served at the altar.

As the silence of the day turned into the deeper
silence of the night, and back again to silent day,
the solitude became unendurable. Only royal
pride prevented Hiram asking some question of
his obsequious custodians. When would the sacrifice be accomplished? Was there no communication for him from Zillah? Could he bribe any
of these bigots to confer with Captain Hanno?
Now he was tempted to rush upon one of the
priests, seize his sacrificial knife, plunge it into
the man's heart, and then into his own. He was
once in this latter mood, and on the very point

of executing his purpose, when the priest who would have been his victim began to mumble his prayers.

"I will wait until the wretch has got through that. He will need all his prayers for his last breath," muttered the king.

The man beat upon his breast and tore his hair, as if in some sacred frenzy. He came nearer to Hiram's chamber entrance, and paused in his walking, with his back to the king.

"The gods favor me for once," thought Hiram. "Now to throttle him and to strike!"

The priest raised his voice in praying, so that Hiram caught the words "Take heart! Be watchful!" A sudden glance at the half-turned face revealed the familiar features of Hanno. All Hiram's self-possession was needed to restrain a cry of recognition. The next day the eccentric priest appeared again, and paused to pray at the same spot. He stretched out his hands towards the Maabed, and, as if addressing the deity enshrined in the midst of the water, prayed thus:

"O Baal Hiram, King of Tyre! keep thine eyes open for the mark of a circle, and follow it. O Baal Melkarth! O Astarte, Queen of Heaven! send prosperity!"

CHAPTER IX

UPON the mainland, adjacent to the island, had stood for many centuries another city, which the people distinguished by the name of Old Tyre. A hundred and fifty years before, its glory had departed, when it fell conquered by the Babylonian Nebuchadnezzar. The dangers of its exposed position on the mainland, as compared with the safety of the island which the Great Sea guarded as a mighty moat, led the Phœnicians to neglect the rebuilding of the old city. Its broken walls, fifteen miles in circuit, were filled with the débris of once proud temples and stately palaces. A few buildings of straggling architecture had been hastily reconstructed with the blocks of stone that made the graceful lines of an ancient mart or fortress. Shanties stood upon the dismantled foundations, and scattered among the ruins were the black tents of traders. A new market-place had been opened close to the shore, where the many caravans that crossed the Lebanons from Damascus exchanged their rich loads for those brought over the sea.

One of the most prominent ruins in Old Tyre

was that of an ancient temple of Baal. Superstitious reverence for the place had prevented its use as a quarry, the fate of so many other ruins. Huge blocks of stone, such as the Phœnician builders were famous for using in their gigantic temples, loaded the ground; and concealed beneath them were subterranean passage-ways, which the priests of old had used in going from one part of the sacred edifice to another, unseen by the worshippers. These were now the abode of jackals, whose domiciles were uninvaded except by the flitting of the bats and the gliding of serpents through the narrower crevices. On the plaza, which had been the court of the old temple, and which was largely unencumbered with débris, rose a dilapidated image of Baal-Moloch.

To Captain Hanno, in recognition of his accession to the priesthood, and as a stimulus to the flagging zeal of others in the class of citizens to which he belonged, was assigned the honorable duty of superintending the preparation for the sacrifice; and he well exemplified the adage, "There is no zealot so zealous as a new one." Under his orders masons relaid the walls of the fire-pit beneath the statue. A gang of sailors rigged chains for the moving of the brazen arms of the gigantic figure. Brass-workers burnished the breast of the god until it dazzled the beholder like a miniature sunset. Sidonian glass-makers furnished great globes, covered with vitreous glazing, for the eyes which glared from the bull's head that surmounted the human shoulders of the monster. Pipes from the fire-pit were to convey the smoke through the nostrils. Piles of wood were brought from the Lebanons, and casks of inflammable oil were placed in readiness near by. Various enclosures were set up for singers, drum-beaters, and trumpeters. Elevated platforms awaited the guilds of civil dignitaries. Lines were drawn within which the priests could congregate according to the different gods they served, and display in pious rivalry, but without confusion, the insignia of their varied worship. This spot was reserved for the devotees of Dagon, the fish-god ; that for Adonis, the god of the seasons. Sadyk, the god of justice, was assigned here ; and next to him his children, the Cabeiri, had their places. Prominent provision was made for the priests of Astarte, the moon-god, queen of heaven, and for those of Melkarth, god of the city ; while the open space directly around the image was reserved for the officiants at the sacrifice.

The day for the solemnity opened with auspicious omen. The sun-god poured down his lustre unbroken by a cloud. Though yet early summer, the rays were intense and burning ; suggestive of the wrath of Moloch, who drank up the springs of water, withered vegetation, and threatened the land with the horrors of a famine by drought, a calamity to be averted only by appeasing his thirst with the blood of nobler victims.

The entire shipping of the port was arrayed in

festive colors. There were vessels not only of Tyre, but from the neighboring cities on the Phœnician coast—Sarepta and Sidon, Byblus and Berytus, Aratus and Joppa—vying with one another in the splendor of the devices by which they exalted their various local divinities, while they attested their common faith in the dread majesty of Baal-Moloch. Trading vessels from Egypt and Greece, and from the far western coasts of the Great Sea also, willingly hastened their coming or delayed their departure that, with reverent curiosity, they might witness the stupendous rites.

The plan for the solemn cortége of vessels that was to convey the victims for the sacrifice from Tyre to the place prepared on the mainland, included a procession around the entire island, starting from the Egyptian harbor, on the south, curving westward and northward through the open sea, thence eastward, passing the Sidonian harbor, and across the narrow space of water to the shore.

This line of movement symbolized the purpose of the whole ceremonial to secure a blessing upon everything that related to Tyre's prosperity—her homes, her arts, her commerce, as well as upon her temples and priests. Along this prescribed course the Phœnician ships were anchored side by side in double rows, between whose bows the sacred barges that conveyed the gifts for Baal should pass. Of these barges there were three.

The first was laden with miscellaneous offerings. There were piles of elegant garments, made of silk wrought on the looms of distant Persia, and the finest linen of Egypt, which had adorned the persons of princely men, or added fascination to the most beautiful women. With such offerings the aristocratic expressed their humiliation before the god, denuding themselves of their pride, even as they divested themselves of their expensive apparel. But as each valuable piece was marked ostentatiously with the name of the donor, a sceptic might have thought that the sinful trait of vanity lay deeper than the soft raiment had touched. Jars of precious dyes were so placed that their dripping contents stained the sea in the wake of the barges, attesting the piety of the makers of such stuffs. Great sacks of ground spices were the offering of a ship-owner whose vessel had gone around Africa and entered the Gulf of Araby, where these precious treasures were procured. These were flung in handfuls to the gentle wind, and loaded the atmosphere with their aroma. There were also great mounds of fruit; birds of rarest plumage; blooded dogs from the kennels of sportsmen; a goat with dyed horns; a sheep with prodigious covering of wool; a splendid horse, the gift of Prince Rubaal; and a bull with white feet, the special offering of the High Priest Egbalus.

The second barge had a more precious freight— seven times seven mothers, each fondling for the last time her first-born son, a little babe that lay naked in her lap. Some of these women belonged to the lowest class, the abandoned sort, whose maternal impulses were hardly above the brutal instinct, and who were not averse to making a religious merit of the infanticide to which they had been sometimes tempted in order to escape the care of their offspring. Others among them were honest, but abjectly poor, and had been persuaded by the priests thus to give their children back to the All-giving Baal. A few made the sacrifice with bleeding hearts. These sat in utter misery, staring as if for relief towards the burning heavens, that gave no token of mercy. Around the group of innocents was ranged a cordon of enthusiasts, who sang in prayer to Baal, and again in wild refrain declared the god's reward to those who willingly gave up their children—riches untold, and new offspring according to desire in number, sex, and beauty; all painless gifts, in compensation for the pang of their gift to Heaven.

The third barge surpassed all in the splendor and costliness of its decoration. About its sides were ranged the statues and banners representing all the gods of Phœnicia. In the centre rose an altar-shaped throne. The royal chair was overlaid with beaten gold. Above it hung a canopy of purple silk, the same that Trypho had dyed for Hiram's gift to Zillah. The king sat on his throne as if he commanded the pageant. His face was white, his lips compressed, his eye steady: a king still, though seemingly done in marble. On his head he wore the ancient crown of Tyre. In his hand was a sword of bronze, its bluish blade exquisitely chased with the symbols of authority, and its golden hilt thickly studded with gems. At the prow of the barge stood Egbalus, arrayed in the most gorgeous vestments of his office, his hands outstretched in continual prayer.

The imposing cortége made its way slowly; the barges being propelled only by priests, whose sacred character was supposed to make amends for their lack of skill in handling the long oars that were affixed to the sides. The tall prows of the vessels that lined the course, as a guard of honor, were surmounted with figure-heads representing the gods; and, moved by the gentle undulation of the waves, these divinities seemed to bow in acknowledgment of the superior honor of Moloch.

CHAPTER X

THUS the sacred regatta moved over the prescribed course to the mainland. Leaving the barges, the priests were marshalled into a vast procession. At the head moved the trumpeters, their instruments pitched to a wailing key, and giving forth long and monotonous notes. They were followed by others, carrying the various articles that were to be offered. Then came the living sacrifices. About the parents who were bringing their children to the god, the singing priests formed a circle, and drowned the weeping in the louder praise they shouted to Baal. The throne of the king was placed upon an open platform, and, with its royal occupant, was borne upon the shoulders of the most noted of the hierarchy; the neophyte Hanno being honored with a place by its side, and with a wand of authority as one of the directors of the ceremony.

During the passage from the landing-place to the presence of the idol, the people were allowed to look upon their vicarious sacrifice. All hatred and wrath had given way to the better emotions of reverence, gratitude, and affection. The crowd

pressed as close to the line as the priestly attendants would permit, and there threw themselves upon
the ground, kissing the spot their king's form had
shadowed, and gathering up handfuls of the dust
for sacred memorial.   He was now their possession
as they had never thought when they called him
their king: for he was their substitute, upon whom
were laid all their woes and fears; and soon he
was to be their god, when, through the mystery of
the fire-offering, he would pass into the sublimer
mysteries of the glory of Baal.

A little way to the front of the idol had been
erected a silken pavilion, covered with devices and
mottoes of religious import, which were elaborately
wrought with needle-work upon its floating walls
of crimson.   This was the Holy Place, into which
the great atoner, leaving his throne, retired from
the gaze of all, that in secrecy he might prepare
himself for the final offering; that, as Egbalus had
said, his soul might first pass into, and be absorbed by, the very being of deity, before his body
should be given to the outward image of the Unknown.   The high priest had declared that so thor-
ough was the acquiescence of the king in his own
immolation that, when he should come forth from
the sacred pavilion and proceed to the flames, he
would not be a mortal, but only the semblance of
his former self; his glory shielded as a cloud shields
the sun, lest the sight should blind the beholders.

As the curtains fell, secluding Hiram in the sacred pavilion, Egbalus kissed the spot where the

6

victim's foot last touched the outer earth. Together with the attendant priests, he then retired from the proximity of the tent, leaving a broad space about it unoccupied by a human being, but penetrated by the gaze of thousands.

A long silence fell upon the multitude. A strange, oppressive awe of what might be transpiring within stifled the very breathing of the waiting throngs.

Then, suddenly, the blare of a hundred trumpets gave the signal for the presentation of the offerings. The inanimate gifts were first placed in huge piles upon the arms of the god, which, being lowered, dropped them into the flames beneath. Next, the living animals of small size were laid bound in his hands. The horse and bull were first slain, their blood poured over the arms of the idol, their hearts thrust into his open jaw, until, shrunken by the heat, they fell into the pit, and were consumed with the remaining flesh.

Then followed a stillness as of Sheol itself, broken only by the sobbing of the women who approached the image, each bearing her child in her arms. One, overcome by her contending emotions, fell fainting, but a priest instantly seized the child, and laid it upon the hot hands that shook it into the flames. Some staggered on with closed eyes, guided and goaded by the attendants. Some sang, in half-crazy ecstasy, the wild refrain of temple hymns, swaying their babes in time with the rhythm, and, without assistance, ascended the steps and presented their sacrifice. As babe after babe disap-

peared through the smoke, new waves of excitement poured over the crowd; hot waves of delirium, burning out humane instincts, and firing that
rage of beasts which is latent in all men. The crowd
yelled in frenzy. The priests, with their long knives,
gashed their bodies, and, filling their mouths with
their own flowing blood, spit it forth again in the
direction of the god.

Then, as the last babe was offered, the grand expectation brought the multitude to silence. Egbalus approached the holy pavilion. He raised his
hand. The note of a single trumpet, finer, sweeter,
yet sadder than any other, floated over the throng.
It was repeated, with louder sound and more pro-
longed. Again it rang forth with full blast, and
was answered by one borne over the water from the
Temple of Melkarth in the island city. Then the
high priest stood with uplifted hands. It seemed
many minutes to the people, whose excitement was
scarcely endurable. Turning to where the folding curtain indicated the entrance to the pavilion,
Egbalus cried with loud voice,

"Come forth, O thou accepted of Baal!"

He instantly prostrated himself on the ground.
The priests in the front row of spectators fell prone
upon their faces. In the crowd every neck was
stretched and all eyes strained to catch the first
glimpse of the sacrificial hero.

But the curtain of the pavilion did not move.
Was not the victim's prayer yet completed? Was
he so absorbed in communion with his god that he

had become oblivious to what was outward? Or did he flinch now at the fatal instant? Perhaps the god had become his own priest and stricken him, or sweetly drawn his consecrated spirit from his body! Was he already dead?

Egbalus rose slowly from the ground, keeping his eyes upon the curtain to note its first flutter. Again he struck his most august attitude, and repeated the invocation:

"Come forth, thou accepted of Baal!"

He prostrated himself as before. But still there was no response.

The high priest rose again. He advanced, and touched the curtain, but, evidently overcome by a feeling that it were sacrilege, or perhaps by the dread of some mystery beyond his solution, or some ghostly power raised by his word, but not amenable to it, and that would not down at his bidding, he withdrew. He beckoned the dignitaries next in rank to himself, among them Hanno, and with them held a consultation. They were evidently as puzzled as he.

A third time the solemn invocation was pronounced, but with the same futile result. Egbalus then, with pretence of bold exercise of his office, but with manifest trepidation, laid his hand upon the curtain. Hesitatingly he drew it aside. For a moment he stared into the shadows. He advanced a step, then suddenly retreated. He looked about him as one bewildered and uncertain how to act. He motioned to the nearest priests. They came reverently, answering the perplexed face of the high priest with looks of equal curiosity and alarm. One by one they looked into the pavilion. Then they raised their hands as if Heaven alone could account for what they saw.

The Holy Place was empty!

"The god! the god has taken him!" said Egbalus, in half-dubious, half-credulous voice.

"The god has taken him!" shouted Hanno, and ran towards the crowd, wildly throwing his arms. "Let us die with him!"

He grasped for his priest's knife. It had fallen from his belt. He beat his breast, and fell in convulsions to the earth. Some of the people fainted with fright. Others covered their heads with their mantles, as if to shut out some stupendous apparition.

At this terrible moment a new portent occurred. The colossal image of Baal shook. Its metal folds creaked one upon another. The ground trembled as if from the convulsion of some subterranean spirit. The idol tottered, and fell half-way to the earth. The priests, wild with terror, ran shrieking into the crowd. Panic seized the multitude, who trod upon one another in their haste to get away from the dread proximity. Many were maimed as they fell among the great stones of the old ruin that covered the ground, and some were crushed beneath the trampling feet, or smothered under the accumulated mass of helpless humanity piled above them. Only when they had reached a distance did the fleeing men pause to look back.

Egbalus alone remained near the pavilion. He seemed to have been transformed into a statue. At length he moved, not to follow the awe-stricken fugitives, but to enter the pavilion! Such halting steps did he take that one might have imagined him drawn by some invisible power which he was trying to resist.

"The god has taken the high priest also!" cried Hanno, who had recovered sufficient self-possession to raise his head and look; but, horror-stricken by the sight, he buried his face in the dust.

A venerable priest advanced from the cowering throng midway the open space, and raised his knife with a loud cry:

"I, too, would come to thee, O Baal!"

He plunged the gleaming blade into his own heart. Scores of knives flashed in the hands of the demented priests about him, as if they, also, were waiting the audible summons to follow.

Suddenly Egbalus reappeared. He beckoned those nearest. He called for Hanno, but the new enthusiasm had proved too much for the neophyte, untrained to such deep emotions, and he lay a heaving heap of unconscious devotion. Egbalus selected two attendants, and with them re-entered the Holy Place. Would the god have more? No; Baal was satisfied; for, see! the three priests emerge, not one of them blasted to a walking cinder, nor ascending in a flame of fire. They talked excitedly. Egbalus lifted his hand.

Suddenly the long blare of a trumpet announced

the termination of the sacrifice. The crowds were not allowed to re-enter the enclosure, but betook themselves, some to Tyre or to their ships, some over the hills to the inland villages, others along the coast—on foot, in litters, on mules and camels and stately steeds—all scattering, to astound the world with their reports of the miracle.

The setting sun flashed its red rays upon the leaning figure of Baal, that seemed to bow in obeisance to the god of day. Only the priests remained to watch until Astarte, smiling in the crescent moon, wrote her benediction with the silvery beams she threw over the scene.

CHAPTER XI

HAD King Hiram vanished into the mystery of Baal? No. He had vanished under a mystery of Hanno.

When Hiram entered the sacred pavilion the place was exceedingly dark by reason of the heavy curtains that enclosed it, and the glare of the outer light that he had just left, for the instant, prevented his eyes from adapting themselves to their new environment. By degrees his power of vision was regained. He observed that the tapestried walls were wrought with the various symbols of worship; the sun of Baal, the moon of Astarte, the fish of Dagon, the star of Adonis, and the like. Beneath his feet lay a rug of silken shreds, pure white. He threw himself down upon this to collect his thoughts; to gather up his strength for the final act in this terrible tragedy. Surely Hanno's hopeful words had been merely to cheer him; they meant nothing, or his friend's plans for his rescue had miscarried. There was now no escape.

He prayed: to whom? He knew not; but still he prayed. For what? Not for himself; it was too late for that. He prayed for Hanno; that, in

the desperation of his love, he might not attempt
to make good his pledge of dying with his king;
that he might be restrained from making a useless
assault upon the priests, or from throwing himself
into the flames. Then he prayed for her who was
more to him than life—for Zillah. He gathered up
his whole soul in a loving thought of her, and laid
it—where? Upon the highest altar in the highest
heavens, if there were any such place where pity
for mortals existed. Then, as the sweet face of
his beloved one filled his imagination, a tear fell—
the first during all these days of agony; for the
bodily humors seemed to have been dried by the
hot fury of his grief. The tear fell upon his hand.
He bowed to kiss it, because it fell for her. As he
did so, his eye caught a spot of gleaming red in the
white rug. Mechanically, without definite purpose
in doing so, he traced the red line as it ran through
the silken nap. It took shape. A wing!—and a
circle! It was only a half-conscious thought—
"The Winged Circle," such as was used as a religious device by the Persians, and was also carved
on the stone architraves of some temples of Astarte.
Then the full thought flashed upon him, "The mark
of the circle!" Hanno's sign! Was it designed?

He raised the rug. A similar mark was rudely
scratched upon a broad stone that lay just beneath
it. He felt the edge of the stone. It moved. A
tilting stone! He lifted it a little. A cool and
dank air rushed out. This, surely, was a door into
some passage! By a little exertion he was able to

swing the stone upon its edge. Adjusting the rug
over it in such a way that it would again cover the
stone when restored to its horizontal position, he
let himself carefully down through the opening.
So strong was the draught of air that he scarcely
needed to feel his way by touching the wall on either
side, but guided himself very much as he had sometimes done when, on a dark night at sea, he helmed
his ship by feeling the wind against his cheek.

He thought of this just for an instant, but it was
long enough to think of Hanno too, as, in their
last sail, they had steered the craft together. He
could not restrain a subdued cry of gratitude.

"Noble fellow! Thy hand is on the other oar,
as thou didst pledge. Thou art the only god that
is left to me!"

For a little way he crawled over and around the
débris that obstructed the labyrinth. Then he
felt the space enlarging. A smooth pavement was
beneath him. With extended hands he hurried
forward. He heard the roar of fire, and knew that
he was passing near to the pit beneath the image
of Baal. A hot gleam shot through a crevice. It
revealed a door of bronze covering an old entrance
into the pit, through which anciently the priests had
been accustomed to feed the flames. The door
moved as he touched its hot surface. He opened
it a little, that the light might illumine the passage.
In the glare he saw several stout pieces of timber
standing upright. These had been recently put in
to brace the great idol, the foundation of which

had given way on that side. Hiram took this in at
a glance—he had time only for a glance, for the
flames burst forth upon him and drove him away
before he could close the door. The fire caught
the timbers, and, a little later, consuming them,
toppled the image above. But of this he knew
nothing, as, taking advantage of the light, he
plunged on through several hundred cubits of open
way.

The passage he had followed ended in a small
chamber into which struggled a ray of daylight.
Here lay a coarse skull-cap of leather and a ragged
chiton—a mere bag with holes at the bottom for
the head and arms, the only garment worn by the
poorest herdsmen. By the side of it was a club of
heavy wood, knobbed with great spikes at one end
—the ordinary weapon with which the herdsman de-
fended himself and his flocks from prowling beasts.
A little wallet contained dried dates and thin cakes
of black bread : another was filled with small coins.

To divest himself of his princely clothing, don
the chiton, and tie the bags about his waist beneath
it, was the task of a moment. Then on he went,
working his way like a mole between the great
stones that, in confused ruin, would have blocked
his progress, had he not been guided by his faith
in the prevision of his friend Hanno.

Gradually the air became purer. It revived his
strength and courage. Light came in through an
opening which was screened heavily by a clump of
bushes beyond it. These guarded the northern

end of the passage from the inspection of any
one without. Crawling through a crevice in the
rock, he emerged cautiously, concealing himself
amid the dense foliage. The bushes grew in a
little cleared space about which were piles of
stone, which had anciently walled a portion of the
temple. He crawled like a lizard to the top of the
stones and raised his head. He was far beyond
the crowd, whose faces were all turned in the opposite direction, watching with absorbed attention
for his reappearance from the sacred pavilion.
Over the stillness he heard distinctly the shrill
voice of Egbalus, as it cried, " Come forth, thou
accepted of Baal!" His impulse for flight was
checked by tragic curiosity. The contagion of the
general excitement caught him and held him almost spellbound. Danger always had for him a
fascination; at this moment he felt it reinforced
by a sudden passion for revenge. Why not join
the crowd, work his way through it, dash into the
cleared space, smite the high priest to the earth,
and hurl his hated carcass into the flames? What
if the priests then cut him into ten thousand
pieces? It would be worth dying for. Why not
be a Theseus to his people, and slay the Minotaur
in the person of its most devilish representative?
His brain reeled with the thought.

A wild cry of the multitude recalled him to his
more cautious judgment. The people surged back.
The great image toppled. Ah! how grimly he
guessed the reason !

The crowd turned in his direction. Was it in flight? or had he been pointed out, and were they cutting off his escape? He griped his club to brain the first who should climb the stone heap behind which he had taken refuge. As some came near he noted their terror-stricken faces, and knew that they were not seeking him in this direction, but fleeing from him yonder where he was a superstitious embodiment of their fears. Then a fiendish humor came upon him. He took the dirty cap from his head, and, bowing towards the distant figure of Egbalus, said:

"I obey, O priest of Baal! Lo, I have come forth!"

He climbed down the farther side of the pile of ruins; paused a moment to rub handfuls of dirt over his hair and face, his clean-skinned legs and feet; then, swinging his herdsman's club, he ran away, outstripping the most cowardly fugitive from the dread scene.

He looked for no new mark of the circle, for the country was well known to him. Often had he dashed over these fields on his horse after the fox. Here, as a boy, he had practised the sling at the running jackals. Yonder lay the road to Sidon, over which, in princely company, he had gone to discharge some duty of state, or more frequently to join in aristocratic revelry with the young nabobs who lived in the favor of Prince Esmanazar. This road he dared not take.

To the east rose the mountains that walled so

narrowly the plain to the sea. In them were hiding-places, but they would be speedily searched.

Beyond the first range, between the Lebanons, a broad valley was open to the north, but that was a highway of traffic. The caravans were passing up and down it. He could not trust himself there, for in every company would be some one whose eyes were sharpened by the hope of reward for his capture.

Galilee was not far away, populated by a mongrel people, composed of the relic of ancient Jewish stock and the colonists who had come from Babylon. To the south was Samaria, and beyond, the land of Judea, her tribes long ago carried away by Nebuchadnezzar, but now returning to fortify again the heights of Jerusalem.

Westward shone the Great Sea, glowing with prismatic colors under the brush of the setting sun. Once upon the sea, he might be safe. But the road that lined the coast would be crowded with those returning on foot or in chariots from Tyre to Sidon. If he could pass them, how could he procure a ship? His present garb would awaken suspicion, if he even talked with any of such a purpose.

Oh, for another mark of the circle! But there was none in the sand that burned his naked feet, and none in the sky, now fiery as with the wrath of the outwitted sun-god.

On he went, scarcely thinking whither, except that the sort of instinct which leads wild animals, when pursued, to double on their tracks, prompted him to turn, making a detour to the east to avoid the scattering crowds; then working his way south, for the first pursuit of him was sure to be north, in the direction of his escape.

South of Old Tyre ran for miles a ruined aqueduct terminating in a reservoir. All the conduits of the latter he knew well, having but recently spent a day in company with an engineer exploring it, with a view of utilizing it in increasing the water supply of Tyre. Here he could be safe until the night darkness threw about him its all-covering shield.

His determination to hide was confirmed by observing two Galli at a distance. They evidently had him in their eyes, for, though their road was different, they kept coming near, as if by subtle purpose. He raised his club, and, balancing it carefully, flung it far in the opposite direction, accompanying its flight with the cry of the shepherds when frightening a jackal. He ran at topmost speed after the missile. As he stooped to pick it up he noted that the Galli had turned back. He was safe from them, but would be safer if he learned the lesson, and made himself invisible. The old aqueduct might become his fortress. Peering out between its disjointed stones, he could inspect the field, and at any moment drop into a conduit and make his exit far beyond.

Night fell about him. Its shadows winged his feet, and its cool, crisp air freshened his vigor as he ran.

In the thickening darkness, a huge object loomed suddenly before him. Startled for an instant, he paused, but a second careful look enabled him to recognize it. It was the tomb of Hiram, his great ancestor, the most famous of all the kings of Tyre. Five centuries had drifted over it, wearing away the very stone as by the friction of the years, but only brightening the fame of him who lay within it.

If the living cherish the memory of the dead, do the dead have no interest in the living? It seemed to the young king as if the very dust within that great stone box must move with pity for him. Would the great king curse him for refusing to become a sacrifice to Baal for the welfare of Tyre? The mighty dead had been a worshipper of the gods of his people, but surely not with such cruel and bigoted frenzy as that of the priests now. The great Hiram had been the friend of the Judean kings, David and Solomon. He had built for them the temple of their God, Jehovah, though the Jews believed in no blood-loving Moloch; nay, they cursed the abominations of the Phœnician worship, as they cursed the other idols of the nations, and swept them from their land. Surely Hiram the Great would be a liberal monarch, were he living. A blessing seemed to drop into the young Hiram's soul from the white form of the marble, that clearcut its shape out of the black night.

He climbed the lofty pedestal, and stood beside the upper shaft. It was but a moment he lingered, yet time seemed to halt, while the olden ages came back and passed in review before him, all grand with Phœnicia's prowess, since first his people taught the nations the alphabet, and pioneered the commerce of the world. Dark clouds came up on the horizon, and blotted out the bright early stars; and so, he thought, death's oblivion had buried one by one his ancestors, the kings of Tyre; yet their glory was untarnished, even as these stars will shine out again, and shine forever. But himself! Would not his flight from death blot his honorable memory in subsequent generations?

Suddenly the clouds parted, and the bright evening-star glowed in the east — the star of Astarte, Queen of Heaven, Goddess of Love. As he watched, it was again obscured. Then Hiram thought of Zillah, whose soul, purer than light, had set in his dark destiny. He clenched his hands as if to crush the edge of the stone beneath them, and swore a horrid oath, in which writhed all the black passions of his being; an oath at the star, at Astarte, at Baal, at all the powers that controlled the world, or at that blind chance that drifted its affairs. Then the star emerged again. It floated into a large lake of blue. Was it an omen? He worshipped it, and called it Zillah. He noted that it floated westward from over the Jews' land. Then he prayed:

"O spirit of Hiram, guide thy son! O spirits of David and Solomon, befriend the son of Hiram! O Jehovah, God of Israel, give me welcome to thy land!"

A wind stirred the dry grass that grew about the tomb. He leaped from the pedestal and ran. Turn-

7

ing from the highway, he threaded a path up a deep ravine. Moloch's fierce beams had drained its brook nearly dry; but in pools he found enough of tepid water to slake his burning thirst, and to wash away some of the heat of his throbbing temples.

Then on! He climbed the bank, that he might straighten his course. He passed a cave. Although he could see nothing within its dark opening, he knew that its walls were carved with symbols of the Egyptian religion, made during the passage of the army of a Pharaoh many centuries before. He prayed to all the gods of Egypt, if any might perchance be sojourning or travelling near. He knew that he believed in none, but, in his extremity, did not dare to admit his incredulity, lest peradventure they might be real; and he needed even the shadows to help him now.

Then on! A moment he stopped to placate with gentle tones a dog startled from sleep beside a shepherd guarding his flock. Again he turned far aside from the path, that he might avoid a tent whose lamp, burning all night, told that all its inmates were living. Inadvertently he came close to a hut shrouded in darkness, from which he was warned by the voices of wailing. He had no sympathy for such bereavement, since Nature, more kindly than men, had only exacted her due, and no horrid idol of Baal stood before the door.

The night seemed interminable, so many terrors massed before him, through which he must cut his way with naked soul. For men and beasts he had begun to lose fear, when suddenly a new menace appeared. The earth seemed to open before him. He descended a step or two cautiously. The ground was hot, and burned his bare feet. Strange! for the night air had chilled all else. The earth was hard and sharp, like the refuse heap near some factory of bronze. Chinks opened. Fire gleamed. Strangling gases were emitted. Had Moloch stirred up the gates of hell to join in pursuit of him? There came a roar not unlike that he had heard when passing the fire-vault of the idol, but deeper and more vengeful. The earth trembled. Great stones rolled down the sides of a precipitous bank, and with them he was hurled headlong. Whither?

"Moloch! Mercy!" was his cry.

Then all was dark.

CHAPTER XII.

A PLEASING light shone through the darkness of that nether world into which Hiram had been so suddenly precipitated. The light was broken by soft shadows, as of gently fluttering leaves. The brightness made his eyeballs ache; the shadows soothed them, so that he could endure to look. Great protecting arms were stretched above him. These assumed the shapes of limbs of a terebinth-tree. Had he passed through the gloom of Sheol into some brighter realm of life? Perhaps the Greeks were right in their hope of the Isles of the Blessed, carpeted with perpetual verdure, gemmed with flowers, and canopied with softest skies. To one of these isles had his spirit floated? This could not be, for over him he clearly saw a dead branch of the terebinth, and there could be no decay in that happy world.

His illusions chased one another away, and were all gone when, attempting to move, sharp pains tortured him, and inflicted him with full consciousness that he was indeed in the body. He was lying upon a couch, soft with feathery balsam tips, and covered with a wolf's skin. This he could feel

beneath his hands. He glanced about him. A low,
but long and rambling, black tent of goat's-hair
cloth stood by, its nearest end just at the edge
of the shadow of the terebinth. The tent poles
and cross ropes were so arranged as to form a
roof of three gables, answering to the interior di-
vision into three compartments. Several rude but
substantially built huts were evidently used for stor-
ing provisions. A stone enclosure served as a fold
for sheep. Without these evidences of more permanent occupation, the tent would have indicated a
settlement of those nomads who, with hereditary
roving habits, have always lodged in the lands east
of the Great Sea ; or of those inhabitants of towns
who adopt this mode of life during a portion of the
year, that they may live among their flocks and
herds on the mountain slopes, or cultivate a tract
of rich meadow-land far away from their ordinary
abodes.

Hiram had scarcely taken in so much of his surroundings, when he was aware that a light form
moved suddenly and silently away from his side.
He caught a glimpse of a white garment—the common dress of both sexes alike among the simple
peasants. Had his observation been more alert,
he would have detected a pair of most gracefully
modelled feet, and limbs bare almost to the knees ;
a head uncovered, except for the rich mass of jet-
black hair that was gathered loosely into a node at
the back ; a face of exquisite contour, swarthy from
exposure, but radiant with health and kindliness.

" Father, he has waked !" rang out a sweet child-voice. And Hiram heard it add, subdued by distance and anxious emotion :

"Father ! He will live again, will he not ?"

A voice, strong and deep, but kindly even to tenderness, responded :

" Jehovah be praised ! I will come."

A heavily built man approached the couch under the terebinth. He was slightly bowed with the years that had chronicled themselves by the gray lines in the long beard which fell far down upon his bare breast. His legs and arms were uncovered, and showed that strength had not deserted the slightly shrunken muscles. His face, though weather-beaten and wrinkled with cares as with years, was a beautiful one, beaming with intelligence and soulfulness ; one of those rare faces that fascinate children, but can command men—such is the combination of affection and dignity they reflect from the abiding disposition behind them. His eyes were deep-set beneath heavy brows, and seemed the home of lofty and generous sentiments, suggesting those crystal springs in shady dells which good spirits have always been traditioned to inhabit.

" The Lord be with you, my son !" was the old man's hearty salutation, as he came and looked down upon the stranger.

" Are you not able to talk ?" he kindly inquired, noticing that Hiram made no response, and unwilling to think his silence discourtesy, as it would have been regarded had the one addressed been fully himself.

Hiram stared at the face of the old man, in painful effort at recollection both of the questioner and of himself.

"Where am I?" he inquired, endeavoring to raise himself upon his elbow.

"Nay, be quiet, my son!" replied the other, laying him gently back upon the couch. "It is enough for this day that you know you are safe, and under the roof-tree of Ben Yusef."

"Ben Yusef? I do not know you." Hiram gazed intently at him, as if to replenish from the intelligent face his own vanished power of thought.

"Ay, Ben Yusef, of the tribe of Judah. You are, indeed, a stranger, not to know the tent of Ben Yusef, of Giscala."

"Giscala? In the Jews' land?"

"Ay, and in Galilee. You must have been badly hurt for so shapely a head as yours to have been knocked out of its whereabouts. I had thought Ben Yusef's tent as well known as yonder rocky pinnacle of Safed, which guides travellers from afar. But who are you, my son?"

Hiram glanced at his own herdsman's clothes. He felt the coarse texture. A tremor shook him, as if from the passing of some horrid dream. He replied:

"I am what you see me."

"Nay, my son, thou shalt not bear false witness, even of thyself," replied Ben Yusef. "A shepherd's feet are not so easily torn as yours have been. Your hair has the odor of ointments that are not of the cattle-pens, and your hands are not hard in the spots where the sling-strings cut. Besides, no sheep would have been so silly as to venture into the crater of Giscala for you to seek them there. The dumb beasts have fled from it for weeks past. The volcano is getting ready to break out again, and the lightest-headed bird will not even fly over it. Only a man driven by some demon to seek death would have plunged into it as you did. Besides, your speech is not that of the herdsmen; nor, for that matter, of any dwellers in the country about. It is that of the men of the coast. Though we use the same tongue, there is as much difference between our accents as there is difference between the grass that grows on these spring-fed meadows and that of the salt marshes by the sea."

Hiram showed evident alarm at these suspicions, and made an effort to rise, that he might venture another flight. The old man gently, yet strongly, restrained him, and placed his head again upon the bolster as he added, kindly:

"Nay, then, do not speak if the truth is not for my ears. Ben Yusef's tree is broad enough to shadow both you and your secret."

"But I must not burden your hospitality," said Hiram.

Ben Yusef knit his brows in evident displeasure, but quickly rejoined, with a smile:

"You shall not burden, but bless me, my son.

Our patriarch Job said, 'The blessing of him that
was ready to perish came upon me.' And never
saw I man that was nearer perishing than you."

The old man raised his eyes reverently to heaven as he added :

"The Lord deal with me and mine as I deal
with this stranger !"

It was the merriest of voices that interrupted
this conversation :

"Abba !"

The syllables flowed with all the sweetness of
bird notes, charged with the tenderness and fulness of human love.

"Abba ! Abba !"

"Yes, my child."

"Shall I bring the drink ?"

"Bring it."

The girl balanced a large jar upon her left hand,
supporting it by the graceful shaft of her forearm,
which in turn rested upon her right hand. The
weight of the jar brought the muscles of her arms
into graceful prominence, and her easy motion betokened that agile strength which is seldom displayed except by those whose freedom of life, as
among peasants of mountain regions, makes work
easy and exhilarating.

"The *leben* is all of the big goat's milk, and, with
the leaven in it since yesternight, should be strong
and quickening. Shall I give the drink ?"

"No, my child. Haste with the supper. Elnathan will soon be in from the fields, and as hungry as Esau. Haste, and the memory of thy mother bless thee !"

As Ben Yusef watched his daughter retiring to the tent, a lusty halloo rang through the air, and a form appeared upon the hill-top. It seemed gigantic, so large a portion did it cut from the glowing western sky beyond; and, though it diminished as it approached, it still showed a strong, thick-set, over-tall fellow, in the first flush of manhood, the down on his chin hardly consistent with the gnarled muscles upon his legs and arms. He came at once to where Hiram lay, and accosted him with a good-natured familiarity which, though rough, did not conceal the essence of gentility that lay beneath it. He took Hiram's hand into his own, and pressed it as if feeling for the fitful pulse.

"I knew you would come to life rapidly when once you started. Judging from your running last night, you have wind enough to outstrip the death angel. I was yonder, watching the crater, when you dashed by me. You made a streak of light through the darkness as a flitting ghost does. I thought you must be Elijah, showing the other prophets how he ran when Jezebel and the priests of Baal were after him; and I believe you would not have stopped short of Beersheba if you had not tumbled into the crater. Couldn't you see it, or smell it, or feel it? Perhaps you had drunk too much leben among the sheep-boys in the mountains. They make it there strong enough to whirl a man's head off; but I never knew it to make one's legs fly as yours did."

" Hush, Elnathan !" interrupted the old man. " Your tongue runs faster than our guest's legs ever did, and makes as great blunders. What news from the mouth of Sheol, for the brimstone on your garments tells you have been there ?"

" The volcano has been less active to-day, father ; but neighbors Isaac and Hosea both think it will break out anew. They remember how it was years ago. The big mound is like the whale with Jonah in his belly. It only wants a little more tickling with the fire to vomit forth."

" Have you watched it all day ?"

" No. As this poor fellow could not tell us what he was running from, I have been searching back on the path he came ; but I can find nothing to harm one." He lowered his voice. " The fellow must have been crazed. No sane man would put that dirty shirt over so trim a body, or wear his hair, which is curled like that of a gallant from Tyre, under the filthy cap I found by him. I think he is from Tyre. They were to have had a great sacrifice—some say of the king himself. This man looks like some courtier who has gone daft with excitement. He surely thought the volcano fire was under some sacrifice to Moloch, for I heard him cry, as he fell, ' Moloch ! Mercy !' "

" Do not breathe that thought, Elnathan," said Ben Yusef. " He is to us only what he seems. The Lord has been merciful to him. In Israel's land his secret belongs only to himself and our God. I charge you, Elnathan, by the Lord God of Abraham, who spared Isaac on Moriah, that you speak not your thought."

The night grew chill. Ben Yusef and his son carried the couch and the sick man under the shelter of the tent. Hiram was exhausted by his excited wakefulness, and soon fell into a slumber, during which the little household partook of their evening meal.

When he awoke he was conscious of the presence of the young girl alone, who sat under the lamp that hung at the doorway of the tent, and who answered his every movement with a look towards him. Ben Yusef and Elnathan sat without. A neighbor joined them. As he was approaching the tent, Hiram heard the father enjoin his son to make no mention of their stranger guest.

" He does not come to us as the angels came to Father Abraham at his tent door," said Elnathan.

" Who knows what form angels take ?" replied the elder. " The angels came to Abraham's tent hungry and thirsty ; why should not one come to us as a sick and wounded man ?"

" From the way the volcano is acting," said Elnathan, pausing to listen to the rumbling earth, " I think he has come as the angels came to Lot in Sodom before the Lord destroyed that place with fire and brimstone. Maybe our guest will startle us before morning with the cry, ' Flee to the mountain !' "

They rose and welcomed their neighbor, with whom they conversed until late in the night, for the imminence of danger from the volcano suggested watchfulness.

CHAPTER XIII

FROM the conversation that Hiram overheard, supplemented by after-information, he learned much of the family history of his benefactor.

Ben Yusef's father had belonged to one of the captive families in Babylon, who, taking advantage of the decree of Cyrus, had returned with Zerubbabel to their ancestral land. Ben Yusef himself was born in Jerusalem; and, though he deemed himself a faithful Jew, had not chosen to resist the charms of a Samaritan maiden, a descendant of the colonists whom Nebuchadnezzar had sent from Hamath to repopulate the land made desolate by the deportation of the people of Israel. When Ezra, the Great Scribe, arrived at Jerusalem with his new bands of devotees, and endeavored to enforce his mandate against marriage with any not of pure Jewish stock, Yusef had opposed him, feeling at first that this was but a device by which the newly arrived would override the descendants of those who had originally returned with Zerubbabel. Though afterwards he became convinced of the honesty of Ezra's purpose, and of the sincerity of his patriotism in wishing to purge Judaism of all

elements foreign to it, he could not believe, as many
did, in the Great Scribe's inspired wisdom in this
regard.   So pure and strong was Ben Yusef's love
for Lyda, his wife, so beautiful was she in character, so true even in her devotion to Israel's god,
and so many blessings had she brought to him,
that he could not expel the belief that Jehovah had
indeed favored their union.   To accede to Ezra's
demand that he should divorce Lyda, or by any
compact separate from her, seemed like striking
the hands which God had extended in benediction
upon them both.   Lyda was not a concubine, as Ha-
gar had been to Abraham.   He therefore would
not send her away, but chose rather to go with
her when she was expelled from the gates of the
city.

But still Ben Yusef was a Jew.   He loved the
traditions and shared the hopes of his people.   He
therefore would not leave the Sacred Land, but
took up his abode in the far northern portion of it,
among the Scythian colonists whom Nebuchadnezzar had settled there.   He built no house for permanent abode, because he believed that the time
would come when he should return to Jerusalem.

Lyda had died.   His first mourning over, he proposed to return to the capital, but was confronted
by the fact that her children would be counted as
of impure blood by the aristocratic and stricter
caste of Jews.   He would not subject them to such
disparagement, and therefore unpacked his already
laden beasts of burden, drove again his stakes, and

stretched his cords. The very names of his children were intended to be a protest against what he
thought to be the narrowness of the Jewish rulers.
" Elnathan " signified " Given of God," and when
the little maiden came he called her " Ruth," after
the famous Moabitish woman, whom the faithful
Jewish Boaz wedded and made the ancestress of
King David.

But no quarrel with the rulers at Jerusalem could
alienate his patriotism or dim his larger hope in the
coming glory of his people. His soul thrilled with
all the good news of prosperity in the sacred city.
He sent his contributions regularly for the temple
service, and, when able, made his pilgrimage "thrice
in the year " to the festivals. When, some twelve
years before the date of our story, Nehemiah had
come from Susa to assist in rebuilding the temple and the walls, Ben Yusef had met him on the
way; indeed, had entertained the new governor as
loyally as his purse and peasant habits made possible. This act had cost him much of the good-
will of his half-heathen neighbors, and forced him
to a more isolated life than before ; for he was now
looked upon as neither Jew nor Gentile.

As Hiram caught partial information of what the
reader now knows more fully, he felt that Ben Yusef
was a man who might understand and sympathize
with him in his expatriation, and consequently rested more complacently. Yet he was persuaded that
it would be wise voluntarily to divulge his terrible
secret to no one. If it were discovered, it would

be time enough to acknowledge it, and claim the kinship which common persecution had made between him and his host.

The night passed in safety. The volcanic activity vented itself beneath the ground, which trembled as if ten thousand chariots were driven over it.

Strength came rapidly to the wounded man. He had prayed to Jehovah, and an answer came either directly from the " God of the land " or indirectly through the invigorating atmosphere of this hill-country; and was not Jehovah the " God of the Hills?" Surely Hiram had heard Ben Yusef singing a psalm of worship as the morning dawned: " I will lift up mine eyes unto the hills, whence cometh my help!"

Ben Yusef again and again indulged his curiosity in such questions of his guest as his sense of hospitality allowed. These Hiram cautiously answered. He admitted that he was from the coast; that he was in disguise and flight because of dissent from the doctrines of the Baalitish religion; that he had voluntarily reduced himself to the humble condition of a herdsman, rather than endure the degradation of his conscience.

To all this Ben Yusef responded with lofty and generous emotion. He eloquently told the story of ancient Israel; of the grand historic triumphs of Jehovah among his chosen people; of the great patriarchs; of the birth of his nation when, under Moses, the people had fled from Egypt; of the valor of the Judges; of the glory of the Kings; of

the sins of the people in admitting Baalitish customs; of the Lord's heavy curse in selling the nation into captivity to Babylon; and of the return
under permission of the Persians, the new masters
of the world. He spoke, too, with prophetic rapt-
ure of the day that was sure to come, when a new
King, greater than Solomon, the Lord's own gift
to his people, would spread the nation from the
Euphrates to the Great Sea; or, as their psalm had
it, "from the river to the ends of the earth." The
venerable man's face shone as he enlarged even
that vision, and spoke of peace and righteousness
filling all lands—even the fields breaking forth into
singing.

The substance of this story of the Jews' land and
people Hiram had heard before; but the old man's
ardor impressed it with such vividness that the listener seemed to see the unrolling scroll of history
merging into prophecy, and could not repress a feeling of the enthusiasm which the speaker conveyed
with his words, his gestures, and his looks.

Two days passed. Hiram had recovered from
the weakness, which came more from the shock of
his emotions than from actual bruises. Ben Yusef
read the thoughts of his guest as he would now
and then suddenly start at some unusual sound, or
hide within the inner room of the tent at the
approach of any neighbor. His observant host
guessed that the patient would be freer of heart
if the day could be spent away from the possibility
of meeting with men.

8

Hiram, therefore, as strength returned, eagerly accepted the proposal to accompany Ben Yusef in searching for some stray sheep upon the mountains. The bracing air and the exhilarating views tempted them on. They climbed the grand pinnacle of Safed. Here, nearly two thousand cubits towards the heavens, no one could follow without being observed. On the summit the old Jew gave wings to his memory and faith, as free and strong as the wings of the eagle that started from its eyrie on the crag. There, to the north, were the waters of Merom, by the shore of which Joshua smote Jabin, King of Hazor. There, to the south, stood Tabor, from behind which Deborah, the prophetess, with Barak for her captain, had deployed against Sisera, when the very stars swung from their courses, and beat the enemy with their baleful omens. Yonder, to the east, rose Carmel, a mighty altar of the Hebrew's faith, where Elijah had drawn fire from heaven to shame the priests of Baal. And there, far beyond, gleamed the waters of the Great Sea, making indentations upon the coast, but beaten back by the great docks of Tyre and Sidon, as Baalism washed away at times the true religion of Israel, but was beaten back by the valor and enterprise of God's true people. Down there, almost beneath their feet, shone the pearly surface of the inland Sea of Galilee, over which hung splendid prophecies yet to be fulfilled; for the great Isaiah had declared, "The land of Zabulon, and the land of Nephthalim, by the way of the sea, beyond Jordan, in Gal-

ilee of the nations. The people that walked in darkness have seen a great light : they that dwell in the
land of the shadow of death, upon them hath the
light shined.''

The old man's purpose had been, at first, only
the diversion of the thoughts of his companion,
for he feared that his recent experience, whatever
it had been, had really affected his mind. But as
he spoke he became himself carried away with his
theme. Hiram easily encouraged him to continue,
and by his appreciative questions led him to speak
of the higher spiritual truths of the Jews' religion.
What he said of the human sacrifices especially
interested his hearer.

"Our father Abraham, living among those who
offered their children to the deity, was once allowed
by the Lord to think that he, too, must offer his son.
To the rocky dome of Mount Moriah he led his beloved Isaac ; bound him upon an altar ; raised the
knife to slay him ; when the Lord's voice cried to
him out of heaven, ' Lay not thine hand upon the
lad ;' and, turning quickly, the trembling father saw
a ram caught by the horns in a thicket, and offered
it instead of his son. That rock is now the base
of the great altar in the temple court at Jerusalem.
All our worship means this — the Lord God is a
Father. He wants no suffering sacrifice among
men. If sin needs atonement, God's own gracious
heart will make it. He wants only man's contri-
tion and love. The Lord is my helper ; not my
hater. The Jews' sacrifice really means that there

is no need of sacrifice, except what Heaven itself shall provide. It is an offering in gratitude, not in penalty; an offering to praise, not to appease, the Judge of all the earth."

Ben Yusef's face beamed with an almost unearthly beauty as he spoke. His voice trembled, but was sweetened, too, by the great depth of his emotion. He uttered no formality of faith. His words were no echo of men's thoughts. They had, as it seemed to Hiram, a double source of suggestion—from heaven above, and from the profound experience of the man's own soul.

Hiram could not help contrasting this peasant with the great Herodotus. The Jew's philosophy seemed deeper than the Greek's. And it was not only philosophy, but an inner life, a feeling, a knowledge. The Greek had pushed away some shadows; the Jew stood out in the light. The Greek's thoughts were formed with beauty, as his statues were carved from the stone; the Jew's thoughts were immense, and untrimmed by human art, like the rocky pinnacle of Safed upon which they stood.

CHAPTER XIV.

TOWARDS nightfall they descended the mountain, and were nearing the home tent.

"Listen!" said the old man, putting his hand upon the shoulder of his comrade. "That is the very soul of our religion—a song in the heart that sends a song to the lips, as the fountain comes bubbling from the full veins in the earth."

A sweet, strong voice rang up through the ravine, to the top of which they had come. Ben Yusef's eyes filled with tears. "So like her mother's voice," he said.

It was Ruth who was singing:

"Jehovah's my Shepherd; I'll not want.
In pastures green he makes me lie,
By restful waters leadeth."

Before the girl stalked a great dog, large enough to tear a wolf. He pricked up his ears, stopped, threw back his head, then with a bound broke through the bushes and climbed the shaly bank to where his master and Hiram were standing. Ruth followed as nimbly as a goat.

"You will be so glad," said she to Hiram, "for somebody who knows you has found you. He described you exactly in face, and said you spoke the tongue of Tyre. He would not have me come to meet you, and when I started followed close behind, until Anax got between us. The dog sat right down before him, and showed his great teeth if the man moved a step."

Ben Yusef glanced quickly at Hiram, asking with his eyes a score of questions without the need of a word.

"Yes," replied Hiram, "I must fly at once. Only shield me by your discretion, as you have by your hospitality."

"You shall not fly from the tent of Ben Yusef," said the old man, with protesting vehemence. "My life will shield you, and, if the danger be great, in an hour Elnathan can summon a score of our neighbors. We have learned, in these troublous times, to combine for mutual protection. One bugle-call over these hills, and, as the stars come out one by one, but before you can count them all are there, so man after man, with ready weapon, will move out from the darkness and surround my tent. And woe to the intruder who cannot give our shibboleth."

"I cannot accept the protection of such brave men, nor yours, since it would surely be revenged by fiends who work in the dark, and who are relentless in their hatred. Let me fly while I may endanger only myself!" said Hiram, gratefully grasping Ben Yusef's hand.

"Wait at least until the night blackens. Secrete yourself anywhere. Elnathan will find you. You

will know of his approach by the hoot of the owl he
has learned to imitate. You may need his knowledge of by-paths. But, above all, in the land of
Israel trust in Israel's God. He has said, 'Thou
shalt not be afraid for the terror by night, nor for
the arrow that flieth by noonday.' 'He that keep-
eth Israel neither slumbers nor sleeps.' Farewell
until brighter days !"

Night fell too rapidly for Hiram to get far away.
Nor was there need, for the base of the mountain
had been torn by earthquake and freshet into a
hundred hiding-places. The chief danger was from
wild beasts rather than from men. He chose a
deep cleft which he observed to have a double
opening, from either of which he could depart if
the other were menaced. He had not waited long
before the hoot of an owl sounded.

" Amazingly natural !" thought Hiram. He had
once prided himself upon his powers of mimicry,
and now he would essay a trial of skill with Elnathan.

" Too-whoo ! too-whoo !" he echoed back.

" Too-whoo !" rang out from a crag quite distant.
A moment later it came again, but this time from
another direction. Then from another.

" The peasant is more deeply learned in bird-
speech than I," mused the listener. " He throws
his voice from cliff to crag, from ravine to tree-top."

Hiram ventured another call. Scarcely had the
sound escaped his lips when the air hummed; a
pair of dusky wings whirred close to his head, and

a black object settled on the edge of the rock above him.

"I did it well," he congratulated himself, "to have brought the bird to me as a mate. Welcome to my nest, Sir Owl, for I think you are a restless soul like myself."

The bird flew away. But other companionship came. A rattling of stones down the ravine told of some one's approach. Hiram's success with the former hoot emboldened him to challenge Elnathan again.

"Too-whoo!" rang and re-echoed.

"But what a shriek!" said a voice not far distant. "I have heard that the owls in these mountains are the ghosts of dead Jews let out of Sheol for a night airing."

"I can believe it, and that they are all damned ghosts, too, if that owl's voice shows his feeling," rejoined another.

The stones rattled again.

"The curse of Baal-Hermon on the traitor's head for leading us on such a road as this," said one who had evidently stumbled and fallen among the rocks.

"Call on some other god, for the mountain god must have spent all his curses in making such a land as this. Try Beelzebub, the god of flies, for it would take a gnat to find the king in these narrow paths, branching everywhere. But I don't believe he went this way. The girl gave him warning. He has gone back, or taken the road to Hazor, and will make for Kadesh and Baal-Gad, and

across the spur of Hermon to the highway for Damascus. We will do better to follow that. The
addle-headed lout at the tent said that was the way
most open, and he must have told the king the same,
for he hadn't wit enough to invent two ideas."

"But we cannot find that path ; at least not until
the moon rises. Let us wait here."

The two men sat down close to one of the open-
ings of Hiram's retreat.

"The sacrifice should never have been at the image of Moloch. Melkarth is Lord of Tyre, and,
had it been at the temple, Melkarth would never
have allowed him to escape."

"If he did escape !" said the other.

"You doubt it, then ?" replied his comrade.

"Yes, for it cannot be proved, and the people all
believe that Baal took him."

"The people be cursed ! But the priests do not
believe it. Baal does wonders, but, so far as I have
seen, he never does wonders that the priests cannot understand. And Egbalus himself shook his
head when we asked him, and looked very wisely
as he pointed to that tilting stone."

"True !" replied the other ; "but Egbalus bade
me explore that underground passage. I did so
until I came nearly under the god, when the way
was utterly blocked. No human being could
have gone farther without being changed into a
ghost."

"If he changed to a ghost, he will change back
again ; and I think some of our knives will find

him to be as veritable flesh as ever butcher cut in the shambles. But, hist! Somebody comes."

"Too-whoo!"

"By the horns of Astarte! The owls are as big as horses here, judging from the way the sticks snap under their feet. An owl-headed man, I think. Back into the crevice!"

One of the pursuers came close to Hiram. In an instant a knife sank from the man's throat to his heart. A sharp cry was its only signal.

"What is it, comrade?" asked the other, feeling his way in to offer assistance.

Hiram, having by daylight observed the turn of the crevice, slipped out of the other opening, and, giving signal, joined Elnathan. A moment's consultation was sufficient for their plan. Each entered an opposite opening of the crevice. As the living priest confronted Hiram, Elnathan's strong fingers were upon his throat. The man struggled impotently, as a sheep might have done in the hug of a bear. They drew him into the open.

"Harm him not," cried Hiram. "He has never harmed thee. His life is mine. Know, thou villainous priest, if it will be any comfort to thee, that thou diest by the hand of thy king. And take my challenge to Moloch himself, if there be any such being in the world of the damned."

The sentence was not completed before the knife had done its double work.

Hiram in a moment recognized his own unwisdom in his hasty speech, and, turning to Elnathan, said:

" I cannot take back the words you have heard. They tell more than I should have told. But, as you saved my life once at the volcano, you can preserve it only by forgetting what you have heard. Pledge me this, as you trust your God for grace."

" Nay," said Elnathan, " I think I shall best serve you by remembering it. I could have guessed as much from what I overheard these two now dead priests say, if I had not guessed it before. The ravine beyond the tent is famous for its resounding walls. The crawl of a lizard can be heard a hundred cubits. These wretches took their supper at one end of the gorge. I was beyond the bend. They might as well have whispered into the end of a shepherd's horn. Your appearance as you lay on the cot under the terebinth, your mutterings in fevered sleep, and what these rascals said to each other, I put together into a story of the miraculous escape of King Hiram of Tyre from being burned alive to Moloch. Now, my good friend, we have no king in Israel. I swear to you, King Hiram, all the loyalty a Jew can offer to any Gentile—the loyalty of man to man. Your secret is mine, and my service is yours. So help me, God of Israel!"

Hiram was unable to respond at once to this. When he did, it was to grasp both the big hands in his own, and say : " But one other man like this lives."

" Ay, my father," said Elnathan.

" And one more," added the king.

He would have kissed the hands of Elnathan, but the noble fellow withdrew them.

The moon appeared at this instant, the leaves and limbs of the trees marking themselves in sharp and moving outlines against her huge red disk, as she shone through the mists that hung over the low-lying lands by the Sea of Galilee.

In the excitement and previous darkness, Hiram had not noticed that Elnathan was strangely transfigured. He was dressed as a Persian soldier. He wore a stiff leather hat, whose round top projected forward; a leather tunic, close-fitting, with long sleeves: leather trousers, which disappeared at the ankles within high-topped shoes. At his belt hung a short sword, or rather a huge dagger. He carried also a spear, the light shaft of which served as a support in walking.

"I have brought you these," said the Jew. "Years ago, when Nehemiah came from Susa to Jerusalem, one of the soldiers whom King Artaxerxes had sent with him sickened on the way and died at my father's tent. These were his trappings. He begged that he might be buried in the winding-sheet, according to the custom of the Jews, whose faith he had embraced. Your herdsman's shirt is not a prudent disguise, especially since some of your pursuers have already tracked you in it. Besides, your very figure belies it. Sword-play and sceptre-holding give a different grace from that of clubbing swine; and it would take full twelve moons to grow a head of hair shaggy enough to make even a sheep look at you without suspicion. Our good King David might as well have played the shepherd with his crown on."

As he talked Elnathan divested himself, one by one, of his martial garments, and made Hiram put them on.

" And now, have I not performed a princely part myself ?" said he, laughing. " For it was our Prince Jonathan who, when he had found out that David was really born to be a king, 'stripped himself of the robe that was upon him, and gave it to David, and his garments, even to his sword, and to his bow, and to his girdle.' "

Elnathan then described carefully the paths leading eastward ; the deep, winding wadies that debouched into the Sea of Galilee ; the rock of Akhbara, rising five hundred cubits, like an enormous castle, cut by nature into a hundred hiding-places ; the towns on the shore of the little sea. He gave the names of men of kin to the house of Ben Yusef, or known to be trusty, to whom Hiram might appeal in case of extremity. To Hiram's repeated pledges to reward him as a king should, when better days came, the Jew replied :

" The Lord is our reward in all things."

" Tell me," asked Hiram, " does your God teach you to do such things as you and your father's house have done to me, a stranger ? for it was not to a king, but to a stricken wayfarer, you did it from the first."

" Yes, it is the command of our God, who taught it by the holy men he has raised up to lead our people. Our patriarch Job said : 'The stranger did not lie in the street : but I opened the door unto the traveller.' "

"But," interposed Hiram, "if the stranger were not merely a stranger; rather one, like myself, of a hostile race, as you Jehovites must regard the Baalites of the coast?"

"In heart you are not of Baal. Our God knows his own; and he has given to some of his people a wondrous power of detecting all true souls. My father, Ben Yusef, through much communing with the Lord, seems to be possessed of such spiritual sight. As you lay under the terebinth, before you came to your senses, my father cautioned us, saying: 'The favor of the Lord is upon this stranger. What we do unto him will be as if done unto our God.' Besides, did not the Lord give your life into my keeping when he bade me look the moment you fell into the crater? Did he not give me daring to go down into its very fires, and strength to carry you out? I have looked into that pit of brimstone since, and surely man alone could not have rescued you. And did not our God, at my prayer, give back your breath, that the hot air had burned out of you? Your life is mine, and must I not guard it as I would my own life? If harm should come to you through my neglect, I would not dare to pray to our God again as long as I live."

"Strange people!" said Hiram, half musing within himself. "In the tent of a shepherd I have learned more than all the world could teach me. I know nothing of gods, but I can pray one prayer to the God of Israel. It is, that he will bless the house of Ben Yusef forever."

"Amen! And the throne of Tyre!" said Elna-than, as the two heartily embraced, and stood gaz-ing a moment into each other's moonlit faces.

Hiram started on his way. He had gone but a few paces, when the Jew recalled him.

"I may serve you further. Let me go with you, or let me follow you, that I may watch for you against dangers."

"It must not be."

"Then give me some sign by which, if evil comes upon you, I may know that you have need of me."

Hiram paused a moment before he replied:

"Then let the sign be the mark of a circle. Fare-well!"

He quickly disappeared through the shadows of the night.

CHAPTER XV

THE morning found the fugitive by the Sea of Galilee. Massive ruins lined the road along its western and northern shores. These were the memorials of the days before the Babylonian captivity. Blocks of stone, pretentious in size and over-ornamentation, evidently dated from the age of the great Solomon. Other blocks were inferior imitations of these, and were made, doubtless, in the times of the later kings. Within the foundations of an ancient palace were loose stone cabins, belonging to the poor inhabitants, who gained a precarious living by adding to the scanty yield of the ground the better gleaning of the sea. Here and there clumsy fishing-boats, drawn upon the beach or floating idly on the water, told of the decadence of the arts and enterprise that had marked preceding times. Only nature was untouched by the degenerating influences of the age; and, fair as upon the day of its creation, lay the water, unrippled by the slightest breeze, mirroring the deep blue of the sky, like an immense piece of lapis-lazuli, in the setting of the encircling mountains.

The silence and motionlessness of the sea imparted themselves to Hiram. The rush of events and the intense excitement of the past few days had almost exhausted the active energies of his mind. As the strained strings of an over-used lyre give no sound, so he seemed no longer able to respond to even the rude alarms of danger. He was fleeing now, not with any sense of fear, but solely with the momentum of past impulses, as the heart sometimes continues to throb and the lungs to heave when conscious life has ceased. He realized his own mental condition. He felt the moral inertia. He said to himself: "I believe I would not move if Egbalus pointed his sacrificial knife at my heart. I could walk into the arms of Moloch." He could understand somewhat how the priests succeeded in preparing their human victims for unhesitating obedience at the fatal moment. He saw how the will becomes paralyzed by the strain of the previous terror, and how the wretched devotees lose the susceptibility to recoil even at the steps of the altar, as the leaves of the sensitive-plant, frequently rubbed by the fingers, no longer shrink at the touch.

In this condition of mind, the stillness of the sea was very congenial to Hiram. It invited him as a kindred spirit. Out upon its placid bosom he could rest, without the necessity of arousing himself every moment to pass judgment on things that appealed to his suspicion. There, too, after yielding himself for a while to the soothing influences that lulled the air and water, he could plan for the future, instead of taking his cue, as heretofore he had been

9

compelled to do, from the movements of his pursuers.   Should he go across the desert to Damascus?
to the plains of Babylon? to the court at Susa, and
throw himself beneath the protecting shadow of the
Great King? to the solitude of the Sinaitic mountains?   Or should he seek the coast of the Great
Sea, and cross to Greece?   Whither, when, with a
few more turns, like those of the hunted fox, he
shall have thrown the Baal-hounds off the scent?

And Zillah!   How her fair face shone in every
bright thing he looked upon, and her frightened,
agony-drawn features stared at him out of every
gloomy object!   There was so much to think about.
And on the sea he could think.   Perhaps Jehovah
would help him think, or maybe speak to him.
Such a beautiful lake as this must be sacred to him
who is god of mountains and water and sky alike.
Yonder where the sea blends with the distant shore,
and the shore rises until it blends with the sky—
surely that must be the meeting-place of earthly and
heavenly influences, if gods ever commune with men.

Musing thus, he observed a fisherman's hut near
by.   One wall had once belonged to some palatial
structure; the others were made of such broken
stones as a man might carry from the heap of ruins
that lay about it.   The doorway of the hut was
faced on the one side with a column of marble; on
the other, with a polished slab of granite.   In front
of the hut was an oven; the half of a huge porphyry vase, inverted, served for the fire-back, and
gave direction to the draught.   On some coals a

woman was broiling fish. On a flat stone, lying half
in the fire, and covered with ashes, a man was bak-
ing thin sheets of yellow dough, to be subsequently
rolled into loaves of bread. Several others were
lounging near, sleeping and bedraggled with the
fishing of the past night. They welcomed Hiram
with a grunted salâm.

"Peace be to you!"

"Peace!" "Peace!" said one and another,
scarcely raising their eyes, as if the apparition of
a Persian soldier were too common to awaken interest. An elderly man, coming from the hut, eyed
the new-comer more attentively.

"Another man from the coast of the Great Sea,
eh! Our Persian masters are hiring Phœnicians
to be soldiers as well as sailors. But it takes more
than change of skin to make a wolf of a fox; and a
man from the coast can never pass with me for one
from beyond the desert. The west wind blows you
fellows inland as it does the salt-water gnats. But
sit by, and the Lord bless you! especially if your
purse is lined with darics."

Though this speech was not assuring, Hiram,
with his recent memories, could not distrust a Jew.
He gave his entertainers some good-natured repar-
tee, though their words had cut far deeper than
they knew.

"Stranger!" said one, "tell us your story of that
miracle at Tyre."

"I have not heard from Tyre for many a day,"
replied Hiram. "I am in the king's business, and

have been going up and down in your land for a time. What was the miracle?"

"Ha! ha! Think of old Benjamin telling the news to a Phœnician who boasts that he knows everything! Why, they were going to offer up some prince or other—or was it a priest, Ephraim? No matter which. Well! the gods saved them the trouble. The sun grew bigger and bigger, and came down nearer and nearer, until he opened his mouth and swallowed up prince, priests, and five-score attendants. I would not believe it but that Ephraim here, who had drunk plenty of leben that same day, says he saw the sun come bobbing down at him while fishing on the lake."

Hiram surprised himself at the heartiness with which he laughed at the story, and matched it with one he pretended to have heard some Jews relate as belonging to their national traditions. "Your great general, Joshua, one day was taken with a chill in the midst of a battle. He could not even give the commands, but only chattered with the cold. Then he bethought him to order the sun to come down and hang just over his head. It floated there like a red-hot shield until he had killed every man among the enemy. But who told you of the miracle at Tyre?"

"Why," said Benjamin, "the priests themselves. Two were along here yesterday."

"They were not priests," said Ephraim.

"They were, though," rejoined Benjamin. "Mother Eve once mistook a snake for an honest

creature; but I know a snake's wriggle and a
priest's wriggle, in whatever disguise they may be.
You could not be a priest of Baal if you tried,
stranger. Your face is too honest. But those fellows yesterday—at least one of them—could not
cast his priest's skin, though he was dressed like a
merchant. He looked as if he wanted to glide
down under the stones there, as they say the Baalite
priests live half the time in the vaults under their
temples, pulling strings to make their gods move,
and talking up through holes to answer the prayers
of the silly people."

"What were they doing here in the Jews' land?"
asked Hiram.

"They said they were searching for a young
Tyrian who had fallen heir to a fortune, who was
travelling hereabouts, and did not know his good
luck. May be you are the happy man."

"I wish I were," replied Hiram, "if for no other
reason than to get rid of a very disagreeable journey. I must cross the lake at once, and go as far
away as Bozrah. The king's business keeps one as
lively as a flea. I must have a boat."

"You have only to pick it out; we have enough
lazy fellows to sail it," replied Benjamin, rising and
looking along a row of boats.

"I would go alone," said Hiram. "I can leave
with you the price of the boat against my getting
wrecked, or being swallowed by this terrific sun of
yours, whose heat must make him thirsty enough to
drink up your little sea."

" Despise not its littleness," replied the Jew. " It is as strong as the very dragon in the sky when it gets to rolling and writhing under the Lord's frown."

" A Phœnician can tame any sea 'twixt Tyre and Tartesus. The heaviest winds that roar over Galilee would be only as the song of a sea-bird to a sailor on the main," said Hiram.

" Leave, then, your money, and sail it or sink with it, as you like," replied the rough fisherman.

CHAPTER XVI.

HIRAM'S experience enabled him to select the best among the boats, though it was one of the smallest. A package of smoked fish, a pile of thin bread cakes, and a bag of dates sufficiently provisioned his craft; and within a few moments he had pushed from shore.

As he did so he observed two strangers approach the group he had left. They conversed a little with the fishermen, then suddenly turned and watched his receding boat. Though several hundred cubits away, he could not mistake the bearing of one of them, who had not the stiff manner of a man used to toil in the fields, nor the firm but elastic step of a soldier, nor the swinging gate of a sailor, nor yet the dignified grace such as is soon acquired by a merchant, whose attire this man wore. Hiram appreciated the keen detective instinct of Benjamin, for he too could not mistake the priest of Baal under that secular disguise. The mental habit of doing everything by indirection comes to impart itself to the physical motions, just as habitual secretiveness and hypocrisy show themselves in the face. Besides, the temple service calls for little use of the muscles, and an old priest's body is not symmetrically developed. That would-be merchant could have come from nowhere but some temple. His every motion seemed a jerk with the bigotry of his business.

Hiram felt a tinge of pride in his powers of observation that was not, perhaps, fully warranted; for, though he had no recollection of having done so, he had often seen this same man among the priests at Tyre. It was a case of unconscious memory.

The other man was not so unique a specimen; indeed, having seated himself while the other was walking about and gesticulating, he was in better concealment. "But crow flies only with crow, and priest with priest," thought the king.

Hiram had gained two furlongs from the shore, when the men came to the boats and prepared to follow him. Only heavier craft than his were left; but there were two rowers against one. They rigged the long oars, one swivelled on either side of the vessel, and each requiring the full strength of a man to wield it. One oarsman was awkward, but the other, by strength and skill, made up for the deficiency of his comrade, and by an alternate strong pull and back-water dip of the blade kept the boat steadily ploughing ahead, and slowly gaining upon the fugitive.

For Hiram to reach the eastern shore before being overtaken was impossible. He laid his plan. It was this: at the moment of contact to turn sud-

denly, and with the prow of his boat crash against
the oar of the inexpert priest, break it, and glide
off, leaving the heavy craft at the disadvantage of
having but one propelling blade. The odds would
then be with him.

Suddenly a dark shadow fell upon the water near
the western shore, just beneath the gap in the hills.
The shadow elongated itself like a serpent emerg-
ing from its hole. Beneath it the water began to
roll in billowy convolutions. The turmoil spread
until, within a few moments, the entire lake was
transformed into a vast caldron of boiling waters.
The storm waves on the Great Sea were higher, but
they were also longer, and more readily mounted
than these. The Galilee boats, too, were utterly
untrimmed for such an emergency, as the fishermen were accustomed to strike for land at the first
sign of a storm, and danger made them alert to an-
ticipate it. But to Hiram the wind-blow was a god-
send. He invoked Jehovah's blessing, and raised
to its place the log that was called a mast, and
swung from it the heavy square sail of goat's
hair.

Let the storm drive him where it would! He
would rather die a victim of the elements than fall
under the gloating hatred of Egbalus's crew of demons. But he did not expect to die. The storm-
shriek was like a bugle blast, thrilling his courage.
He shouted in triumph as he went bounding over
the waves. A Tyrian king! A sea king, indeed,
was he!

In the exhilaration of the moment he almost forgot his pursuers. But glancing back through the dense spray, he caught a glimpse of a heavy prow not far in his wake. Above it hung a great sail that seemed like some black-winged spirit driving it onward to fulfil its accursed mission. The vessel disappeared an instant in the blinding mist, only to reappear a full length nearer. A moment more, and fate would ring down the curtain upon this tragedy.

But Hiram determined that the exit should be a climax, if there were any ghostly spectators to applaud; and drawing his dagger, he caught it in his teeth, and waited. Fast as they flew, the waves rolled faster, and poured over the low stern of his vessel. Crossing a shoal, the huge billows mounted higher, and one of immense size hovered an instant in air, like the jaw of some great behemoth pursuing its tiny prey, then fell upon the boat, swallowing her in its remorseless maw.

Hiram was prepared for this, and, being a tireless swimmer, kept afloat while he was flung through the breakers. His pursuers came on. Being higher in the stern, the great waves caught and hurled their boat across the shoals. Hiram cursed all the gods when he saw that, and even taunted Jehovah as the hated craft flew past him.

But a moment later he became as pious a Jew as he had been a blasphemer; for the flying boat suddenly stopped; her mast bent forward; she swirled, careened, and sank.

Hiram could not see the shore through the blinding spray, but the billows were wings for him, and he was sure of holding out though the entire lake were to be crossed.

The wind in an instant died away. The spray as quickly ceased to fly from the broken crests of the waves. The billows rolled, but seemed to have lost their force. They lifted him gently, and allowed him to glide onward. The shore was there, not a hundred strokes distant.

But what was his consternation to see, scarcely three boat-lengths from him, a swimmer as strong as he. It became a race for life. Hiram had kept his dagger in his teeth. He dived, intending to come up beneath his antagonist and plunge the blade into his body. But either he miscalculated the distance, or the man, discerning his purpose, had swum out of harm's way.

It was now a question which should first reach the shore and seize his opponent with fatal advantage. Hiram's strokes were tremendous, surpassing those that had won him the match so often in the harbor of Tyre, before the dignities of the crown had forbidden his taking part in such sports. But they were now of no avail. His competitor kept abreast with him. They reached the shore almost at the same moment. Hiram, striking a better footing, was first out of the water. Seizing an enormous stone, he turned to crush the skull of his enemy before he could gain a foothold on the shelving beach.

"My king!   My king!" cried the man.

Hiram dropped the stone in bewilderment.

"Hanno!   As sure as Baal—as Jehovah lives, it's Hanno!"

CHAPTER XVII

A N hour later a white chiton might have been
seen hanging heavily in the sultry air from the
limbs of a juniper bush, that grew out of a sandy
mound between two great boulders on the eastern
shore of the Sea of Galilee. Under the shelter of
the rocks were two men, the one having on only a
pair of leather trousers ; the other, but for a close-
fitting shirt, entirely nude. This was not the most
decorous position in which to find the King of Tyre
and his aristocratic nobleman ; yet they both
seemed supremely, even hilariously, happy. King
Hiram had completed the story of his adventures ;
and Hanno, donning his chiton, entered upon the
account of the events that had occurred recently at
Tyre.

The priests, he said, after consultation, and with
some misgiving as to their policy, agreed to encourage the popular belief that King Hiram had been
bodily translated to some heavenly world by the
favor and power of Baal. They boasted thus a
greater miracle on the part of their god than those
reported in the olden times of the exploits of Jehovah in Israel, who took Enoch, Moses, and Elijah

away without their seeing death.   For several days
the Tyrian populace held high festival in devout
celebration of this astounding event.   The city was
given over to orgies that drained much wealth into
the coffers of the priests.   Half the jewels of Tyre,
and heaps of coins, were stored in the Temple of
Melkarth.   A hundred skins of choicest wine were
poured into the sacred lake around the Maabed.
So many men offered themselves for the priestly
occupation, expecting miraculous reward, that some
of the shops of the artisans were closed for lack of
workmen, and many ships were delayed in sailing
because they were unmanned.

Perhaps Ahimelek was the most ostentatious
donor, "unless," said Hanno, "I myself surpassed
him in extravagant zeal.   Three ship-loads of dye-
stuffs I emptied into the Egyptian harbor, empur-
pling the water, and staining the stones of the quay
with royal tints against the time of our king's return.

"The priests were not long in discovering the real
method of your disappearance, but to have confessed it would have brought the whole affair into
such disrepute that the people would have torn Egbalus and the rest of us to pieces."

"But was your hand not suspected?" asked
Hiram.

"I think not.   I anticipated that I too should
have to flee, and prepared to do so; but the falling
of the foundation of the image, through the acci-
dental burning of some wooden supports, com-

pletely blocked the passage from those who investigated it; and I have since removed every royal rag
you left in the vault beyond.

"Egbalus summoned a few of the more cautious
and desperate, among whom I was surprised to find
myself, and revealed his own view and policy. The
shrewd old fox was certain that you had escaped by
some ruse. You must be tracked and killed, even
if you had gone to where the Nile begins in the
melting of the mountains, or had become a savage
in the islands of tin. Priests were despatched to
Greece, to Susa, to Damascus, to Memphis, and
Thebes. A dozen are tracking this Jews' land. I
volunteered in such fine frenzy—this fresh gash on
my breast is the mark of my vow—that Egbalus
hugged me to his villainous heart, and called me a
true son of Baal, and offered me the fairest girl born
of his concubine Tissa for wife when I returned.

"I thought to go out alone. But I knew little of
these inland roads, so yoked myself with old Abdemon, the shrewdest of all the priests. He was poor
in tramping, and weak of arm, but had the wiliest
head for this sort of business. He knew every path
in the Jews' land. I felt sure that he would get
your foot-prints, unless you had taken to flight in
the air; so I joined with him. He struck your
trail at once. He scented you near the crater of
Giscala, and put the two devils you spoke of on
guard there, while we watched here by the sea."

"He was drowned when the boat sank?" asked
Hiram.

"Yes, he sank like a stone. If he had swum a stroke I would have choked him in the water. Indeed, when I saw your boat go down I drew a dagger on him, but before I could use it our boat was in the same straits."

"But what of Zillah?"

"There is nothing to report, except what was known to all before the day of the sacrifice. Her father had made a close alliance with Egbalus. Believing that you were doomed, he offered his daughter to your cousin Rubaal, and pledged the same dowry as he had pledged to you."

"That shall never be!" cried Hiram with impatient fury. "I will return to Tyre, steal my way into the city, cut the throats of these wretches, and flee with my betrothed."

"You shall return, but not now."

"Why not now? I cannot, I will not, wander about like a cowardly fugitive."

"Wait at least, my king, until you get the mail on your hand to strike the great blow that will shatter all this horrid tyranny at once. No harm can come to Zillah. It was because I knew your hot blood and quick determination that I sought more eagerly to find you, and prevent your sudden return. Trust me in Tyre. The marriage with Rubaal cannot take place until the next festival of Astarte and Tammuz. A hundred things may happen before that. Patience! and then not mere vengeance, King Hiram, but your restoration, and the renewed splendor of your power! I believe in it, and if the gods will not send it, we will make it. Loving you as I do, I am not risking my life merely for yours, but for your crown as well. Tyre must be saved, made rich, powerful, the mistress of Sidon, the queen of the Great Sea, the conqueror of—"

"Peace! peace! good Hanno. Let's first think of how to save a whole skin, instead of gilding a new crown. But see! your boat has floated, and is drifting this way."

Hanno looked sharply at the distant object.

"And, by the mouth of Dagon! old Abdemon is on her, clinging to her bottom."

"I will smash his skull with the very stone I had selected for yours," cried the almost frantic king. "If I cannot dispense justice in my own kingdom, I can here."

"No, no," said Hanno; "leave him to me. Get you gone out of sight. If he has seen you I will put him out of the way. If he has not seen you, he will confirm the report that you were drowned. That will recall all the priests from pursuit, and leave the field free for us to work. Hide away!"

Hanno plunged into the sea, and swam to the floating wreck. Abdemon was barely alive. He had ceased to cling, and was lying limp across the bottom of the upturned boat. The sea had subsided, else he had been washed off. It was nearly another hour before Hanno was able to work the wreck to the beach and carry the nearly unconscious priest ashore.

10

As Abdemon recovered his senses, it was plain that he had seen nothing of what had occurred.

"The Cabeiri have avenged Baal," cried he. " I could have died willingly after I saw the sea swallow up the traitorous king, but I could not bear the thought of being myself drowned in the same water. Baal be praised! Baal be praised!"

"And now," suggested Hanno, "we must hasten back to Tyre with the news. The sooner the search ceases, and the priests return, the less danger of suspicion by the people. Baal has taken his offering, whether by fire or water it matters not that the crowd should know."

"Baal be praised!" echoed Abdemon.

"Could you not return alone?" asked Hanno. I, as a new priest, and one assigned by our most worshipful chief to the superintendency of our temple property, would learn of the practices of worship among these tribes of Ammon and Moab. And then I would visit Jerusalem, where these Jews are rebuilding their temple. I may learn much that will add to the splendor and impressiveness of our worship."

After some further consultation Hanno's plans were approved by his fellow-priest. They talked about the renovation of temples and the coming glory of the priestly guild, when the wealth of Ahimelek should augment the treasury of Melkarth.

Near nightfall a fisherman rowed Hanno and Abdemon across the upper end of the Sea of Galilee to one of the little hamlets there, and under the starlight he brought Hanno back to the eastern shore.

CHAPTER XVIII

THE veracious chronicler of the adventures of King Hiram is compelled to pass over in silence a period of several months. As certain rivers disappear, and flow for a distance beneath the ground, so the course of events, as directed by the discreet and wary Hanno, was for a while inscrutable. We will follow it, however, from the point where it came again into the daylight of observation.

Since men began to travel on the earth, innkeepers have been noted for the courtesy, tact, and assiduity with which they have reaped the rewards of their business. On a certain day Solomon Ben Eli, innkeeper at Jericho, in the valley of the Lower Jordan, found all the above-named qualities of his disposition exercised to the utmost. This was the day before the opening of the annual Feast of Tabernacles at Jerusalem, during the seven days of which celebration the men from all parts of the land came together at the Sacred City.

The hostelry at Jericho—called Beth Elisha, in honor of the prophet whose miraculous cruse of salt once healed the spring hard by, which now supplied the town with delightful water—was a long, low building, rambling, and diverse as the various generations which had successively built upon it. During the night all its rooms and ingles had been crowded with pilgrims from up the Jordan and beyond it. Early in the morning, long before the sun had looked over the beetling cliffs of Moab, the multitude poured forth into the court-yard. They were clad in gay garments of many colors, and were not unlike the variously plumed doves which came out of their adjacent cotes, and filled the air with their flapping wings and querulous cooing. The shed that enclosed the opposite side of the yard discharged a more turbulent crowd of horses and camels, asses and mules, which were kicking and rumping one another in the attempt to get their noses into the great stone trough that stood in the centre of the court. The crisp air resounded with the unedifying matins of mingled grunts, neighs, and brays, which were far from being reduced to harmony by the shouts of the drivers.

It was easier for the host to seem ubiquitous than it was for him to command in himself such a variety of tempers as the occasion required. He must placate those who grumbled at their reckoning; hasten his laggard servants; adjudicate the quarrels of guests over the uncertain ownership of bits of harness; must smile, yet frown; beam knowingly, yet knit his brows in simulated perplexity; be patient, yet keep the sharpest eye and quickest tongue; and shift all these aspects in such rapid succession that they seemed to be simultaneous. We may forgive this prince of innkeepers if for a moment he did not maintain to perfection his manifold part. Such was the moment when a servant announced to him that Rabbi Shimeal, the most noted man in the synagogue at Jericho, would speak with him at the gate.

"A pretty time of day for him to come ! I'll warrant he has been up all night owling it over some verse of the law. Or he wants a gift for the synagogue. Tell him his affairs must wait until I can get this holy crowd off for the Temple," was Solomon Ben Eli's petulant response.

The servant soon returned with the statement that the Rabbi Shimeal must have his assistance in providing a beast to convey to Jerusalem no less a personage than Ezra, the Great Scribe, who was a guest at the rabbi's house, and whose animal had given out under the terrible heat of the previous day, as he had journeyed through the villages of the Jordan plain, pursuing his holy work of inspecting the copies of the Law used in the newly established synagogues.

Solomon Ben Eli was shocked at this news, as if an angel's wing had brushed his face.

"Heaven forgive me !" said he, making low obeisance before his servant, in obliviousness to the fact that that son of Gibeon was not the great man of God himself.

"But this is unfortunate," he added, rubbing his hands nervously. "I have not a horse left, nor a camel, and not even an ass."

The attention of the bystanders being drawn to the host's dilemma, a marvellous spirit of sympathy with him and of devotion to Ezra was instantly displayed. Every one urged upon his neighbor the duty of self-sacrifice, as if each were ashamed of the others for allowing the Great Scribe's detention or even inconvenience.

"If my horse was strong and handsome, like yours," said one, "I would gallop at once to the rabbi's. Mine is but a spavined beast, and it would be a disgrace for the holy man of God to bestride him."

"I would instantly offer my steed," responded the other, "but he is poorly broken, and the Scribe —be it reverently spoken—is too old to control him. I could never forgive myself if my beast were the cause of Ezra's breaking his holy neck among the rocks of Cherith."

A young man stood by who was noticeable from the fact that his garments were richer in texture than those of most of the pilgrims, though he was not arrayed for the festival. His cloak, which he drew closely around him as a protection from the chill morning air, was that of a traveller. Beneath it he wore a belt, which supported both a sword and an inkhorn, and thus indicated the trade of merchant. The short black beard about his lower features was balanced by a head-dress of black silk, which was bound about his brows with a purple cord, and fell down upon the back of his neck and shoulders. He was plainly a Phœnician, but con-

fessed that many months had elapsed since he had
been to the coast. For his identification and safety
from the imposition of petty officials in the various
lands he might have occasion to traverse in following his trade, he carried a letter issued by King
Hiram of Tyre, and bearing the royal seal. Similar letters were borne as passports by all the captains of vessels and masters of caravans who represented the genuine business houses in the cities
of Phœnicia; and by these credentials they were
distinguished from the irresponsible adventurers
who, in the convenient disguise of travelling merchants, infested all those countries.

The young merchant, observing the perplexity of
Solomon, the host, addressed him :

"If his Excellency the Great Scribe will accept
the courtesy of a stranger, let him take any of my
beasts."

"Thanks, noble Marduk !" replied the innkeeper, in grateful relief. "But I regret that my own
people are thus rebuked by a Gentile."

"Nay," replied Marduk, "I would not rebuke
your people. They have each only one riding-
beast, while I have many. My animals are lightly
laden, and we can distribute the burden of one upon
the others."

"And, I bethink me, the Scribe will ride upon
nothing but an ass," replied Solomon. "He
cites the growing infirmities of years as his ex-
cuse. I will convey your courteous offer to the
rabbi."

"And bid him say to the Scribe," added the Phœnician, "that if he can delay his departure until the crowd has preceded us, my party will gladly bear him company."

CHAPTER XIX

A N hour later the inn-yard was deserted, except by a single group of persons who, notwithstanding their exceedingly diverse appearances, were preparing to depart together. There was the party of Marduk, which, besides the merchant himself, consisted of Eliezar, a Damascene, a shrewd tradesman to whom were intrusted the details of the business; and there were half a score of others who filled the various offices of the travelling camp—cook, tent-maker, camel-drivers, muleteers, and the like. With their clattering tongues and jangling accoutrements, as they ranged their various beasts for the journey, they were in unique contrast with the company of Jews who had accepted their convoy.

Chief among the latter was Ezra the Scribe. He was slight in natural stature, which was further diminished by the bowing weight of years. Long gray forelocks hung down from his temples and mingled with his beard. His forehead was high and straight. His face showed the incipient emaciation of advancing years, being sunken beneath the cheek-bones. Restless gray eyes twinkled in their deep setting, and suggested his undiminished brightness of intelligence. His whole aspect betokened great amiability and kindliness of disposition, united, however, with rigid firmness of conviction and powers of patient endurance. One who was over-critical in reading the countenance might perhaps have pronounced it lacking in indications of that self-assertion and daring which fit a man for leadership in troublous times. Marduk said to himself: "That man would never make a soldier; though he might make a martyr."

The Scribe was accompanied by two young men. One was Malachi, whose face, though not beautiful, was strangely prepossessing. The deep weather-tinge did not take from it a sunny brightness, a sort of translucency due to habitual high and pure thinking. His head, however, seemed to over-weight his body. His eyes were large, and wide open; and, while really fixed upon one's face, gave the impression of being focused upon something beyond or within one. His brows were heavy, and, at times, seemed to project until they dropped new shadows upon his face, whose lines contracted under the intensity of painful thoughts. As Marduk afterwards noticed, Malachi was often absent-minded; indeed, was never entirely otherwise. While engaging freely in conversation, he was never fully engaged by what was said; and, though he contributed more than most men to the elucidation of various subjects, one felt that he reserved more than he gave; that he was a critic rather than a participant in what was going on. He seemed to be two persons; the greater personality unexpressed, but observant and waiting.

Marduk was not surprised at the innkeeper's information that Malachi was the favorite pupil of Ezra, and that the Scribe did not hesitate to pronounce the young man's spiritual discernment as something akin to the prophetic gift. He even had said that, when he prayed for the renovation of Israel, he could not avoid associating his hopes in some way with the career of his young disciple.

Malachi's companion was in every respect diverse. Marduk noticed first of all this man's fine physique. He was robust and muscular; round-headed; red-haired; rollicking, yet quick-tempered; impudent at one moment, and apologetic the next. For instance, while Malachi reverently bowed his head, and waited until Ezra was first seated on his beast before mounting his own, his young comrade seemed to forget his obeisance, and, without ceremony, almost lifted the Scribe in his strong arms, and placed him in the high saddle upon the rump of the ass. Then, at a bound, he was astride his own restless charger.

Solomon Ben Eli whispered to Marduk that this young man was Manasseh, grandson of the High Priest Eliashib; who might one day come into that office himself—that is, if he could curb his restless disposition as effectively as he curbed his steed.

The good host also ventured the further information that Ezra loved Manasseh, and had said that he was "only like the Sea of Galilee, which often hides its transparent depth beneath a ruffled surface."

Solomon added to this his own criticism : "If Manasseh once settles down, he will make just the man to reform Israel. He has immense will and courage, and draws the best young blood of Jerusalem with him. But if he does not change, he will be only like a stout centre-pole of a tent that is not well set, tottering in the wind, and endangering the whole, however strong may be the cords and stakes. It is a pity that he and Malachi cannot be rolled into one, be thoroughly mixed, and then be evenly divided into two again, as the flour and the butter in the making of two cakes."

Solomon parted with his guests, as they passed from his gate, with that versatile courtesy which innkeepers and politicians alone acquire to perfection. He reverently kissed the hand of the Scribe. He bowed with great respect to Malachi. He gave Manasseh a whisper that provoked his merriest laugh. But he pressed his hand heartily with Marduk's—perhaps the sensation of the merchant's generous darics had not yet left his own palm.

The cavalcade once on the road, Ezra made his grateful acknowledgment to the Phœnician for the use of his beast.

"I would you had selected a nobler animal!" said Marduk, smiling at the picture of the greatest man of the Jewish nation sceptred with a donkey-punching stick, having declined the service of an attendant to propel the beast from behind.

"The little ass and I will be good friends," replied Ezra, facetiously. "His short steps will not jostle my thoughts. An attendant might make havoc in my meditations by punching him at an unfortunate moment."

Then he more seriously added: "Know, good Marduk, that the ass is a most honorable beast. There is a prediction among us Hebrews that, when our Great King shall come, he will make his triumphant entry into Jerusalem riding upon an ass. And, besides," resuming his pleasantry, "our Psalmist says, 'A horse is a vain thing for safety,' as you will be apt to find out before we get through the rocky ravine between this and Enshemesh, unless your steed's feet have been trained like those of the goats."

"I am told that the way before us is noted for the license taken by robbers," said Marduk. "My company will therefore be a safe escort."

"I accept your company heartily," replied Ezra, "but will need no protection. It is now many years since I came from Babylon. I then refused to ask of the Great King an escort of soldiers, for the hand of our God is upon all them for good that seek him. From that day I have never borne a weapon, nor had an armed attendant. I have gone safely throughout the land, and even among the Jews scattered abroad, and have found no evil; nor will I ever.

"But the route we are taking will be of interest to you, I think, without the hazard of carnal adventure. The deep gorge we are entering, and up which we must climb some three thousand cubits before we reach the high ground of Olivet, takes its name from the brook Cherith, and is famous as having been the hiding-place of our prophet Elijah, where he was fed by ravens during a terrible famine that came upon our land according to his prediction. It was during the reign of King Ahab and his Sidonian wife, Jezebel, a priestess of Astarte, who made Israel to sin in following Baal. But pardon this unkind allusion to the worship of your people. I would not wound another's convictions, however strongly I might hold my own."

"Do not apologize for it," replied Marduk. "One should speak of his faith freely in his own land; and I think also in all lands. Therefore, I venture to make an argument for the Phœnician faith, assuming the recent news from the coast to be true. Your land is famous for its miracles, but Tyre just now seems the special arena for divine exploits."

"You refer, doubtless, to the alleged translation of King Hiram?" replied Ezra. "I have not investigated the story; nor do I think one needs to do so in order to judge of it. It is, even in its own assumption, totally different from the miracles of Israel. Ours were openly wrought by God, with his high hand and outstretched arm. All people could judge them; as the dividing waters of the Red Sea and Jordan, the sun standing still in heaven, and the like. But the marvel of Tyre was wrought, I am told, within a cordon of priests who carefully surrounded the place. Now, a miracle wrought for priests is apt to be a priest-wrought miracle. But—"

The conversation was interrupted by Marduk's horse suddenly taking fright, losing his footing on the narrow path, and nearly precipitating its rider into the brook Cherith, which gleamed, a tiny thread of white water, far below. As by dexterous management he enabled the horse to recover himself, Marduk laughingly admitted that he was enough of a Jew now to believe the Psalmist's saying about the horse being a vain thing for safety, at least in such places as this.

"But what have we here?" he cried, leaping from his beast. "This earth did not give way itself. The path has been dug under, and only the surface shell left. It is a prepared avalanche; and, by the rays of Baal! there is an ambushment below. See! the villains are skulking back into the hills. They were to tumble us and our baggage down there, and then pluck us at their leisure."

Ezra raised his hands in prayer, and repeated: "We thank thee, O Lord, for the fulfilment of thy promise through thy servant Moses: 'Surely He shall deliver thee from the snare of the fowler. He shall give his angels charge over thee, to keep thee in all thy ways, lest thou dash thy foot against a stone.'"

The Phœnician was as much impressed with the

beauty and tranquillity of the Scribe's faith as with
the horrible catastrophe that had so nearly over-
whelmed them; especially as he recalled Ezra's
statement that so his God had always delivered
him.

CHAPTER XX.

FROM this point of the journey Marduk insisted on riding ahead with Manasseh, lest new dangers might await them. That sort of clairvoyance which generous souls have in detecting congenial spirits quickly put these two young men at ease with each other. Their horses were not unmatched in strength and nerve, and caught from their riders a sense of good-fellowship. Scarcely waiting their masters' will, they dashed together up the steep ascents, raced across the open spaces, and waited impatiently with tossing manes and pawing hoofs for the laggard train. Their riders ran many a tilt of wit and braggadocio, rivalling each other in their stories of adventure. The merchant related exploits in many lands; enough to have made the reputation of a veteran soldier, sailor, and merchant combined.

"It is a pity you are not a Jew," said Manasseh. "We have some quick blood at Jerusalem that would mix well with yours. You see this dagger!" tossing a bright blade into the air, and catching it deftly by the handle. "Father Ezra there does not know that his good boy goes armed. I keep this just

11

as a memento of an escapade some of us youngsters made from the walls of Jerusalem one night. We sacked a camp of Samaritans who had come too near us and blocked the road to the north gate. Every day these half-breed marauders sent some insult to our people; but never after that night. Nehemiah, our governor, thought that he and Ezra had prayed them away; and so these saints stole our credit."

"I am part Jew," replied Marduk, "for I belong to all nations. See, here are my credentials!" producing a handful of coins. "The golden ring of Egypt, the double-stater of Greece, the daric of Persia, and the shekel of you Jews. One metal, many shapes; so man is one, nations and customs many; and, for all that you and I know, one God, and many notions of him. El, Bel, Baal, Jove, Jehovah, the same metal in thought, but stamped with different dies. All gods are one."

"Say rather that One God is all," interposed Malachi, who had ridden up just in time to catch the last sentence.

The party halted for rest and lunch at the upper end of the ravine of Cherith. The travellers were awed into silence by the view here presented. The ravine is a jagged cut in the earth, nearly five hundred cubits deep, in places scarcely wider than the tiny brook that glides like a shining serpent at its bottom, and winds down, with a thousand turns, for miles, until it debouches between awful cliffs into the open valley of the Jordan.

Refreshments were furnished from the well-stocked hampers of the merchant. The mules and horses were unladen and tethered. The ungainly camels crouched down for relief under their loads. After an hour's rest the Jews proposed to take their leave of their kind patron of the road, and hasten on to Jerusalem. The merchant's beasts should not be hurried, but Manasseh avowed that Ezra would rather die of exhaustion on the road than be left outside the gates of Jerusalem after sunset on this particular night, which was that of the preparation for the great Feast of Tabernacles.

The parting of Marduk and Manasseh was not until the latter had exacted a promise from the Phœnician that he would become his guest while in the city. The Jews joined with others of their nation, pilgrims to the city, who had halted for mid-day rest, and who now made their way towards En-shemesh joyous with their songs, such as:

"I was glad when they said unto me, Let us go into the house of the Lord. Our feet shall stand within thy gates, O Jerusalem, whither the tribes go up, the tribes of the Lord, unto the testimony of Israel, to give thanks unto the name of the Lord."

Scarcely had the pilgrims disappeared over the hill-tops when two men were observed climbing up through the ravine. They rode upon mules. One was old; the other a stalwart youth. Eliezar, the Damascene steward of Marduk's camp, recognized the elder one as he drew near, and ran out to meet him.

"Why, it is Ben Yusef of Giscala! And this is the fine lad whom I last saw the height of a kid! The air of Galilee grows big men, as it grows big hills."

"But what brings Eliezar here?" asked Ben Yusef. "Was not the northern country of Syria large enough for the sale of your merchandise?"

In a few words Eliezar narrated how that, from being a private peddler of such goods as a meagre purse could buy, he had come to be the viceroy, satrap, tirshatha, prime-minister, or whatever term of speech might suit the office, of no less notable a merchant than Marduk, famed in many lands for his great enterprise—Marduk of Tyre."

"Of Tyre!" exclaimed Ben Yusef. "Then Elnathan and I would speak with him."

Marduk had eyed the new-comers with that keenness which a merchant acquires in recognizing the sort of men it will pay to deal with, and had turned away to give orders for the reloading of his beasts, but approached the strangers on hearing Ben Yusef's remark.

"I am Marduk of Tyre, and your servant," said he, bowing with indifferent courtesy.

"My lad has acquaintance there, of which he would inquire," replied the old man.

Elnathan walked a little way with Marduk; and, as they turned, the latter was heard to say:

"I can give no information, for my route has been from Egypt across the desert of Arabia. Nor can I offer you encouragement, since it may be

some moons yet before I again visit the coast.
But if your Galilean flocks are well fleeced we may
some day strike a bargain for their wool."

Ben Yusef and his son, with suitable apologies
for their intrusion upon the great merchant's privacy, and with familiar parting from Eliezar, went
their way towards Jerusalem. Marduk's party followed.

CHAPTER XXI

THE last glow had faded from the western sky as Marduk looked towards it over the shoulder of Olivet. But there burst upon the view of the Phœnician a scene of weird magnificence. The stars above seemed to reflect themselves in hundreds of lights that gleamed along the hill-side, and from the valley between Olivet and the city. In sombre contrast with these, the walls of Jerusalem, with their regular outline broken by the temple and scattered turrets, rose black as a rayless night. But as Marduk gazed, the temple suddenly blazed as if with volcanic brilliance. It seemed like some massive altar in the midst of flames that had fallen upon it out of heaven. Every graceful architectural line was revealed, every burnished plate of gold and brass glowed in the fire. Only the outer surface of the city walls remained unillumined, and in their immense mass of darkness made the contrast startling and sublime.

Marduk's awe did not stifle his Phœnician curiosity; and, leaving his men to arrange his camp, he turned towards a couple of Jews who were engaged in erecting a booth near him. They proved to be Ben Yusef and his son. The venerable man was evidently inclined to be communicative, if one might judge from the low tones in which they conversed, as they walked among the booths and back into the shadows of Olivet. Anon they stood by Marduk's tent, while the Jew pointed out the objects of interest, and explained their significance.

"There are in the court of the temple two enormous lamp standards, each fifty cubits in height, and supporting four immense basins of oil. The garments worn by the priests during the year have been twisted into great wicks, and now at a signal have been suddenly lighted. See, too, hundreds of hand-torches are being waved by priests who crowd the court! The night gloom that first hung over the city symbolled the moral and spiritual darkness which we Jews believe hangs over all the nations, as our prophet Isaiah said, 'Behold, darkness shall cover the earth, and gross darkness the people.' The bursting illumination, throwing its glare for leagues through the night, expresses our faith that the truth of Jehovah shall shine forth from Judaism and fill all lands, as Isaiah also says, 'Arise, shine; for thy light is come, and the glory of the Lord is risen upon thee. And the Gentiles shall come to thy light and kings to the brightness of thy rising.' "

"But what mean the sudden shouting and singing?" asked Marduk.

"Listen closely," replied Ben Yusef, "and you will hear the Levites, who stand on the fifteen steps

leading from the women's court. They strike their
harps and cymbals as they chant the fifteen Songs of
Degrees, some of which you may have heard the pilgrims singing as they were coming up hither. See!
they are dancing over there; and soon the whole
city, and these multitudes outside, will join the innocent revelry. It is a sin not to be merry to-night.
The man whose griefs have made him shun the face
of his fellows must be neighborly now. The stranger must make a comrade of the one next to him.
Our God is a happy divinity, and men may share
the joy of the Lord."

Marduk did not sleep that night. Most of the
hours were spent in the company of Ben Yusef and
Elnathan. They wandered among the booths, which
the Jew said were everywhere, not only in the fields,
but in the city, wherever there was space enough in
the streets, in the house-courts, on the roofs, on the
walls. Indeed, the stone city and the stony hills
about were mantled with an artificial forest of palm
and pine, olive and myrtle.

"But," asked Marduk, "how dare so many Jews
leave their homes to come hither in such times as
these? The Samaritans and other enemies of your
nation must take advantage of this."

"No," replied Ben Yusef; "our God, who stopped
the mouths of the lions when our prophet Daniel was
thrown to them by Nebuchadnezzar, stops the wrath
of our enemies at such times. When our three annual festivals were set up, ages ago, in the days of
Moses, Jehovah promised: 'Neither shall any man

desire thy land when thou shalt go up to appear before the Lord thy God thrice in the year.' I leave
my own little girl alone in my tent in far Galilee,
fearing no evil for her until I return."

All night long joy echoed from the walls and over
the hills about Jerusalem. With the first pale shim-
mer of daylight over Olivet came a hush. The people stood by their booths, with faces turned towards the city, in silent expectation. At length a
sweet note floated out from the temple precinct.

Ben Yusef pointed to the distant forms of two
priests who, leaving the temple, advanced eastward
across the court, carrying great silver trumpets.
Reaching the wall, they suddenly turned their backs
to the east, and shouted in loud tones these words :
" Our fathers once turned their back to the sanctu-
ary, and their faces to the east, and worshipped the
sun-god : but we will lift our eyes to Jehovah."

Soon a thick column of smoke rose from the great
altar in the temple court, and outspread above the
sacred precinct like a canopy, its edges fraying in
the scarcely moving air, and, as Marduk said, " floating some fringes of its blessing to the good heathen
beyond."

" Yes," replied Ben Yusef, " for during the week
of festivity seventy bullocks will be offered—a
round number for all the nations of the world."

CHAPTER XXII

SCARCELY had the Phœnician inspected his own camp, and eaten his breakfast, when Manasseh approached. His coming was heralded by a commotion among the people, who everywhere recognized the aristocratic descendant of the high priest, his well-known freedom of life and liberalism in opinion rendering him at once the most popular and unpopular of the young men of Jerusalem. He insisted upon acting the part of host to Marduk, or at least of guide for the day.

"Our Jewish customs will interest you; and, in turn, I would learn from you the ideas of the many peoples you have come to know in your travels, so that our obligations will be mutual and equal, to say nothing of your courtesy yesterday," was the argument by which Manasseh overcame the Phœnician's scruples. Together the young men mingled in the crowds, each carrying the lulabh, a bunch of myrtle and palm entwined with a willow spray.

At the temple they saw the two processions, one headed by a priest bearing in a golden pitcher water from the pool of Siloam, the other by a priest car-

rying a pitcher of wine, which they poured together
at the base of the altar. Manasseh explained this
beautiful ceremonial as an oblation of gratitude for
the rain that fertilized the fields and for the yield
of the vineyards.

They afterwards joined with a multitude in front
of a raised platform, from which was an almost continuous reading of the ancient laws of Israel by
different persons. The readings were only interspersed with brief interpretations by rabbis of repute.

The deepest interest was manifested when the
venerable Scribe, Ezra, mounted the platform, accompanied by Malachi. The former began to speak,
but his voice was not heard beyond the group im-
mediately about him. It was evident, however,
that he had said little beyond commending to the
people his disciple Malachi.

Marduk was surprised at the awe with which the
young interpreter was received. But this surprise
did not remain as Malachi spoke. Such simplicity
combined with elevation of thought, such reasona-
bleness with rapt fervor, such practicality with deep
spirituality, the Phœnician had never heard before.
He felt the spell of the speaker's eloquence, and
was about to join the crowd as they murmured
their Amen to a special appeal to conscience and
faith, when his thoughts were interrupted by Manasseh's hand upon his arm :

" Come, good Marduk, this can hardly interest
you. You are to break bread with me."

To Marduk's hesitation to inflict his heathen presence upon the household of the high priest at such a time, Manasseh explained that he lived by himself during the festival. He had pitched his booth upon a house-top. According to custom, every Jew was to keep open table.

"And lest your humility should again object to becoming my guest," said he, laughing, "I will tell you that we are enjoined at such times not to invite our own family or particular circle, but to share our provender with the stranger, the poor, and the fatherless. And you are a stranger—I hope neither poor nor fatherless."

"Yes, especially poor," said Marduk, jingling coins in his wallet. "So with that understanding I will go with you, provided you will also feed figs to a spavined ass if we find one on the way."

"There is one of our customs I do not like," replied Manasseh, drawing his arm through that of his friend, "especially when I am hungry. An old saw has it that devout people will hasten to worship, but return to their homes with lingering feet; so you see all these people crawling along when their bellies would fly. Mine is as empty as the whale's was when he had ejected Jonah."

As they walked leisurely the Phœnician remarked: "If there are bigots among the Jews, you are not one of them."

"I trust not; but it is because I believe more than most Jews."

"Believe more? One would imagine less."

"On the other hand, I believe more. I believe the Lord is too great a God to be confined to Jews' notions. They belittle him. I love Ezra for personal reasons; but I wish the Lord would take him to heaven in a chariot of fire, if he would only take along our Tirshatha, Nehemiah, to drive it. Nehemiah, you know, is in Susa now. I hope the Persian king will keep him there. Nehemiah is a bigot. He insists on driving out of Jerusalem every woman whose blood is not of the purest Jewish stock, forcibly divorcing her from her husband, and disinheriting her children."

"What argument can they advance for such harsh measures?"

"Oh, the need of pure blood; the fact that Solomon got into trouble through marrying foreign wives; the fact that the children of mothers who were Gentiles would not be stiff enough in keeping up strictly Jewish customs. I admit that the mixing of bloods has not strengthened pure Judaism of late, and that some whom Nehemiah calls the half-breeds are pulling up as fast as he plants. I am not a rebel, not a traitor to my people, because I want to see the Jewish religion broadened and liberalized, until you Baalites even can worship at our altars. Our old prophecies speak of our light enlightening the Gentiles. But how can that be if we shut our light in the stone lantern of our own notions and customs?"

"Does Malachi hold closely with Ezra and Nehemiah?" asked Marduk.

"That I cannot say. I hope not, for Malachi is the coming power in Jerusalem. He seems inspired at times; and, for that matter, he once told me he thought he was; that he felt the impulse of thoughts that came from beyond himself. He said something like this: 'At times my holiest feelings seem unholy; my highest thoughts grovelling. A sense of the law of the Lord binds my sense of right, as a vast crystal holds within it some speck of dirt that glistens.' He says, also, he has impressions he cannot utter; as if he stood in the presence of some glorious being who was coming to be the King of Israel. He cannot shake off the feeling. But here we are at my booth."

CHAPTER XXIII

THE two young men turned in at a little gateway leading from the street, entered a small court, and climbed a stone stairway that ran up the outside of the building to the roof. A booth of four upright poles, covered with brush and leaves, made a shelter from the noon sun that was beating hot upon the stone parapets. The repast showed that Manasseh was as free in living as he was in thinking. The richest condiments and wines of various vintages were used in a familiar manner, and evinced that Manasseh was in no need of instruction in the art of feasting from even the travelled Marduk.

The perfect day overhead, the magnificent landscape of the hills roundabout Jerusalem, a Samaritan banner far off towards the north, which waved its harmless defiance to the streamers that floated from the hundreds of booths in the Valley of Jehosaphat and on the slopes of Olivet—and perhaps the generous flow and mixture of wines—warmed the hearts of the young feasters into familiarity and confidence.

"Manasseh, you would make a superb high priest, only your Urim and Thummim should have, instead of the twelve stones for the tribes of Israel, seventy gems for all the rest of the heathen world, for whom, I understand, you offer seventy bullocks during this festival. Now, I am in the merchandise business, and can trick you out with them. But I am afraid these stiff Jews will never give you the breastplate, unless you repent. Tell me frankly why you show so much heat about the Jews not being allowed to marry foreign wives. Your blood is clear enough from Aaron."

" I stand for the principle of the thing, Marduk."

"That is good," replied the Phœnician. "But perhaps you would like a heathen girl thrown in along with the principle, as this good Bethlehem wine is spiced with something that grew in Arabia. A handsome fellow like you, who goes prowling about among the Samaritans, must have seen fairer flesh than is caged in Jerusalem. I suspect that some Moabitish Ruth, like the one your great Boaz married, has tempted your patriotism. Eh? Or some Egyptian, like the priest's daughter your mighty Moses picked up? Why not start a harem of beauties, as Solomon did? Come now, tell me your secret—for you show no such gall about any other subject."

Manasseh got up, walked to the parapet and leaned over, as if searching for his answer in the stony street below. Coming back to the booth, he slapped Marduk on the shoulder, with—

"Well, since you have guessed, I will confess it. And, Marduk, to be bold about it, you can help me."

"I? Why, of course I can. I have decked out many a maiden, and can present you yours in all the elegance of the Queen of Sheba, who, you say, fell in love with that other gay Jerusalemite, King Solomon. What will you have? Pearls from the lands beyond the Euphrates? Diamonds that were once in the crown of Kassandane, the blind queen of Cyrus the Great? Silks from Damascus, dyed in the purple of Tyre? Ointments and perfumes of the newest fashion in Athens? Give me your list."

"I wish I could buy these," said Manasseh. "But you forget that we Jews did not steal the treasury of Darius, when we came back from Babylon. Yet there is something more valuable than any of these I would get first."

"Why, what an ambitious fellow you are! I have mentioned the rarest trinkets in the world. What more would you have? Name the article: I will try to get it."

"Agreed! get out your tablets."

"Agreed! what is it?"

"I want the girl."

"Ho! ho!" laughed Marduk. "Your love is like heat-lightning; it has flashed, but struck nothing. You would like me to bring you a statue, such as one of our Tyrian kings made, which was of such marvellous beauty that it came to life, and jumped into his arms."

"No," said Manasseh, "mine has life, but I cannot get her into my arms."

12

"Hum-m-m!" ejaculated Marduk, taking his turn in walking to the parapet and looking over.

He brushed some troubled wrinkles from his brow as he turned towards his friend. He slapped Manasseh on the shoulder.

"I will do it, if possible," said he.

Manasseh had closely watched Marduk's action, and baited a question with a similar suspicion.

"Would you not like me to help you? I have wondered what led a thriving merchant like you to go through our land; for our people are too poor to buy your wares. Some Jewish maiden? Eh? Let's make a compact. I will help you to yours, if you will help me to mine. There is lawful precedent for your marrying a woman of my race. In our annals we read that when King Solomon would build the temple, King Hiram of Tyre sent him a famous artisan, who was also named Hiram—for it seems that half the babies of your town are called by that name : I wonder how you escaped the common title—and this workman, Hiram, was the son of a Tyrian man by a Jewish woman. And here is Tobiah, the Satrap of the Ammonites, who is now honored with rooms in our temple, much to the grievance of Ezra. He married the daughter of one of our best citizens, Shechaniah. So tell me the dove that you are swirling through our skies to pounce upon, and I will help you in any honorable way. If Nehemiah should return, he could not forbid your marriage. All he could do, if by any means he acquired the power

he aims at, would be to drive you from the city.
But if you can help me to the possession of my
dove, I can offer you a royal refuge, for I shall
have a power that even the Tirshatha could not
long dispute."

"Oh! I see it all," said Marduk, "you would
be son-in-law to Sanballat of Samaria. But do you
have the heart of the maiden? Indeed, have you
ever seen her? She is reputed to be of queenly
beauty, but of an untamed Moabitish spirit. Woe
to you if you catch a tigress for her spots!"

"Seen her? Ah, my dear friend, when you go to
see her on my behalf you will not need to tell my
name, but just let her look into your eyes. She
will see me pictured there by your very thought of
me. Seen her? Ay, by daylight, and moonlight,
and, best of all, by eyelight, when our lashes touched.
There are exits from Jerusalem that few know, and
I have more than once been reported sick in my
chamber, when I was in the tent of Sanballat."

"Say no more," said Marduk. "I will help you
to a soft place in the Samaritan's palace, and to
the soft arms of the fair Nicaso: and you will
help me—if I want you to?"

"It is agreed," eagerly cried Manasseh. "Bring
out the parchments."

"No, we will not write it, lest the flies read it
and buzz it into the ears of men."

"Crack a stone then, and each carry a half, in
pledge that each will fit himself into the other's
plans, as one part of the stone fits into the other."

A broken bit from the stone parapet that surrounded the roof was cracked in two. Each placed a piece in his wallet, and, with many wishes for mutual success, the young men parted.

CHAPTER XXIV

THE town of Samaria crowned the hill that rises from the centre of a magnificent valley, like an inverted cup in a lordly dish. Far away to the east stand the mountain walls of Gilead and Ammon and Moab; while on the west stretch the uplands of Ephraim and the gleaming waters of the Great Sea. The nearer hills, terraced into gigantic steps, and ordinarily luxuriant with vineyards and fig gardens, were now covered with rankest vegetation of wild growth, at once nature's rebuke and invitation to the husbandman.

The old palace of Ahab, built with bankrupting magnificence by that renegade king of Israel, had long since fallen to ruin. Hard by stood a sarcophagus in which had once rested the spice-embalmed body of some fair princess, but which was now the feeding-trough for a herd of swine. A superb pillar of porphyry, polished until it had once reflected the gay lights that flashed about it, was now a scratching-post for the cattle that roamed at will through the valley.

Since the Persian king had appointed Sanballat, the Moabite chieftain, to be satrap of Samaria, the

land had been somewhat improved. The bats had
been frightened out of the niches in the palace. The
storks no longer sat enthroned upon the stately
columns, nor posed upon one leg, with drooping
wings, looking down lugubriously upon the passer-
by—the symbolic funeral directors of dead em-
pires since time began. The great cedar roof that
once spanned the hall had been succeeded by a
double awning of canvas—the outer covering of
black goat's hair, the inner of white linen, upon
which were wrought tapestries whose gay colors
compensated for their rude forms.

By the side of the grand doorway, with its enormous lintels and cracked cross-piece of stone, stood
the tall banner-staff of the satrap, in sight of a hundred tents which sheltered the standing army of
Samaria. This band of braves was composed
chiefly of Moabitish men, swarthy, long-limbed,
with treacherous looks, as if seeking to repel the
historic taunt of their ill-begetting as a race from
the incestuous daughter of Lot. Their officers
were lithe and gallant Persians, each one of whom
boasted the various deeds he would have performed
if the last expedition against the Greeks had not
been chiefly a naval affair. More plausible, perhaps, were their stories of hair-breadth escapes in
their adventures connected with the harems of Babylon and Susa.

Sanballat, the satrap, was not in military mood
as he reclined upon a long divan in his pavilion.
Seated upon the floor beside him, fondling his long

beard, was a young girl. A glance could detect their relationship. The stiff black bristles that stood upon the man's head were surely of kin to the raven locks that fell softly about her temples. Both had the same jet eyes. In hers the pupils contrasted finely with the pure white balls; in his they were set in blood-shot orbs. Her forehead was low and broad, but moulded as if by some sculptor; his was of the same outline, but knobbed, as if with fiercer passions, and wrinkled by a hundred cares, no one of which had as yet dropped a shadow upon her brow. The father's straight lips were slightly arched in the daughter. Her lips won by asking; his evidently gained only by commanding. His skin was tanned and roughed by years of exposure to the elements, perhaps discolored by excessive use of wine; hers was bronzed by the kissing of the Syrian sun, but not enough to hide the healthy blood that tinted itself through, and displayed her beauty in all the delicate shades of blushes. The crimson upon her cheeks and temples was just now of a deeper hue than usual, as Sanballat was saying:

"My Nicaso must let her father keep charge of her heart. The satrap's daughter shall not be as other maidens, the prey of any fine fellow whose manner may be pleasing. Such a face and form as yours, to say nothing of your lineage, would gain you admission to the court of Susa or Memphis. Old Orpha, your nurse, tells me that you talk overmuch of some young swain. I do not ask who, for none worthy of my fair one lives in Samaria."

"I believe you," replied the girl, playfully pluck-
ing a gray hair from his beard. "No one in Samaria is good enough for the great Sanballat's
daughter. I will sell for too much; for—a satrapy
of all Palestine, if Artaxerxes likes my looks! or for
an alliance with the new king of Tyre, if the daughter of the rich Ahimelek dies broken-hearted because Baal will not send back her Hiram."

She leaped to her feet, and, catching up a timbrel,
gracefully performed the movement of a dance.

"By Astarte!" cried the satrap, "such a woman
never graced this place since Jezebel. Aha! no
little Ahab shall catch my wild pigeon. Have a
care, Nicaso, who sets a snare for you!"

Her laugh rang merrily. "Be sure I shall keep
myself bright and safe, like a new coin in the box,
for the day of sale."

She looked between the swinging curtains.

"But here comes one handsome enough to be
cup-bearer to you, father, when I have bought you
a throne. I will begone. Only don't sell me through
him. He is a merchant. One, two, three camels
heavily laden, and himself on horseback. He could
trinket me out fit for Tammuz himself, I have no
doubt. And, father," she threw her arms fondly
about his neck, "just a necklace, or an anklet, or
an armlet, or a cap of coins! I will sell better for
an ornament."

The girl disappeared through the rear of the pavilion into the palace enclosure. Sanballat rose to
welcome his visitor at the entrance.

The traveller dismounted from his horse, and made a low salâm, which the satrap returned as cordially as his reserve of official dignity permitted.

" I am Marduk, servant, if you will permit, to my Lord Sanballat," said the stranger.

" Ah, Marduk of Tyre! Your fame as a merchant has come before you. Welcome good Marduk of Tyre."

" I hardly deserve the title ' from Tyre,' for many months have passed since I worshipped Melkarth in his temple there. I am rather a citizen of the world. The Isles of Greece, the Nile to the Cataracts, the shores of the Red Sea, the lands of Ammon and Moab, and even Jerusalem might claim me."

" The more welcome, then," replied Sanballat. " The proverb says, ' A travelled man is a wise man,' but it ought to have said, if he did not linger too long in Jerusalem ; for only fools are there. Shake off the dust of the Jews' land, and make one of us, good Marduk."

Servants relieved the stranger of his upper garment and sandals ; they brought water and washed his feet. Others offered refreshments, of which Sanballat partook with his guest.

" And what land pleases you best ?" asked the host as they lingered over the cup of wine.

" No land is fairer than Samaria, my lord. Your fields are richer than I have seen for many a day. The vale of Shechem, by which I entered your domain, is a place where the gods might be pleased to abide with men. As I looked up to the heights of Gerizim I could well believe the legend that there, rather than on the hill where the Jews have put their temple, the great Father Abraham offered the sacrifice of his son."

"A sacrifice that Jehovah would not accept," said Sanballat, sneeringly; "but he preferred a ram as something nobler than a Jew. Baal did accept the sacrifice of the heroic Prince of Tyre. Ah! he was worthy of the god's feast even without being roasted—eh, Marduk? But don't take offence. I meant no irreverence to Baal. I believe in Baal as much as you do."

"I do not doubt it," replied Marduk.

"Yes, I worship Baal," continued Sanballat, scarcely pausing. "That is, as a Moabite I worship Baal-Chemosh; but in this land of ancient Israel I have to keep on good terms with Jehovah, or, as I should call him, Baal of Israel."

"That is wise," replied Marduk. "I have studied closely the strange people at Jerusalem. They are truly possessed by their God. Jehovah is a reality among these hills, whatever he may be elsewhere."

"Yes," said Sanballat, "Jehovah is a god of the hills. Baal can't match him there. But down on the coast, in your country, Jehovah cannot keep a foothold."

"Have you noted," interrupted Marduk, "how the power of the Jews is growing? Thousands of them, once scattered among all countries, are returning. They are bringing with them great wealth, and

are building the waste places. The enthusiasm for
revived Israel is like a disease that floats in the air
over many lands, and fastens on those who are sus-
ceptible ; and every Jew from Babylon to Gades is
in the catching condition. I wonder that you do
not make an alliance with them, and reap in their
harvest, my Lord Sanballat?"

"Reap their harvest! That I would—with a
torch. Think you, Marduk! I have offered these
miserable Jews my friendship. Even offered to help
them build their city. But their ass-headed stub-
bornness would not listen to me. There was a time
when I could have cut all their throats, and yet I
spared them."

Sanballat strode up and down the apartment.
When he had worked off the froth of his passion
the native cunning of the man asserted itself, and,
sitting down close to his guest, he studied his face
for a moment. "You said, Make an alliance? Is
it possible?"

"Possible! Why not?" replied Marduk. "Only
Ezra and Nehemiah have heretofore prevented, and
now Ezra is like an old dog who keeps his spirit
but has lost his teeth. He cannot hold on to affairs long. And as for Nehemiah, the Tirshatha,
he is enamoured of the feasts at the palace of Susa,
and shows no sign of coming back."

"The Tirshatha! A curse on that mongrel Persian and Jewish dog!"

Sanballat took another turn about the room, as
uneasy as a chained bear with a dog snapping at

his legs. The exercise clarified his half-drunken wits, and he resumed the council.

"Ezra's teeth may be broken, but that whelp Nehemiah's teeth are sharp enough. But for him I should now have my palace on the hill of Zion, and my soldiers be encamped in the valley of Jehosaphat. Then, think of it, Marduk! mine should be the satrapy from Syria to Egypt."

"The thing is possible yet," replied Marduk. "There is no ruler now at Jerusalem. The high priest's family are chief in influence. They are jealous of Nehemiah, and do not want him back from Susa. They are ready to strengthen themselves in any way. They are already scratching the ambitious itch of Tobiah, the Ammonite. They have torn out the walls between the priest's chambers to make state quarters for his Impudence in the very temple itself."

"Humph! Tobiah cannot help them," said Sanballat.

"But he can help himself by them," replied Marduk.

"He shall not."

"Why not?"

"Why not? Why not?" Sanballat was again upon his feet, and shook his fist in the face of Marduk, as if the guest were the hated Tobiah. "Why not? Because"—he fairly shrieked out his spleen —"because he is an Ammonite. Moab must have the ascendency in this land, so far as Persia allows either of us to rule. The blood of every man of

Moab would turn to adder's poison if Tobiah were anything higher than the servant of Sanballat."

" Then prevent him."

" Prevent him! I shall, or may the fire of Chemosh burn me! But, good Marduk, tell me how you would do it?"

" Why, by offering better alliance with the priests myself. The rising man in Jerusalem is Manasseh. He is grandson of Eliashib, the high priest. He is as astute as Nehemiah, and more popular. If the Tirshatha does not come back, Manasseh will be proclaimed governor. If Nehemiah should return, Manasseh, by virtue of his priestly rank, must be the man of his right hand."

" Grandson of Eliashib? Then he is still young, and unmarried."

" Yes."

Sanballat took a long turn about the apartment. Seating himself again, he put his head close to Marduk's.

" You have seen my daughter?"

" I have heard of her beauty. It is famed everywhere. Good blood will come to the cheek as well as put strength into the arm. They say she is a sprig of yourself, my Lord Sanballat."

" Woe to the man that should say differently," replied the Moabite, feeling the flattery. " Is Manasseh comely, well built, strong; or a sleek priest that dare not draw a knife but on a bullock?"

" No man is better gifted in body or mind than Manasseh. Far be it from me, a stranger, to sug-

gest such a thing to my Lord Sanballat ; but since
you have first mentioned it, I make bold to say
that there is no alliance so permanent between
rulers as an alliance of blood. As the blood gives
a common life to all the body, and prevents the
parts from falling asunder through disagreement,
so it is with an alliance of blood among nations.
Besides, such a union with one who is to be high
priest would modify the strictness of the Jews' religion, and lead to some common code of worship
in which Jehovite and Baalite might unite. I fore-
see from that a new Syria, its people one, its ruler
Sanballat, and its great temple here in Samaria, or,
perhaps, upon Mount Gerizim itself. All Phœnicia might be brought into such a confederation.
Think of the riches of Tyre and Sidon, the strong-
hold of Jerusalem, the great tribes across the Jordan, perhaps Damascus, all under the suzerainty of
Samaria !"

Sanballat was carried away with this conceit,
which it was evident Marduk had only revived in
his mind, not suggested. He strode to the palace
front, and looked out over the hills. His eyes
widened as if taking in the vision of his new empire. Marduk followed him. The satrap put his
arm fondly about his guest.

"You speak as the Jews say Daniel did in Babylon when he told the king his dream, for what you
say has been my waking vision for years. yet I have
breathed it to none. And why should it not be accomplished ?"

"It may be, and you yourself have suggested the first stitch in the new fabric—the union of your house with that of the high priest."

"Well said, Marduk! Well said! I would see the young man. No father can fix the stars for his child's destiny until he sees if they reflect themselves brightly in her heart. If Nicaso should evince repugnance to the Jew, or he should not be taken with the charms of a Moabite—"

"Impossible! Impossible to either, when they meet! Two such comely persons must love at sight. Besides, they could not resist the wooing of great state necessities, ambition for the glory of rank and power, and the praise which we can make sure each shall hear of the other, even before they meet."

"Marduk, you are a statesman, worthy of the repute of your King Hiram, whom Baal has taken to himself; for they say he was the wisest man that ever sat in the council of Tyre. Draw up the compact, Marduk. You merchants know the form. We will study it at our leisure, for you are to be my guest until you return to Jerusalem with authority to consummate the union of Nicaso and Manasseh; of Nicaso and Manasseh! The names sound well together. Ay, the union of Samaria and Judah, of Sanballat and all Syria!

Sanballat was in high spirits. He ordered a jar of the wine of Hebron, "the only wine the King of Persia will drink, but not too good for Marduk and the Satrap of Samaria, of Syria." He called for his captains, and distributed among them a skin of beer, the brewing of Damascus. Dancers were summoned; men who, balancing pitchers and jars of water upon their heads, took their steps dexterously between the waving blades of swords; and women who exhibited every possible grace of motion with their bodies, while allowing only the slightest motion of their feet. Horsemen performed marvellous exploits. The camel-drivers added their share to the hilarity by attempting to imitate these equestrian movements upon their awkward beasts. A score or two of asses were forced into orchestral braying by tickling their noses, and brought to a sudden silence by twisting their tails.

As the crowd withdrew to regale themselves with a largess of leben, the daughter of the satrap appeared. Her maidens spread an elegant rug, wrought on the looms of Tehera, a gift to the satrap from Artaxerxes.

Nicaso's entire person was covered with a long veil. Though it was supposed to hide her features, it coquettishly revealed not only enough to assure Marduk that the fame of her beauty was warranted, but also to make him feel that her part of the entertainment was not altogether due to obedience to her father's wish, but was also a gratuitous compliment to his presence.

A harp was brought to her. To its accompaniment she sang a song based upon the legendary love of Solomon for the Shulammite maiden, his wooing, and her rejection of royal favors through constancy to her shepherd lover. Nicaso's voice was exceedingly rich and flexible. It well represented the gentler sentiments; but was startlingly effective in its deeper tones, which were adapted to the wilder portions of the song, and suggested an untamed element in the singer herself.

"A glorious bit of womanhood," thought Marduk; "but I would rather Manasseh had the responsibility of owning it than I."

He turned to speak to the satrap, but that worthy, overcome by the abundance and mixture of drinks, was fast asleep, if not drunk. It will be well to drop the curtain briefly upon Samaria.

13

CHAPTER XXV

TWO hours' ride south of the Phœnician city of
Gebal, which the Greeks called Byblus, the
river Adonis pours into the sea the water it has
gathered from the melting snows and living springs
of the Lebanon. Every year the banks of the stream
were thronged with multitudes that swarmed out
from Tyre and Sidon, Byblus and Sarepta, and all
the fishing hamlets and farm villages from Aradus
to Joppa. These people were pilgrims to Apheca,
the source of the sacred river Adonis.

It was the month of Tammuz, when summer bursts
with fecund life upon the land of Syria. The change
of the season was thought of by the Syrians under
the pleasing myth of Astarte and Tammuz; or, as
the Greeks told the story, of Venus and Adonis.
When summer yielded to winter, stark and sterile,
this was Tammuz, in his strength and beauty, slain
by the wild boar. The returning spring-time was the
resurrection of the fair divinity under the embraces
of the yearning goddess. The water of the river,
reddened by the earth that mingled with it, as the
melting snows from the Lebanon overflowed the
channel of the stream, was it not Tammuz's blood?

Several months had elapsed since the events heretofore related. The ruddy tide of Adonis River had already sent out its annual invitation for the festival. The report had been duly repeated that the star, which was none other than Astarte herself, had been seen to pass over Lebanon and fall into the pool of Apheca, the fountain-head of the river.

The joy of Astarte and Tammuz, now restored to each other's arms, was especially honored by love-making between the sexes. The innocent play of sentiment among the simple-minded people would naturally have degenerated into grossness, even had there not been prescribed the sacrifice of maidenly modesty upon the altar of Astarte, as a preliminary to legitimate marriage. The renown of the festival of the Syrian goddess drew not only worshippers, but the curious and the vile, from all parts of the world, as insects are attracted by light and by foulness.

The banks of the river Adonis were adorned at places with the memorial tombs of the god, wrought not only with the highest Phœnician art, but in many cases with the touch of the more delicate chisel of the Greek. Interspersed among these permanent ornaments of the sylvan stream were the tents of the pilgrims, whose rich canvas and streamers contrasted gayly with the sombre rocks of the deep ravines and the dense shadows of the overhanging trees. These tents the wealthier folk pitched for their noontide rest or for the night, as they journeyed leisurely towards the river's fount.

A pavilion larger than all others, and which excited the gaping gossip of the passers-by, was that of the household of Ahimelek of Tyre. Indeed, next to the marvels of the goddess herself, the visit of Zillah was the chief notoriety of the season at Apheca. She was to engage in the ceremonial which not only marked her entrance upon womanhood, but which was to be especially preliminary to her marriage with Rubaal, the presumptive king. By ancient custom the queen of Tyre was also ordained a priestess of Astarte. The splendid rites of Zillah's institution as such were to follow the less seemly ones. This would have drawn to her tent the curiosity of all, even if the tent had not concealed the person of one who had been the affianced of King Hiram, whose translation to the estate of the gods surely omened some miraculous blessing upon her who would have been his queen and bride.

The priests of Melkarth had joined with those of Astarte in fanning the popular interest in Zillah's investiture, as it was understood that the greater part of Ahimelek's dower would go into their coffers; for Rubaal, her prospective husband, was but the priesthood crowned in the person of its tool.

To Layah, the handmaiden of Zillah, the strange taking-off of the king, whatever it meant, was the profoundest disappointment of her life. She had thought so long of him as her young lord, had served him with such devotion when she served her young mistress, that she had now no object in life but to join with Zillah in her mourning, or to comfort her as a mother would comfort her broken-hearted child. From the marriage of Zillah with Rubaal she shrank, and would have detested it even if her mistress had been able to put off her old love for the new.

"To-morrow, Layah, is the day. It has come at last."

Zillah raised her face to her companion's. It was very fair; more winsome than ever before. It had been growing in beauty; but of that spiritual sort of beauty that awakens pain together with admiration. Her eyes were deeper set; more lustrous, but with a far-away look, as if the light that kindled them came from beyond the common day. Her face was thinner, its lines harder and sharper. "A typical face for a priestess!" old Egbalus said, as once he saw her. "A sufferer's face!" thought Layah every day, and a hundred times a day, as she saw beneath it the tragic features of her mistress's soul.

"Do you hold to your resolution, my lady?" Layah asked, her voice trembling, scarcely making the words articulate.

"Yes—at last! at last!"

Layah threw herself on the ground at her mistress's feet. She remained for a while as one in prayer. At length, raising her face, she cried:

"O my lady! have I influenced you to this decision? Tell me truly, as Astarte lives! as Baal-Hiram lives there in the sky! tell me, truly, have I led you?"

"No, Layah, you have not. It was the covenant
I made with him who was Adonai to me, my lord
Hiram! my god Hiram, if Baal will! Baal will
take us both. Hanno himself, and he is wisest of
all the priests, assured me that we should not always be separated. I asked him directly if at the
festival of Adonis I might not go to Hiram. He
replied that in the lore of the priests such things
are said to have occurred, and bade me be true to
Hiram, and watch; and, furthermore, he gave me a
sign of the divine will. But I may tell it to no one;
not even to my faithful Layah."

"If," said Layah, "I have not persuaded you to
the deed, tell me now, before the gods, have I
sought to dissuade you?"

"No, my dear Layah, you too have been true to
my lord Hiram. You have not hindered me from
my holy sacrifice to him."

"May I have my reward, then, from the hand of
my mistress?"

"Ask what you will, Layah."

"Let me go with you, if merely human creatures
may enter the world of the gods. Perhaps I can
serve there. They have slaves there, have they
not? The sky has flecks in it. Why may not I
be with you? I know that Baal-Hiram will let me
come with you."

"No, no!" cried Zillah. "It must not be. If I
live after my body is dead—and who can tell?—
let me think of you as living here. I will come
back often, and bless you: or I will watch over

you as the moon gleams upon us. And if I do not live again, let there be one heart in this world to mourn for me. I have none other than thine, my dear Layah. My father does not love me, except for the riches I may bring him. To you I give these. See! This armlet was Hiram's gift. Let me put it on you. This necklace you shall wear. Do not deny me this favor, or I shall believe no one on earth loved me."

The two women remained much of the night weeping, or in grief too deep for tears: Zillah prayerful and resolute, the comforter of her hand-maiden; as if the poor girl's sorrow were for some other misery than that of her consoler.

CHAPTER XXVI

WITH the dawn all was astir. From behind rocks and trees the curious stared as Zillah's litter was carried along. At every spot where the path widened, so as to allow them to gather in crowds, many people prostrated themselves as if before a sacred ark. The day was yet young when the denser throngs indicated the immediate vicinity of the holy place. The servants of Ahimelek had gone before Zillah and prepared her pavilion, so that when she stepped veiled from the litter she entered alone the seclusion of her own chamber.

A vast amphitheatre of rocks, rising almost perpendicularly hundreds of feet, abruptly closes the valley of the Adonis. A deep and dark cave opens at the base of this precipice, like some ominous portal of Sheol itself. From its black jaws issues the torrent, hailing its first glimpse of the light with wild roar, like that of some beast startled in its den by the flash of the hunter's torch. Tossing high its mane of spray, it leaps wildly down from ledge to ledge, until it stretches itself for its long race through the deep ravine below. Its course is lined with trees—gigantic oaks, their limbs gnarled and torn, like those of veteran gladiators, by conflict with the storms of centuries; tall pines whose lofty tufts at noonday throw shadows, like patches of night, into the gorge below. Nature here seems to resent the intrusion of men, and drops a sense of solitude among the noisy crowds, or lifts them in spite of their revelry to an awe of her own vast mysteries. It is a spot where men, if they have no genuine revelation, are tempted to invent gods; to shape them into phantasies of overwrought imagination, and clothe them in the shadowy habits of their fears.

Close beside the Fountain of Adonis rose the Temple of Astarte. In front was a quadrangular court, in the open portion of which the throngs of votaries walked, and beneath whose cloistered sides they rested in extravagant ease and sanctioned vice. In the centre of the court stood the great conical stone, the symbol of deity, on the top of which, twice a year, a chosen priest sat and presented to the divinity the prayers of those who sent their petitions up to him winged with sufficient gifts to warrant their flight to the goddess. White doves flitted through the air, perched upon the projecting stone-work of the porticos, and flocked on the marble pavement regardless of the convenience of human beings, whose superstition made reverent space for the birds which Astarte had chosen to be her favorite symbol. The cooing of the doves, intermingled with the softest notes of flutes floating lasciviously from hidden places, melted into the murmur of the stream. The natural perfume of plants and flowers was supplemented by the incense of rarest spices, which loaded the atmosphere with the illusion of some other world beyond the shores of Araby the Blest.

Back of the great court an ascent of steps led to the temple. Folding gates of bronze guarded the sacred precincts from unhallowed intrusion. Gilded beams held aloft the roof of cedar, carved with grotesque symbols.

The statue of the goddess stood colossal in size and exquisite in form and decoration. In her right hand she held the sceptre, in her left the distaff; for, while she swayed the hearts of women, she was at the same time the patroness and rewarder of their domestic industry. On her head was a tower of gold, whose gleaming spikes well imitated the rays of the sun by day. But at night her peculiar glory was revealed. Then the sacred stone that was set in her crown glowed with mysterious light, and filled the temple with soft rays as of the moon. The central gleam from the stone followed the beholder as an eye, shooting the beam from the omniscience of the goddess into the very soul of the devotee. A statue of Baal sometimes floated in the air, and invited the questions of worshippers, to which it gave oracular response by swaying forward if the answer were affirmative, and backward if a request were refused.

There were varieties of worship adapted to the caprice of all comers. Some bent over the pool, where the torrent, issuing from the cave and plunging from the ledge, makes its first halting-place. Into the swirling waters they cast jewels and gems. If these sank to the bottom, they were presumed to have been accepted by the divinity; if they were cast up by the swift and turbulent eddies, the worshipper retired without assurance of favor. Perhaps the devotee did not confess to himself the selfishness of his motive for making his offering of goodly weight; nor did the priests confess to the people the motive with which every night they dragged the pool and took up the sunken basins they had placed in the bottom.

In the temple court were daily hung some golden caskets containing the hair and beards of young men, their first manly offering to the goddess, whose favors they entreated with the fair sex; and other caskets or bags of golden thread held the similar offerings of the maidens.

A less attractive sight was that of one who had sacrificed a sheep, and, while its skin was still warm with life, placed its head upon his own, tied its forelegs about his neck, the greasy inside against his face, and, doubling his body so that he could kneel upon the lower part of the skin, prayed to the Sheep-goddess — one of the appellations of the Queen of Heaven.

The most imposing offering was that of the Fire Night, the preparation for which occupied many days. A large area in front of the temple court was filled with standing trees which had been cut from the sides of Lebanon, and made an artificial grove. The offerings of devotees were hung among the branches—rich jewels, and the handiwork ornaments of the poorer class; garments of priceless stuffs, and the discarded only raiment of some pauper; birds of all plumage, some in cages of bronze or carved alabaster, some tied by strings to the trees; wild animals, the captive pets of the hunter; sheep, and at times living bulls, swung in girdles from the stancher branches of the trees. The combustible nature of the wood was augmented by smearings of resinous matter gathered in great quantities in the forest.

After the images of the gods had been carried about the grove, at a given signal torches were applied at many places simultaneously. Then there burst through the night a spectacle of wildest magnificence. The spark sprites sprang rapidly from the lower to the topmost limbs of each tree; then roofed the intervals with arches of fire; then flung far and high over all a hundred sheets of flame, banners and streamers that signalled the event to the very sky. The intense heat so rarefied the air that, though scarce a leaf quivered on Lebanon, a mighty wind was created, which swayed the forest around, whose roar answered back the roar of the burning timber. This was not unreasonably interpreted by ignorant people to be the response of nature to the honor paid to its queen.

The day on which Zillah reached the shades of

Apheca was the one devoted to mourning for Tammuz. The box containing the image of the god had been borne on the shoulders of six priestesses of Astarte, followed by a procession of maidens with dishevelled hair and torn garments, who threw handfuls of ashes into the air, and filled the grove with their wailing for the brief widowhood of their goddess. At nightfall the coffin was buried. As at the time of real death the lights are extinguished in the house, so now every tent was darkened. Only sounds of lamentation floated through the ravine and among the sacred trees, prompted at brief intervals by the lugubrious wailing of a trumpet blown in the temple precincts.

With the first blush of the new day all was changed; hilarity took the place of mourning. The woods rang with shouts and song and merry laughter. The image of the god was exhumed, and carried in the arms of dancing women to the temple. On this day maidens, hoping to be married before the year elapsed, gave their hair in offering to Astarte or their persons to the embrace of strangers. The latter was the more sacred service, the performance of which could not be omitted in the case of one highly born or ambitious of entering the aristocratic circles of matronhood. The women entered the booths prepared. With locks entwined into the conventional sacred node, arrayed in elegance rivalling that of the bridal raiment they hoped to wear, glittering with the gems that betokened their dowry, they sat and waited for the rite.

CHAPTER XXVII

LAYAH was fully persuaded of the determination of her mistress to destroy herself, and, notwithstanding Zillah's commands to the contrary, was resolved to imitate her heroic example. This purpose was strengthened by her fears of Rubaal's vengeance upon her in the event of Zillah's suicide. Her handmaiden would be suspected of collusion with the unhappy lady, and certainly be charged with a criminal neglect in allowing such a deed. Her penalty would be death, unless Rubaal and the priests invented for her something worse—sale for the ship-harem of some rude sea-captain, transportation to the tin-mines of the Cassiterides, or physical torture in some prison. In contrast with such possibilities, her mind became fascinated with the idea of standing erect, raising her arm adorned with the wristlet which her mistress had given her, striking the sharp blade into her breast just beneath the heavy pendants of the necklace that Zillah had worn, and falling dead by her side — a brave self-sacrifice to her love for her mistress and her fidelity to the royal house of Tyre.

The two women went together to the shambles

of Astarte, both closely covered with the long veil, which concealed their faces and forms. No word passed between them, except Zillah's repetition of the oft-said vow: "The dagger before the stranger!"

At the shambles they stood a moment in endearing embrace, then silently separated. Zillah entered the booth designated by the insignia of the house of Ahimelek. Layah entered another adjacent, which communicated with that of her mistress; an arrangement which allowed the toilet service of a maid without apparent intrusion.

The day passed. The general reverence for the person of the betrothed of the now deified Hiram, together with the awe that was felt for the person of one who was to be a priestess of Astarte, restrained the most wanton from approaching Zillah's retreat.

Night shadows had already climbed the precipitous sides of the valley, crowding the sunlight before them, until the day gleamed only in the tops of the tall pines that fringed the crest and seemed to mingle with the sky.

The priests had noted the immunity of Zillah's apartment; that no one had approached it. They were concerned about the issue. A group of several strangers had been observed during most of the day sauntering about the temple court. These were approached by the priests, who evidently offered them money to assist in the accomplishment of the rite. After a few moments of apparent entreaty with them one of their number said, " I will go ;" and, stepping from the group, walked to the apartment.

"Handsome enough for Adonis himself !" observed a priest.

"How the eyes of Rubaal would turn green to see him !" rejoined another.

" He looks like a Jew," said a third.

" That cannot be," replied the first speaker, "or he would have bargained with us for a heavier price upon his service."

The strange man approached the curtain of the apartment and hesitatingly drew it aside.

Zillah sprang to her feet. She was clad in the white robe of a priestess of Astarte. One who believed that Hiram had entered the estate of the gods would have declared that Astarte had herself entered the person of this woman. Her look was superhuman. An unearthly passion burned in her eyes. Her whole frame seemed to glow with the radiation of her soul, as a lantern globe with the light that is centred in, but not contained by, it. Her attitude, as she retreated a few steps to the rear of the little room, was majesty itself. Her jewelled hand held a dagger at her breast. She pressed it until the blood trickled beneath its gleaming edge, but, in the ecstasy of her mental mood, she was evidently unconscious of pain.

The man raised his hands in entreaty against the intended deed. He stepped towards her. She retreated farther, and stopped his approach by the

very spell of her gesture as she raised her left hand
and bade him stand. He tried to speak, but she
silenced him by her words :

"Go! tell the priests that I offer myself to my
Adonai Hiram, whose spirit calls me."

A look of agonizing terror came upon the intruder.
He hastily threw back his outer garment, and point-
ed, speechless with excitement, to his own breast.
Upon his white chiton glowed a ring of crimson.

Zillah's dagger fell from her hand.

"The circle!" she cried, and dropped into a swoon.

A slight scream as of an echo to Zillah's cry rang
from the adjoining apartment of Layah. It was a
tone of mingled determination and pain, shrill, brief,
and followed by the sound of one falling to the
ground.

Silently the man waited. At length Zillah raised
her head. She gazed around her in a daze.

"He is not here, my lord ! my Hiram !"

Seeing the man, she added : "O cruel dream!"
and reached for the dagger that lay on the ground
beside her.

The man seized it first. The action fully aroused
her to the reality of her position.

For a moment the two stared at each other in
mutual perplexity. They were parts of an enigma
which neither understood, though each held a portion of the clew.

Zillah was the first to break the silence.

"What is your message to me by the mark of the
circle ?"

14

"You know its meaning better than I," rejoined the stranger, bowing in profound respect.

"Am I to go with you?"

"I am to do your bidding, my lady."

The man made obeisance, touching the ground with his forehead. "My life is pledged to bring you to him who wrought the symbol on my breast."

"And he?"

"Marduk, of Tyre."

"I know none such. Is he not Hanno, the priest?"

"I only know him as Marduk, the merchant of Tyre."

"Tall, with shaved head, and eyes full of subtle wisdom?"

"No. Of my own stature, with hair black as the raven's; of open face. His beard conceals a scar of a wound received in fight."

"A scar! Is he a man? Is he not a god?"

"More godlike than any god of the Phœnicians; yet a man, indeed."

Zillah sat motionless, her head pressed against her hand in deep thought.

"I cannot understand it," she said, at length. "Mystery! mystery! Oh, I do not know—I cannot see!" and she stared into the shadows as one walking in sleep.

"Nor I, my lady. I only know that I am here to obey you. Command me!"

"And I will obey the sign," said Zillah. "Let me look upon it again. 'Tis a circle, surely; and 'tis blood-red. I must follow it."

" And follow me ?"

" Yes—to him ! to him !"

" Let me leave you, then, my lady. You will
know my face or my voice ; for I must let no eyes
but yours look upon the symbol. To-night I will be
beside the pavilion. Another will accompany me
whom you may trust, for we both serve a man we
love ; one to whom we have vowed secrecy and service."

" Before what god have you vowed ?"

" Before no god, but by all that is meant by
man's honor. And, by all that is meant " — he
paused before he added—" by all that is meant by
the sanctity of womanhood. I swear by the life I
have saved this hour—and I know of nothing more
sacred, since what I have witnessed—I swear that
no harm shall come to you. If mistake has happened in the person of her I seek, or in him you
seek, I swear by your own life to return with you
to your father's house. Can I do more ?"

" I will follow the mark of the circle wherever it
may lead," said Zillah.

The stranger withdrew from the apartment. The
priests met him without. They led him to the clerk
of the temple, before whom he took the oath that
the sacrifice to Astarte had been rendered.

Zillah sought the adjacent apartment of Layah.
Upon the ground lay the prostrate form of the girl.
A pool of blood told the story of her sacrifice, not
to Astarte, but to friendship ; to that love of woman for woman, holier than the debauched heathen-

ism of the world ever conceived or tried to express through its rituals.

Zillah flung herself upon the body: "It is too much! too much! O my Layah! my sister! my mother! speak to me!"   She kissed the silent lips, that seemed to smile at the touch, and gave into hers the last lingering warmth that had been life.

Scarcely knowing what she did, she took up the dead girl's veil and ran from the apartment; not through her own, but directly into the court. With stumbling feet she sought her pavilion.

"There goes her handmaid," said a priest.

"A graceful shape, which the veil cannot hide. The new priestess will come out soon," said another.

CHAPTER XXVIII

ZILLAH'S soul now impelled her to hasten her flight. She must not be captured. For what could she live in Tyre but to grace the pride of Rubaal, insolent as he was insignificant? Then the memory of Layah, who had given her life to encourage her in fleeing such a fate, would be a perpetual rebuke. She would see the dead girl's face always in remonstrance. Layah would become to her a jinn, a demon, her human love turned to ghostly hate.

Nor was this all. Zillah conceived of herself as having broken faith with Astarte in not rendering the sacrifice. She could not now be a priestess of the goddess. Astarte, if a real divinity, would strike her dead the first time she attempted to minister at her altar.

But Hiram had not believed in Astarte; why should she? It was possible that Hiram was living. The scar? It must be so. If not, the circle which priest Hanno had told her to follow surely indicated his will. Her human affection led her to seek him. If he were dead to earth, and, as the priests said, taken to Baal and become a god, he surely would have prevented any misuse of the symbol he had given her. It must lead to him, to some mountain-top, or some cave where gods have been known to meet with men.

There was but one course open to her. It was flight. She knew not whither; but, if the worst came, she had the last resort still left. She could join Layah and Hiram anywhere, at any moment; and, suiting her action to her thought, she felt in her bosom for a phial containing the poison with which she had intended to accomplish her suicide if anything prevented the quicker work of the knife. It was there. Drawing it out, she looked through the ruddy liquid, and apostrophized it thus:

"You will befriend me! Red, like the blood of Layah! Red, like Hiram's circle! True friend, if men prove false! We cannot misunderstand each other!"

She kissed the phial, and put it back into her bosom.

It became quite dark, except for the lanterns that hung from the trees and the torches that the revellers were carrying. She stepped out into the night, closely veiled.

A voice, that of the stranger, greeted her. It did not startle her. She had become familiar with it, though so few words had it uttered, because they had been words of kindness and confidence. Strange though it was, it was the only voice in all the world that she dared to hear now. She must trust it. What else was there to trust on earth or in the sky?

"I am ready. Lead! I will follow," she whispered.

It was not difficult to avoid detection, there were so many veiled and masked figures flitting among the lights and shadows of the sacred grove. Zillah felt confident of safety, at least from the priests, should they seek to detain her; for her quick eyes could not fail to notice that there were others in league with her guide. Two men almost kept pace with her. Sometimes one went ahead, and, making a way for himself through the thicker throngs, left it open for her. Or, if attention seemed drawn to her, one of these mysterious attendants dropped behind her, and blocked the way until she was beyond the sight of the curious.

A little way down the ravine, where the crowd was thinner, a litter was in waiting. As she entered it, the two men she had observed lifted it, and, turning abruptly from the river, climbed the steep bank. As they reached the bluff and placed the litter upon the ground a fourth person joined the party. His stay was but for a moment. He threw his arms about one of the bearers of the litter.

"All the gods be praised, and especially Jehovah of the Jews, this time!" said he, putting his hand upon the shoulder of the guide. "But I must away. This is no place for me, the future high priest of Melkarth! Ha! ha! But now you have the goddess herself enshrined in a litter, you will have safe journey. For a while Baal and Jehovah watch between us, good Marduk." The speaker was gone.

The guide lifted Zillah from the litter; and as he held her by the hand, he placed it in that of one of the carriers.

"Marduk, have I kept my covenant with you?"

Marduk's reply was not to him. A whispered word, and Zillah lay speechless in the arms of the Phœnician merchant.

The men withdrew as from too near proximity to some holy scene. Four horses were brought. As Zillah was lifted to the saddle, the Phœnician mentioned the names of his comrades, Manasseh of Jerusalem and Elnathan of Galilee, who in turn kissed the hand of the maiden and mounted their horses — Elnathan guiding the way, and Manasseh following, while Marduk rode by Zillah's side. The moon burst brilliantly from behind a mass of clouds.

"Astarte's parting blessing!" exclaimed Elnathan.

"No, Astarte goes with us," said Manasseh, remembering the scene in the shambles. "A fairer goddess than Phœnicia ever dreamed of!"

Great was the commotion in the Grove of Adonis late that night. It was reported that Ahimelek's daughter had not been seen to come from her apartment, though her maid had returned to the pavilion. As the hours wore on, the anxiety of the priests led them to search the place. There lay

the girl upon the ground. The armlets and necklace were assumed to identify her; and such was
the dread the common people had of a dead body,
that no one of the domestics from Ahimelek's household had ventured to look upon her face.

The priests ordered that the body should be left
where it had fallen until swift couriers had run to
Gebal, where Ahimelek had taken advantage of the
coming exaltation of his daughter to the priesthood
of Astarte, to demand the monopoly of supplying
the provisions that were sold to the caterers at
Apheca during the festival—a source of enormous
revenues. His presence at Gebal had been sufficient to secure the discomfiture of all competitors
for the trade, and many of his ships had exchanged
their cargoes for the gold of the venders at the dock.
Just before the priestly couriers brought him the
news of Zillah's supposed death, a messenger had
come from Tyre to Gebal, conveying a letter which
had been discovered in her chamber after the family
party had left their home. It read:

"MY FATHER,—A daughter's obedience is sacred while
the life he has given her remains. But I cannot endure the
severity of your command. With your permission I once
gave myself to King Hiram. I cannot recall this betrothal.
To him I shall go. This will explain anything that may occur at the festival of Tammuz.   ZILLAH."

On reading the letter, Ahimelek's rage knew no
bounds. He cursed his daughter aloud in the
hearing of the bystanders. He cursed the name
of Hiram, and defied him to appear to him as god

or jinn or ghost. He even challenged Baal himself to thus circumvent the will of the richest man of Phœnicia—one who held the welfare of the state religion at his disposal.

"Let the Temple of Melkarth fall! Let the image of the god rot!" he exclaimed, in his insane rage.

Other couriers then arrived bringing the news of Zillah's death. "Killed by her maid, who has escaped," they explained.

The remnant of fatherly instinct asserted itself for a moment in Ahimelek's breast.

"My daughter! My daughter!" he cried, sitting upon the ground, and covering his face with his hands. But the gentler mood gave way to his wrath, as on the Fire Night the flames in the grove of Apheca caught the unburnt trees.

He held the letter in his hand, which trembled with his frenzy. Bewildered with his anger, he read it aloud.

"She has slain herself!" he cried. "Curse! curse! A father's curse upon the suicide! She has robbed me of my riches, of my honor. And you priests, see you not she has robbed you? robbed Melkarth? robbed the king? robbed Tyre?"

Then, as the fire dies down when resinous matter has been consumed, so he buried his head in his hands and moaned.

"My child! my Zillah!"

The priests waited his commands. By custom one who betrayed Astarte on such occasions was thrown into the pool of Apheca. With difficulty they aroused the wretched man to understand the situation. He stared stupidly at them for a time. His mind was evidently giving way in the fierce contention of his grief and rage. Suddenly he rose, pale with passion.

`"Her body to the pool!" he shouted, and fell as if dead upon the floor.

Upon the return of the couriers the priests held counsel. They judged that there could be no doubt of the suicide. Her letter to her father proved it. Or if she fell not by her own hand, her maid was only an accomplice, and executed her mistress's purpose. The honor of the goddess demanded some disgrace to be shown the body of one who had flung such contempt upon the entire worship of Astarte. The whole Phœnician world would hear of it; it must hear of Astarte's vengeance also. Besides, the father's command could be quoted as inspired directly by Baal. Sudden insanity was believed to be an over-exaltation of the mind due to divine influence. Surely Ahimelek's raving was sufficient evidence that the hand of the god was upon him,

The body of the supposed Zillah was lifted from the ground by men who averted their eyes, that they might not be polluted, or even blinded, by the sight of the unhallowed thing. They thrust the corpse into a sack, and plunged it into the pool. Men were deputed to watch it as it emerged from the great caldron and floated down the stream, and to follow it, carrying with them poles with which to dislodge it from the rocks and fallen timber that might obstruct the river, until the body should be lost in the waters of the Great Sea.

CHAPTER XXIX

THE fugitives from Apheca rode as rapidly as the sure-footed horses could pick their way in the moonlight up the side of the western range of Lebanon, and at dawn looked down upon the majestic valley of the Litany. The weariness of the journey, and the attendant excitement, could not altogether destroy the impressiveness of the marvellous scene.

Thousands of feet below them lay the green meadows. Far across to the east rose the other range of Lebanon, a mighty wall delaying the sunrise. Among its snow-covered peaks the rays of morning poured, as the white foam surges over the breakers and between the jagged rocks on the Syrian coast. Tongues of snow filled the high ravines, and, diminishing as they descended, carried the illusion of an overflowing reservoir of light. Below the lustral crest, the rocky sides of Lebanon were black in shadow; here gashed by the ceaseless plunging of cataracts, there beetling with crags, like castles which had borne the assaulting storms since chaos. High against the mountain's base the immense amount of detritus made a sloping mound of soil, rich and green like a bank of emerald.

The valley of the Litany which lay between the two Lebanon ranges had been for ages the gateway of Syria from the north. Down through it had poured the vast armies of Assyria and Babylon, devastating Syria and Palestine on their way to the great objective conquest, the land of Egypt. Now it was dotted with the caravansaries of traders, the camps of Persian soldiers, halting *en route*, and the black tent villages of the farmers who thus congregated for mutual protection in the midst of the fields and herds they were watching.

Midway across the valley was a little city, whose buildings clustered about a temple, each of whose enormous stones was clearly marked to the eye miles away, so immense were they. These stones had been consecrated by the blood of human sacrifices. This was Baal-bek, the city of Baal. Not far from it Marduk pointed out his tent, a white cone just distinguishable in the distance.

On the mountain brow they took their morning meal, with which Elnathan's well-filled hamper supplied them. For an hour Zillah must rest. The cloaks of the men made her couch. It would be well for her to sleep; but the over-excitement of the day and night could not be allayed at the call of expediency. She could only promise to lie still if Hiram were by her. Manasseh and Elnathan assumed the duty of picket guards, and wandered back over the road they had come, to give warning in case of pursuit. Of this, however, they had little fear, at least for that day, as they had chosen a path which would hardly be thought of by others; the way of flight being naturally down the river Adonis, where one could be lost in the crowds and easily take to the sea; for the escape of such a person as Zillah would be thought of in connection with some wide preparation looking to future abode in a distant Phœnician colony, or perhaps in Greece or Egypt.

Zillah's chief fear was not danger from men. The superstition of her religion still held a partial spell over her mind which no resolution could break at once. The habitual thoughts of a lifetime will linger and impress us in spite of our calling them unreasonable. Zillah felt that she had challenged Astarte. In her keen imagination, the indignant eyes of the goddess were turned upon her. They burned her. She could not rest. But there was a counter-spell in the kiss of her companion, which would have gone far to exorcise these demons of fear and religious anxiety, even had he never uttered his stout words of disbelief in the whole system of Baalism.

Zillah's spirit was strong and self-assertive to a degree seldom shown by women or men, else she had never proposed to herself, and followed so nearly to completion, the project of self-sacrifice rather than submit to the custom of Astarte. But when with Hiram, her whole soul, her opinions as well as her will, became plastic to the touch of his thoughts and purpose. His soul was the mold into which her nature, melted by the fire of her love, ran and reformed itself. That Baal had not received him to an estate of divinity lessened not a whit her real reverence for Hiram; it only destroyed the sense of awe with which she had come to think of him. His loving humanity was more to her now than even her ideal of his godhead had been. He was her Adonai, her lord indeed. If he had diminished in magnitude, he had come nearer, and so was greater to her. Her heart worshipped and adored, though she did not call it worship. Simple love had wrought all this. Surely love must be divine to perfect that relation between human creatures which formal religion only aims to accomplish between the soul and a god!

Zillah looked into the face of Hiram as he bent over her, and thought something like this: "Oh, if a god were like him! If I could feel towards the divinity as I feel towards him! Then I would be a priestess indeed!"

"Have no scruple nor dread concerning Astarte," said Hiram, divining her thoughts. "Have I not found out that our religion is all a lie? My absorption into Baal the priests knew to be no more a falsehood than are all their teachings. Hanno is less false to them than they are to the people. See yonder pile they call a temple. From here how small in comparison with the mighty height of the mountains back of it! That little cloud of white smoke and incense from the fire they keep always burning, how insignificant under the white glory of the morning that bursts over Lebanon and fills all the sky above us! How cruel the sacrifice of bird or beast or child seems in a world which the real God has made so beautiful and filled with the sweet air! And how good he must be to have ever thought of making such a creature as my Zillah, and giving me eyes to see her and a heart to love her!" He bent low, and worshipped her with a kiss. "If there be any god, he is one of kindness, who hates cruelty, whose deep abomination must be for such things as you and I have escaped. I would live alone with this thought, and be inspired by it to happiness, if all the world believed the contrary."

"Do any people believe as you—as we—do, dear Hiram?"

"Perhaps no people do; but I am sure that some persons do. I met a man in Jerusalem who helped me to my faith, vague as it is. The Jews have sacrifices and many forms of worship; but one Malachi, whom some day you shall know, sees through all forms. His God is only a spirit—a spirit of right and love. The forms of religion with him are only like our letters, the shape suggesting a meaning that we put into it. Who would think that this"—drawing a few marks on the rock—"meant my love for you? So little can express so much! But to whom does it express it? Only to you and me, who feel our love. So the forms of religion represent great thoughts. But for whom? Only

15

for those who have first felt them. Malachi was
looking one night at a lamp flame very intently,
and I asked :

"'What part of the flame is the most beautiful?'

"Manasseh, who was with us, said, 'He sees only
the smoke that wreathes itself above it, for he is
always brooding of gloomy things.'

"'No,' replied Malachi, 'I like to look through
the centre, where it has no color, before the flame
has got red.'

"So he sees religious ceremonies : he looks
through the transparent centre of them. He talks
of Jehovah's goodness and pity as if he felt them.
He loves his God, and so knows Him. But he fol-
lows all the foolish ceremonies of the Jews. For
that matter, few break away from the customs in
which they have been brought up, as we have
broken away from ours. But see, the sun comes
over the mountain!"

Instantly Zillah rose from her recumbent position, and, bending her body, so that the first rays
might fall upon her brow, began a morning prayer
to Baal.

Hiram interrupted her with louder voice. "O
God of all the Baals—of Jove! of Jehovah! God
of all the world! bless us, thy children, and guide
us this day!"

It was deemed advisable that Marduk should
not travel farther in company with Zillah, lest any
suspicion that might have attached to either should
lead to the identification of both. Marduk there-

fore proposed to go directly to his camp under the
walls of Baalbek, where he should remain for a
few days: while Zillah should accompany Manasseh and Elnathan southward to the home of Ben
Yusef.

The sun glared fiercely upon this latter party as
the day advanced. Towards noon they sought the
shade of a terebinth grove; but, on coming near,
they found it already occupied by various parties.
Manasseh, going forward alone, discovered that one
of the companies was the suite of a Persian officer
whom he had met at Jerusalem, now going to the
Jewish capital to collect the tax due the Great King.
The young Jew was cordially invited to join them.
He declined to leave his companions, whom he described as Elnathan, son of Ben Yusef, whose home
he must visit, as he had been deputed to gather
information regarding the names of the families
that had returned from Babylon under the original
firman of Cyrus. The young man, he said, was
travelling with his sister. The genial disposition
of Manasseh, together with the fact that he belonged to the highest rank at Jerusalem, as a member of the high priest's family, led the Persian to
gain his companionship by extending the hospitality of his camp to Elnathan and Zillah. This was
a sure protection from all pursuit, as such a company would not be suspected. At the same time,
the stricter customs of the Persians regarding the
presence of women forbade any curious inspection
of Zillah's appearance. She remained veiled while

upon the march, except as she conversed aloof from the company with Elnathan, and was served with the utmost hospitality in a tent that was pitched for her private use.

On the third day they reached the sea of Galilee, where the party halted, while Manasseh saw that his charge was safely under the tent of Ben Yusef, and presumably made all necessary inquiries into the genealogies of the house of that worthy. The record which he showed to the Persian was long enough to have carried the family back, not only to the days of the Captivity, but to the life of the great patriarch Yusef himself.

CHAPTER XXX

SLOWLY the hours dragged while Zillah awaited the coming of Hiram. Elnathan was as faithful to his charge as the huge mastiff was to the care of little Ruth ; and there was very similar communication between them. The young Jew's eyes searched all the paths over the hills that converged at the family tent ; his ear was quick to detect any approaching step ; and he eagerly ran to meet every one coming, lest some interloper should spy out the strange guest. Then from a distance he would watch the Phœnician lady as she walked, or sat under the great terebinth. The part he had taken in her rescue had reacted in a strong fascination for her. How many romances he wove about this beautiful woman !—a different one for almost every hour, but all terminating in her flight, and all involving himself as in some form her protector. He had felt a sort of proprietorship in her destiny, as he did in that of Marduk since he had saved his life at the old crater ; yet it was a proprietorship of absolute unselfishness, of obligation to cherish and guard, such as a father feels in his child.

Beyond that, Elnathan could not go. To admire Zillah's loveliness, of which he now and then caught a glimpse, seemed unlawful for him; for that belonged to her lover alone. He scarcely ventured to speak to her, lest his words might be a sort of profanation. He could only wonder and watch. She was his queen, and every fibre of his soul thrilled with loyalty.

Old Ben Yusef had much the same feeling as his son; but his curiosity was absorbed in his tenderness. Tears came into his eyes as he looked upon Zillah's face, now shadowed with trouble, now ecstatic with yearning. That there had been some barrier to her union with Marduk was enough to revive memories of his own early life, when his now buried Lyda, an alien from Israel, had cast her lot with his. His tent-home, the home of an outcast from the family of Judah, was itself a memorial of the triumph of love over traditionary proprieties; and it seemed as if the God who had blessed his married life had now sent this Phœnician maiden to his care.

Ruth did not need to catch the sentiment from her father and brother. The fresh impulses of her own young womanhood went out unreservedly to their guest. Zillah's need of sympathy quickly responded, and from the first greeting the two were in closest sisterly relation. Ruth's presence was a perpetual salâm, a benediction of peace and quiet to Zillah's perturbed soul. The Jewess, though only a child, was old enough to respect the privacy of the Phœnician's thoughts, and made no inquiries, content to find her way to the other's heart, and to feel that she brought comfort to it.

But there was one respect in which the kindness of Ben Yusef's household failed. Zillah could not rest. There was but one pillow for her, and that was the breast of Hiram. Why did he not come? A strange listlessness passed through her. All the third day of her sojourn at Giscala she hardly spoke, but talked all the night long in her sleep.

The fourth day brought the welcome visitor. El-nathan made the rocks ring again as from the adjacent hill-top he signalled Marduk's approach. Ben Yusef ran to meet him as if he had been a son. Even Ruth left the side of the Phœnician, and tripped far away to greet him.

But Zillah moved not from her seat under the terebinth. As Marduk came near and extended his arms in eagerness, she stared at him with stony eyes. Then a faint smile passed over her face. Her body swayed against the trunk of the tree, and would have fallen had not Marduk caught her.

"A passing swoon!" said Ben Yusef. "The gladness has been too much for her. Some wine, Ruth!"

The swoon passed. Zillah rose, and, wildly flinging her arms, cried, "I will go. I will go to him! See! this—this shall take me to him!" She felt for something in her bosom. Raising her clenched hand, and with a shrill cry, "I come, my Adonai, Hiram!" she fell again. They brought the unconscious form into the tent.

Moments passed, which to the watchers dragged themselves as if they had been hours. Hours passed, heavy and slow as nightless days. Days lapsed into weeks. But neither day nor night brought rest to the disordered brain of Zillah. Her tongue ran incessantly; now uttering some fear: "The priests! Moloch! Save him!" Now some pleasant illusion: "He comes! No need for a crown! See the rays about his head! Baal crowns him with his own beams."

Day and night her phantasy ran in one or other of these grooves. There was no sleep, only brief lulls in the wild storm of delirium. After some days, Elnathan brought a physician from Samaria, an attendant on the household of Sanballat. He murmured over the tossing body some magical incantations. These failing, he prescribed the usage among the tribes beyond the Jordan in cases of high fever; namely, to wrap the patient in wet cloths. Under this treatment she caught some periods of quiet sleep, but only to awake again in the world of ideal torment or ecstasy.

Her lover was almost equally insane at times with his grief. He accused himself of being the cause of her death through his attempt to rescue her from the shambles of Apheca.

"No, no," old Yusef said at such suggestions. "The Lord gave man wisdom. For the use of so much as he receives the man is responsible. What happens beyond our wisdom is the Lord's dealing, not man's. You did as you thought wisest and best. Afflict yourself with no censure. Say now with our Psalmist, 'It is the Lord. Let him do what seemeth him good!'"

At times Marduk would stare at the sky, as if questioning whether this were not some curse of Baal. Then he would pray to Jehovah, into whose land he had come, to defend him from the assault of his old enemies, the gods of Phœnicia. But this mood was of briefest duration—only in moments when his grief made him forget his scepticism. Once he inquired of Ben Yusef if it were not possible that, through ignorance of the ways of the god of the land, he had inadvertently offended.

"The ways of the Lord are those of every honest man's heart," replied the patriarch.

"Is there no sacrifice I could offer? Behold all I have! Let it be burned! Nay, I will lie myself upon the altar willingly."

"Remember our Psalmist," Ben Yusef would reply. "'Thou delightest not in sacrifice and offering, else would I give it. The sacrifices of God are a broken and contrite heart.' If you have sinned, my son, confess it in your thought, and let us pray the Lord for his mercy."

One day the old man stood facing the south, and raised his hand. His white locks floated in the breeze, while thus he prayed, using the words of Solomon at the dedication of the first temple: "Moreover, concerning a stranger that is not of thy people Israel, but cometh out of a far country for thy name's sake: hear thou in heaven, thy dwelling-

place, and do according to all that the stranger call-
eth to thee for : that all the people of the earth may
know thy name, to fear thee, as do thy people Israel."

Three weeks had passed. The patient had steadily declined in strength. She could no longer toss
upon her couch, but moved only her hands under
the impulse of her restless soul.

One day she lay very quiet. Ruth scarcely left
her side. Suddenly a sharp cry rang through the
tent. It was that of the watcher. Entering, the
men witnessed a scene that confirmed their worst
fears. Ruth was leaning over the couch, and gaz-
ing with fixed stare upon the face of her patient,
from which the fever flush had vanished. The
pallor and rigidness of death were upon her. Her
eyes were lustreless, the balls upturned.

"Quick! quick! the draught!" The physician
forced some drops through the stiffening lips. The
eyes remained fixed.

"It is over! O Jehovah! I would have served
thee! Cruel as Baal art thou!" cried Marduk,
throwing himself across the couch.

"Hush!" said old Ben Yusef. "The doors of
Sheol open. Upbraid no one here; not even thy-
self. 'The Lord gave. The Lord has taken away.
Blessed be the name of the Lord!'"

The old man's trembling voice almost belied the
submissive faith expressed by his words, for in a
moment he too bowed his head and sobbed.

Ruth held the cold hand in hers, as if to force
into it the warmth of her own life. So intense was

her yearning look that it seemed as if her soul
would break through her countenance and reani-
mate the face of the dead.

The silence was only for a moment, but it seemed
a long time until the physician spoke.

" The doors of Sheol are closing again, and
she—" He watched intently his patient's face as
he completed the sentence slowly, and as if waiting
to verify the words as he uttered them : " She—
has—not—passed them."

There was slight twitching of the eyeballs. They
resumed their normal position in their sockets.
There was in them a soft gleam, as of recognition,
not of the watcher, but of something very distant.

" The life throbs again in her wrists," cried
Ruth, covering the hands she held with her kisses.

Zillah's eyelids fell, but it was in sleep. The
breathing became regular.

" The fever has burned itself out ; but it has
burned up branch and stock, and left nothing but
the root of life," said the physician.

A long sleep followed. At first consciousness
came in lucid moments only. Then these periods
lengthened until they became continuous.

Only Ruth was permitted to enter the sick-cham-
ber. Zillah would look at her intently, evidently
dividing her thoughts between wonder and admiration for the beautiful face of her attendant.

" Where am I ?" she would ask.

" With me," would be the reply.

A kiss upon her brow was enough to restore

perfect tranquillity, and with a smile the patient would go to sleep.

"What do I hear?" she one day asked.

"They are chanting our praises to the Lord for your recovery," said Ruth. "Listen!"

Old Ben Yusef was evidently the precentor, and the strong voice of Elnathan followed, accompanied by the well-known accent of Marduk:

> "Bless the Lord, O my soul: . . .
> Who healeth all thy diseases,
> Who redeemeth thy life from destruction."

"Shall I sing to you?" and the sweet child-voice sang:

> "Jehovah my shepherd is."

So the time passed, except that, after a few days, Marduk took his place by the couch. One day he bore Zillah in his arms, and laid her upon the cot under the terebinth. Then he told how he had lain there with the same little angel of Jehovah watching him, the gentle Ruth.

The pure air of the hill country of Galilee; the simplicity of life among the peasants; the uplifting influence of their faith, so sublime, yet so consoling and soul-freeing; and the love of one whose heart was welded to hers in the fire of their mutual afflictions — these were the medicines which did more to bring health to the invalid's cheeks than all the arts of Egypt and Greece could have accomplished.

To remain themselves as peasants, communing

with nature, with no cares beyond those of the fields and the flocks, was a pleasing dream that the lovers repeated to themselves, with such variations as the landscape has of cloud and shadow and color, while it remains the same in substantial contour.

But the project could not be realized. The sense of great duties he owed to his people impelled the Phœnician to think of a larger world. This may have come partly from his natural habit of mind and training, for he was born to rule, and nature left this birth-mark on his character as clearly as she depicted royalty in his face and bearing. He conceived a lofty ambition of reforming the religion of the Phœnicians into something conformable to reason, and inspiring to man's better impulses ; purging its impurities and follies in the fire—let us confess it for him, since he did not confess it to himself—the fire which should be a veritable burning of Egbalus and many of his band of priestly bigots. Besides, he was bound to make this attempt in loyalty to Hanno, who had saved him from the cruelty of Moloch, and Zillah from the shame of Astarte, not for friendship's sake alone, but for his country's, and for the glory of the throne of Tyre. The wealth which he carried with him as the Tyrian merchant, Marduk well knew came from the private fortune of his friend ; and honesty bade him return it in the only way in which it was possible to do so, by regaining his lost rank and inheritance as the acknowledged leader of his people.

CHAPTER XXXI

THE time came for Hiram's departure from the home of Ben Yusef.

"There is one favor more I would claim from the hands of my protector," said he to the old man. "You have been a father to us; we would have a father's blessing in making us one. Let me receive my bride from your hands."

"Let me look into your eyes," replied Ben Yusef. "Now as Jehovah liveth, and as thy soul liveth and feareth the curse of its Creator, answer me truly. Does any other woman than this one hold your vow? Our first father Adam commanded that 'a man should leave father and mother and cleave unto his wife, and they twain should be one flesh.'"

Marduk, following the custom of oath-taking among Jews and Phœnicians alike, placed his hand beneath the thigh of Ben Yusef and declared:

"As Jehovah liveth, no woman but this one ever heard vow from me."

"And she? Is she thy betrothed, and thine alone? Does her father live? and has he given his child into thy keeping? For I can stand as father to her, only as I am assured that I transgress no sacred law of fatherhood among Jews or Gentiles."

" Her father once solemnly betrothed her to me according to the laws of our people," replied Marduk. " In his presence I placed upon her hand the ring of betrothal she wears."

" It is enough," said Ben Yusef. " And may this woman bring thee the blessing that my own Lyda brought me when I took her from the tent of Terah, her father !"

Several days later the home of Ben Yusef was transformed into a place of festivity. The old terebinth was hung with garlands. A booth was erected at a little distance from the family tent. Though very simple in structure, it was lined with rich stuffs that well depleted the stores of Marduk, the merchant. These were arranged by Eliezar, the Damascene, whose ingenuity had never before been so taxed to fill the order of any merchant as it was by the order of Marduk to prepare the nuptial tent. The broad divan was covered with that rare fabric of white wool, grown on the slopes of the Lebanon, and called "damask" from the looms of Damascus, that weave its fine fibres, and prepare them for the rich red color of the dyer. It was curtained with lace, the handiwork of a Syrian peasant woman, and into the elaborate pattern of which had gone many years of her toil. She could have indicated certain knots that were made when her eyes were full of tears for some affliction ; others wrought when her fingers flew nimbly as she hastened her daily task in order to meet some expected pleasure. Oh ! if one could only unravel the secrets of the lives of the workers, and tell the thoughts they had as they toiled, as one can unravel the stitches, what history we would have ! — a thousand times larger and a thousand times deeper than that preserved in the annals of our kings !

There was a mirror of polished brass, set in a frame of silver, the craft of Sidonians. And such a toilet of necklaces and ear-rings, of gemmed brooches and hair-pins, of bracelets and anklets ; such a collection of tiny vases of rock crystal, of bronze, of glass, of alabaster, all containing kohl for coloring the eyebrows, or salves for the lips, or perfumes for the clothing. There was such a ward-robe of shawls and tunics, veils and sandals ! Even Eliezar could not describe them all, for he had left the selection of these to Hador, the haberdasher to the King of Damascus.

During the day Zillah had been invisible. The mysteries of her apartment in the tent of Ben Yusef we must leave to the imagination of our fair read-ers, and to the knowledge of Ruth, who waited upon her.

As the day waned, many shepherds of the neigh-borhood, with their families, came to join in the fes-tivities ; for to salute a new-made bride was thought to bring blessing upon one's own household.

Just as the sun went down, Marduk emerged from his booth, arrayed in gay robes, and crowned with myrtle entwined with roses.   His garments were redolent with myrrh and frankincense, and verily, as Solomon described the comely bridegroom, with "all the powders of the merchant."

The peasants formed in procession to escort the bridegroom from his tent to that of Ben Yusef, at the door of which, as it was her temporary home, he would receive his bride, and conduct her to his own dwelling.

Scarcely had the procession begun to move, when it was suddenly halted by an exclamation of surprise and caution from Elnathan. On top of the hill had appeared a band of horsemen. Elnathan darted into the great tent, and reappeared with a number of swords, knives, slings, and such bludgeons as made every tent an arsenal in those troublous times. The peasants were quickly armed, even some of the women taking weapons.

Elnathan advanced to meet the intruders who had halted upon the hill-top, as if they were reconnoitring the scene, or waiting for others to join them. One of the horsemen was clad in the dull russet leathern suit which indicated a Phoenician soldier. Another wore a white, closely fitting tunic and the projecting cap of a Persian. A third was dressed more as one of the wild rovers of Moab, in big turban and flowing burnoose.

The three awaited Elnathan's challenge, and answered it with, " Peace be with thee !" then dashed down the hill-side with a cry in three diverse tongues, "Marduk! Marduk! Marduk!"

16

"Hanno!" cried Marduk, and had nearly pulled the Phœnician soldier from his horse before he caught the admonition of his friend, and repeated louder: "It is Captain Beto of Sidon, as sure as Baal lives!"

"Just as sure!" was the response. The second comer was a stranger to Marduk, but at once recognized by Elnathan as the Persian officer in whose escort he had come down the valley of the Litany. The third was a Sidonian soldier from the house of Sanballat. A few words sufficed to explain their coming.

It was necessary for Hanno to communicate with Marduk concerning matters that could be safely intrusted to no one else, so he had assumed the disguise of a soldier and sought his friend.

"But I would never have found you in this retreat, though I thought I knew the way from your description, had it not been that I fell in with these good men, and discovered that this noble Persian, who was returning from Jerusalem to Susa, by way of Samaria, was directing this servant of our Lord Sanballat to find Marduk. But woe betide the man who interrupts a marriage ceremony! Let us all be friends of the bridegroom."

The new-comers joined with the merry peasants. The procession was re-formed, and, with Marduk at the head, approached the great tent.

Ben Yusef met them at the door. He held

Zillah by the hand. She was clothed in white, relieved by needlework of gold. Her robe was gathered at the waist by the kishshurim, or wedding girdle, to be loosed only by her husband. Her hair was unbound, flowing in a cascade of glossy jet. A crown of gold, beaten into the shape of ivy leaves, was on her head. She wore a veil that hid her features, but fell about her form like a phosphorescence, concealing the sharper folds of her attire, but revealing their lines of grace.

Ben Yusef, placed the hand of Zillah in that of Marduk, saying:

"Take her according to the law of Moses and of Israel."

Then he added the blessing of the elders at the ancient marriage of Boaz and Ruth:

"The Lord make the woman that is come into thy home like Rachel and Leah, which two did build the house of Israel."

Then Ruth pushed aside the veil just enough to kiss her, and, holding the bride's cheeks between her hands, repeated the extravagant blessing the family of Rebekah used when they gave her to the patriarch Isaac:

"Thou art our sister: be thou the mother of thousands of millions; and let thy seed possess the gate of those that hate them."

The little crowd of peasants had in the meantime lighted flambeaux and small hand lamps. Elnathan marshalled them into a procession, which, making a detour over the hill-side, returned to the booth of Marduk. Here the couple entered. The crowd gathered under the terebinth, where, with feasting and songs, they made the night merry, until the east dropped its gray dawn upon them without a cloud—which they interpreted into a happy omen for the newly wedded—and, with a hundred shouted well-wishes to the merchant and his bride, they dispersed to their homes.

The Persian officer rejoined his own company. The soldier from Sanballat, who carried a letter to Marduk from Manasseh, set out upon his return. "Captain Beto" seemed to forget the proprieties of the occasion, and made himself a companion of Marduk and his wife during almost all the first day of their wedded life. The three sat under the terebinth, or walked together over the hill; the devoted couple apparently as deeply interested in their visitor as in each other.

Whether their interest in "Captain Beto's" talk was warranted or not, we must leave the reader to judge. He told of events in Phœnicia, some of which are recited in the next chapter.

CHAPTER XXXII

AFTER Ahimelek's horrid curses upon his daughter, he remained in a stupor during the day and night. When the morning broke, the servants found him sitting in a corner of his apartment in the inn of Gebal with his arms folded as if clasping some object, and talking incoherently:

"Don't go, Zillah, my pretty one! There now! Sleep again! You will not hate your father when you grow to be a queen, will you? Kiss me again. A curse! a curse! a curse on him who will touch a hair of my Zillah! What are those men pushing with their poles? Save her! Give her to me, Layah!"

Then followed a long period of weeping. Like a child, at last he cried himself to sleep.

Late in the day he awoke. He was a changed man. His hair had grown perceptibly whiter. His face was ashen-hued. From middle life he had passed suddenly into senility and imbecility. The terrible excitement had seemingly burned out his brain.

For some days he refused to leave Gebal. When at length he set out, and came to the river Adonis, he was held by some spell from crossing it. As his litter-bearers rested by the bank. he leaped from his carriage. and ran hither and thither. searching with wild eyes into every pool.

He then made them convey him to the coast, where the ruddy waters of the river mingle with the Great Sea. There he paced the shores. wringing his hands. now praying. now cursing. Egbalus and Rubaal were especially the objects of his imprecation.

They brought him to Tyre. He shut himself in his house. For days he was invisible. Captains in the harbor delayed their sailing. awaiting orders from him as the owner of their craft. which orders never came. Merchants from Sidon. with whom he was interested in joint ventures. returned enraged at his neglect of most pressing business.

The first to gain access to him was Hanno. From boyhood Ahimelek had known and liked the genial comrade of young Hiram : and now that he must have some one to speak with. yet feared everybody else. he bethought him of Hanno.

There was something of the old-time welcome of Ahimelek as his guest appeared.

"Enter. my son ! my boy. Hanno !" said he, throwing his arms affectionately about the stalwart young man. Then he looked at the dignified form. the serious face of the visitor. and. as if suddenly recollecting himself. made profound obeisance. remaining with head bowed for a moment.

"My Lord Hanno ! priest of Astarte, to be

high priest of Baal-Melkarth! I worship your presence."

"Simple Hanno, if you will," was the reassuring reply.

The wretched man put his hands on Hanno's shoulders and scanned his face, as if making an effort at recollection.

"I—I knew you when a child, did I not? In this room you have played. With these same old swords and helmets you have played. Hiram and Hanno played, and I—I let them. I never told them not to play."

"Yes, you were a good friend to me and—to Hiram."

"Was I?" said the man, with delight. "And you have not cursed me, as a priest have not cursed me, because I was good to you when a boy? And you will not curse me?"

"No! no! noble Ahimelek! There have been cursings enough. But you sent for me?"

"Ah, yes. I remember. Hanno! priest Hanno!"

He drew his friend to him, and studied his face again, as if half in fear that sudden lightning might flash from it and blast him.

"Hanno! priest Hanno! can you see the gods?"

Hanno hesitated a moment, as if balancing his reply between honesty and some plan he had of using the superstition of Ahimelek, and then replied:

"I have seen all the gods there are."

"Have you seen Hiram, Baal-Hiram, since—the sacrifice?"

"Yes."

"He really lives?"

"Yes."

"Is blessed of Baal?"

"Yes."

There was a long pause. Ahimelek's face went through a series of contortions. With husky, hesitating speech, looking against the blank wall, as if questioning himself rather than his visitor, he stammered out:

"And Zillah? She went to Hiram?"

"She is with Hiram."

"You can see her?"

"I have seen her."

"Does she curse her father?"

"No, she is too happy with Hiram for that."

"Baal be praised!"

Raising his arm, he would have embraced Hanno, but his emotion was too much for him, and he fell across the divan.

Hanno lifted him kindly, and clapped his hands for a servant, who gave Ahimelek a cup of wine.

The old man was soon in loquacious mood.

"Captain Hanno, they are robbing me."

"Who?"

"Egbalus, King Rubaal, my captains, my camel-drivers — everybody. They will have every ship, every jewel, every daric. Save me, Hanno! I'll pay you well. Come, see what they would take!"

He drew one end of the divan away from the wall, took out a panel of the carved wainscoting of the room, and from a little chest drew by main strength a heavy bronze box.

"In this are more precious things than elsewhere in all Phœnicia. For years my captains have been commissioned to purchase the most splendid gems. Some of these singly cost all the freight of a bireme to Gades."

Then he whispered, as he tapped the box lovingly with his finger:

"The great diamond of Xerxes, that the Persians are searching for, is here. A handful of rubies, too, that a Greek gave me, to keep my ships in the far western sea, so that the Persian levy would be lessened. Ah! if my ships had been at Eurymedon, the battle might have gone differently. And you should see the gift of Megabyses for my influence in keeping the men of Tyre from going to help the Sidonians when the city was besieged. Oh! I have been a great man, Hanno, in my day; quiet merchant Ahimelek, as they thought me; a great man! a great man! And the harvest of forty years is in that box. Did you hear what young Ezmunazer, Prince of Sidon, is having carved on the coffin they are making for him? It is, 'Curse the man that moves my bones.' I have guarded this box with all the spells the witches know of, and put ten thousand curses upon him who should touch it. But now, Hanno, they are going to take it away."

The old man cried like a whipped child, and clutched his treasure-box.

"Who can take it without your consent, Ahimelek? Our laws will prevent any robbery by day, and you have strong watchmen by night," said Hanno, encouragingly.

"No, but look here! read this!"

He drew from a heap of papyrus and parchments a document. It proved to be a copy of his dowry agreement in espousing his daughter Zillah to Rubaal. He pledged to the prospective king the equivalent in gems of a thousand minas of gold, together with half the revenue of his ships; making Rubaal withal partner in all his enterprises. With this enormous price he thought to buy into his own family the throne of Tyre.

"But your document is surely invalid, since your daughter has not become the wife of Rubaal," said Hanno.

"Such were but the just interpretation; but Rubaal holds that from the day of the espousal the dowry was due; that it became his then, the death of Zillah being as the death of his real wife. And the great counsellors all hold with Rubaal. The Shophetim can assure me of no relief. To-morrow they come to make good the claim. To-morrow! Oh, good Hanno! priest Hanno, help me!"

Hanno thought a moment, and replied:

"Ahimelek, is Rubaal king yet? He has not been crowned, and may never be. Let this be secret between us. I am assured that the Great King,

Artaxerxes, has expressed displeasure with Rubaal; and surely the Tyrians will not crown a king who will not be recognized at Susa and receive the appointment as suffete under Persia; otherwise Persia would send an officer of her own, and our king would be in disgrace. Tabnit of Sidon, too, refuses to recognize Rubaal. We dare not break with our brethren the Sidonians. I assure you, Ahimelek, that Rubaal will never be crowned. You must not allow this wealth to come into his hands. Never!"

"How can I prevent it? They will force my house. It may be this very night. And once possessing this, they will have money enough to buy the pleasure of the Great King."

" The gems must be secreted," said Hanno.

" But where?"

" Out of the land; under the care of some other god; for Baal will show them, as he shows everything, to his priests. They should be sent across the seas, or over into Jehovah's land."

" To hide them in some cave, or bury them in some wood? No, no. I would not rest day or night lest they should be discovered."

" Put them under the care of the god of the land, then. I can arrange that matter as priest of Astarte with the priests of Jehovah."

" Will you deal with me truly?" said Ahimelek.

" As truly as Baal lives."

" Swear it."

Hanno stood out in the centre of the room,

where a sunbeam fell through the bronze-latticed window. With the light on his face, he kissed his hand to the sun—the customary oath before Baal, the sun-god.

The old man opened the bronze box. But as his eyes caught the lustre of the gems, he closed it again and sat upon it, asking Hanno a hundred questions, and taking from him again and again the oath before Baal, invoking curses of Baal-Hiram and Zillah, and every ghost and jinn that ever walked the earth, upon his proving false or allowing the gems to go to any other than their rightful owner.

CHAPTER XXXIII

A S Hanno, under the terebinth of Ben Yusef,
narrated the substance of all this to Hiram
and Zillah, he bade them feel the tough leathern
suit, like that of a Phœnician soldier, in which he
had disguised himself. The stiffness of the leather
served to hide its uneven thickness, for its lining
was quilted in tiny blocks, each of which was
nubbed with some precious stone, or padded to
protect some delicate setting or cluster of gems.
He twisted a bit of iron from the end of his sword-
hilt, and poured out a handful of diamonds. He
mimicked the tricksters who draw pearls from various parts of their bodies, except that he left the
pearls and emeralds and rubies in the hand of Zillah, and possessed no power of the wizard to make
them vanish. He grew hilarious.

"Come!" said he. "Let us play the chase by
the robbers. I will be the victim. You shall
catch me and take me to your own den—the booth
over there—and flay me alive—for all this skin belongs to you."

But Zillah could not be provoked into mirth.
Hanno, in narrating the events that followed her

escape from Apheca, had not told her of her father's curse, reserving that part of the story for Hiram's ears alone. She was oppressed by what she thought of as her own unfilial conduct; and in her mind Hanno's zealous interest in their behalf had led him into robbery. Hiram's sympathy with her awakened scruples in his own mind that perhaps he would not otherwise have thought of.

"I cannot take these things, good Hanno," said he.

"Why not? They are yours, and have been for more than twenty moons. Indeed, you should not only take them, but demand usury on them, too. Recall Ahimelek's dowry contract with yourself. You told me it was for a thousand minas, and for a half of all the revenues of his ships; the same as this contract with Rubaal. By the laws of Tyre all this comes with your bride. That he villainously sought to kill you, to break his daughter's heart, does not touch this fact under law, however it may affect your feelings. I did not steal these things from him, for they were not his, and have not been since the day of your betrothal; or if there were any doubt of that, they are not his since your marriage. And, by the name of Jevovah, into whose land you have come, to no other hands than yours shall they be given! Besides, you are not merely Hiram and Zillah; you are the king and queen of Tyre. They belong to your throne. Loyalty to your throne compels your retention of them."

"Nay," said Zillah, "your own pledge was to put them into some temple, under the protection of the god."

"The true temple of God is a man, and that temple's true revenues are the man's rights," said Hanno, oracularly. "I will fulfil my pledge best if I leave them at your feet, and go back to Tyre. I will then kiss my hand to the sun, and swear I have done my duty."

"Hold!" interrupted Hiram; "it may be that Manasseh can help us in the matter. He is of the priestly line, and perhaps can find a safe place in connection with the temple at Jerusalem. We need a better guarded treasury than our pockets. But you have not asked the news from Samaria that the messenger who accompanied you brought. I will read it:

"'*Manasseh, son of Ioiada, of the tribe of Levi, to Marduk, son of Baal, and to my lady Zillah: Greeting!*

"'My wedding with Nicaso, daughter of Sanballat, satrap of Samaria, will be on the seventeenth day of the seventh month, which is Tisri. My lord Sanballat bids me welcome you among his most honored guests. My own summons may be best read in your thoughts, O my friend, for thou knowest my heart. My salutations to Elnathan and the house of Ben Yusef!'"

The following day the Phœnician party left the hospitable home of their Jewish host. They proceeded southward by the Sea of Galilee, striking the road that leads by Mount Tabor. They encamped for the night near the western slope of that beautiful mountain. The sunlight that lingered on its symmetrical crest when the dusk filled the plain about them they interpreted into a good omen, notwithstanding that it was a superstition of the religion of the sun-god.

As the morning broke, they observed that a large camp of Persian soldiers had been formed near them during the night. Inquiry revealed the fact that this was the escort of Nehemiah, the Tirshatha of Jerusalem, who was coming from Susa, where he had been for several years, having assumed that the affairs of Jerusalem were sufficiently settled to allow his return to the Persian capital —a place that, although he was a Jew, still held many of his interests, and where he was allotted a high rank as the former cup-bearer of the king.

The Tirshatha was accompanied by a detachment of Persian cavalry, whose horses were tethered between the tents. By the central pavilion stood the tall spear; floating from its head the ensign of the commandant. Smoke wreathed from a score of fires, where the morning meal was being prepared.

At a sudden bugle blast the entire scene was transformed. The tents fell; the fire was trampled out; horses were harnessed; camels knelt to receive their burdens. In a few moments the gallant cavalcade, followed by the baggage train, and guarded at the rear by a detachment of horsemen, crowded the road.

As they passed the camp of the Phœnicians,

now ready for the journey, the Tirshatha sent his messenger to learn who were his neighbors. Upon hearing they were merchants, he bade them join his party, and invited Marduk to ride by his side.

The Tirshatha was mounted upon a superb horse, equipped with expensive trappings embossed with gold; his bridle of silk inwoven with threads of gold; the saddle cloth a rich purple embroidered in gold. The rider's habit was in keeping. His purple tunic was adorned with flower-work, as were his flowing trousers. His sword-hilt was of gold, studded with gems. A massive chain of gold was about his neck. He wore the conical cap projecting forward at the top, as if to make a shade for the face. The officers of his suite were in array approximating in splendor that of their chief.

Marduk returned the cordial salutation of the Tirshatha as he rode up to his side.

Nehemiah opened the conversation genially.

"Marduk, a Phœnician merchant? The name is new to me, except that on this journey I have heard it spoken with respect. I thought I knew all of your trade who were accustomed to visit our Jews' land."

As he said this he gave a quick glance with penetrating eyes into the face of Marduk—a glance that took in every feature.

The Phœnician felt that there might be some suspicion in this, and deftly foiled it.

"Your people are increasing rapidly in wealth under the stimulus of your government, Tirshatha;

and many merchants who used to trade elsewhere are now attracted hither. You will see many strangers at Jerusalem, my lord."

" Your compliment is more kind than considerate," replied Nehemiah. "Our people have little wealth as yet, and cannot buy much of such rare goods as you evidently carry."

" Yes, but by buying and selling my wares they make gain."

" You are going to Jerusalem, then, sir merchant ?"

" To Samaria first."

" Oh ! to deck out Sanballat's daughter for her wedding?" said Nehemiah, with a sneer.

" I believe she marries one of your people."

" Yes, but it is most ill-advised," replied Nehemiah, with undisguised ill-humor.

" How? Any alliance between Samaria and Jerusalem must strengthen both."

" Nay, it is an alliance of clay and iron that makes the iron brittle. Our people, Marduk, are of peculiar customs, religion, and mission. Again and again have our old kings tried to widen their prosperity by widening their alliances, but have always failed. The Persian government is wiser. It does not seek to make all the provinces it conquers to be alike in their laws and worship. It allows each nation to retain its own, and only asks loyalty and tribute. King Cyrus commissioned us to return from Babylon and rebuild the temple. So did Darius, and so Artaxeres has sent Ezra the Scribe and myself to reconstruct our own peculiar system. We condemn no other people by maintaining the pure blood of our own. Over yonder is the ruin of the palace of Jezreel. You know the place, perhaps its history. One of our kings, Ahab, married Jezebel, daughter of one of your kings of Tyre ; but it wrought only trouble. We are now crossing the great battle-plain of Esdraelon. Every Jew thrills at its sacred memories. Deborah and Barak here conquered Sisera, the general of the Canaanites. Yonder is Gilboa, where Saul and Jonathan fell fighting the Philistines; and there is the valley of Jezreel, where Gideon vanquished the Midianites. All these were battles for our integrity as a people, and especially that no other God than ours should be worshipped in our land. Even a Phœnician, with your legends of a thousand years, must respect the lessons of our history. But let us not dispute, Marduk. What is the news of your country by the sea ? Will Rubaal get and keep the crown, think you ?"

" Why not ?" asked the merchant.

" At Susa he is not thought of with favor," said Nehemiah. " The sacrifice of the former king, Hiram, is regarded as a cruelty that Persia must frown upon, even if she allows freedom of religion ; and the other Phœnician kings are afraid of the precedent of allowing the priests to have such influence that a king's life is in their hands. Therefore the kings are all opposed to Rubaal, and the Great King would not antagonize them. He de-

pends too much upon the Phœnician fleet to alienate their loyalty."

The Tirshatha plied Marduk with questions regarding all the lands adjacent, the condition of
roads, names of the chief men in the towns across
the Jordan : to which questions the merchant gave
uncomfortably meagre responses. His ignorance
occasionally brought those keen eyes of Nehemiah
to a suspicious scrutiny of his countenance.

As they parted company, the Tirshatha remarked to his chief officer :

"That man knows both too much and too little.
Have an eye upon him."

The following day the Phœnician took the short
road from Dothan to Samaria, while the Tirshatha's party kept to that running by Shechem, and
leading them more directly to the Sacred City.

CHAPTER XXXIV

THE hill of Samaria was in a blaze of color. Every tent of the army of Sanballat floated its gay streamer. Rivalling these were the displays of the various chieftains of neighboring tribes, who had come to honor with their presence the wedding of the Samaritan princess. The extravagance of Oriental fashion vied with that of martial splendor; gaudy turbans with polished helmets; brilliant robes with gleaming breastplates; palanquins of fair women with the mail of the heavy war horses. Furlongs of bright cloths hung from the trees, and draped the stone columns that still stood as the relics and reminders of the glory of this old capital of Israel. In cool nooks were skins of wines, while troughs were overrunning with the new-pressed juices of apples and grapes. There were jars of confections, spiced to kindle the thirst that the free-flowing liquors were to quench. Games, dances, songs, the thumbing of stringed instruments, the whistle of pipes and the ringing of trumpets, gave vent to the spirit of abandon among the motley crowds of people.

Sanballat entertained within the palace the

great chiefs, whose spears, adorned with their various insignia, were stuck into the ground, in semicircular array, in front of the grand entrance. There was Geshom, the Arabian, and a score of braves from Idumea, Moab, and Philistia, who lounged at the tables. Even Tobiah, the Ammonite, was not forgotten; indeed, his presence was a special pleasure to Sanballat, whose magnanimity rose with the conviction that he had at length circumvented his rival in gaining alliance with the Jews. These worthies drank to one another, and to one another's gods : to the sun-god, to Baal-Shâmayim, lord of heaven ; to Melkarth of Tyre, to Chemosh of Moab, to Milcom of Ammon, to Moloch of Philistia, to Dagon of the coast, to Succoth-benoth of Babylon, to Nergal of Cuth, to Ashima of Hamath, to Nibhak and Tartak of the Avites, to Adranmelech and Anammelek of Sepharvaim, to Jehovah of the Jews, and to Astarte, the goddess of love. With clinking cups and hilarious shouts they invoked the blessings of all gods upon the bride and groom. They drank until they knew not to whom they drank, each one making a god of his own belly. Then they bepraised every one his own possessions and prowess, and they scattered oaths and blows; indeed, all had a right merry time, as the proprieties of the occasion and the rude manners of the age and people prompted, until the soberer servants removed both the viands and the guests together.

At nightfall the hill of Samaria seemed a mass

of flame. Torches flared upon the palace walks; bonfires filled the grove with ruddy light, amid which the trees and the moving people seemed like weird spectres.

A bugle blast sounded from afar. The crowds gathered near the open roadway that led to the palace. The clatter of hoofs was soon heard, nearer and nearer, louder and louder, while shouts rent the air. A band of wild riders dashed up the garlanded avenue. The soldiers and populace battled against them with waving torches, tufts of grass, and shrieks of mimic rage. The cry of the assailants was—

"Manasseh! Manasseh!"

They pressed up to the palace front. Some, dismounting, beat upon the gates. These were flung wide. In the opening stood Sanballat, surrounded by as many of his noble guests as were able to get upon their feet. With angry voice the Satrap demanded the cause of this irruption. A chorus of hoarse voices replied:

"Nicaso! Nicaso for our Lord Manasseh!"

Sanballat parleyed with them.

"Would you rob a father of his only child?"

"Yes," was the response, "and of a hundred only children. One for each of us if they were like Nicaso." And a score of witticisms, some sharp, some scurrilous, were hurled at him.

At length, with well-feigned fear, Sanballat led forth his daughter. She was elegantly robed and crowned. A spirited horse, superbly caparisoned, was led to her side. Without awaiting the proffered assistance, Nicaso leaped upon his back. The horsemen led her captive, followed by a procession of maidens who wailed in feigned lament the fate of their comrade, amid the amorous gibes and jokes of the young men. They brought Nicaso to the happy bridegroom's tent.

Thus far they had followed the custom of the East-Jordan tribes in mimic seizure of the bride.

Nicaso, however, delighted in breaking through all proprieties. The flashing lights and shouts excited her wild blood, and, instead of dismounting to receive the embrace of her new lord, she dashed away from the crowd, crying, "Let him have me who can catch me!"

Her horse was sure-footed and keen-eyed, and galloped among rocks and through by-paths without the guidance of even the single rein that his mistress threw upon his neck. Down among the tents of the soldiers, out on the high-road towards Shechem, back through the woods, now flitting like a spectre in the darkness, now all agleam with her bejewelled crown and robe as she passed some bonfire; thus the daring girl led, and yet eluded, the pursuing crowd.

Manasseh, though surprised at this unexpected postponement of the moment when he should clasp his fair possession, really admired the adventurous frolicsomeness of his bride, and accepted her challenge with equal spirit.

Was it the happy guidance of some goddess of

love, or the quick eyes of Nicaso that watched his coming, that brought their horses together at two converging paths? Their beasts reared and plunged at the shock, like two waves clashing in counter seas. Nicaso's steed galloped away riderless.

Cries rose: " She is thrown !"

In fact, at the moment of the collision she had thrown herself from her horse fairly into Manasseh's arms, and, with crown awry, hair dishevelled, her black eyes flashing with merriment, a magnificent picture of wild queenly beauty, was borne by her lover to his tent.

As she jumped to the ground some portion of her clothing caught upon the trappings of the horse, and she would have fallen had not Marduk extended his arm and relieved her.

" Marduk, you have fulfilled your part of our covenant," said Manasseh. " Let me take my bride from your hand, as you took yours from mine."

The bridal pair disappeared in the nuptial tent.

For seven days the festival was kept up. Then the young Jew set out for Jerusalem with his bride. The Phœnician's party accompanied them. Nicaso's wardrobe burdened as many camels as did the merchant's wares. Among his rich robes was stored a strange article for such a collection — a heavy leathern suit of a Phœnician soldier.

CHAPTER XXXV

THE spacious residence of Ioiada, son of the high priest Eliashib, was ordinarily a rendez-vous for the aristocratic circles of Jerusalem. The fashion of the city seized the occasion of the home-bringing of his daughter-in-law, the bride of Ma-nasseh, and the feastings that celebrated it, to throng his court and chambers with such gayety as had not been seen since the return from the land of the Captivity.

The repute of Nicaso's beauty, the romance of such an alliance between a priestly house of the Jews and the family of Sanballat, their ancient enemy, set the tongues of all classes going. The multitude hailed the event. They were wearied with the exclusiveness they had been forced to maintain as respected their intercourse with neigh-boring people. Shopkeepers were delighted, for, in the train of Sanballat's daughter, came men and women from all surrounding tribes, and Jerusalem seemed about to become again an emporium of trade, as in the days before the Exile.

Marduk was solicited to open a bazaar in the chief street of the city with the assurance of doing a thriving business in foreign stuffs, for which the good people of Jerusalem had taken a sudden and violent fancy. But for reasons best known to himself, the Phœnician merchant chose to pitch his tents without the walls. Yet here he apparently did a lively trade; for scarcely a day passed that did not bring a camel or two down from the north, or a horseman up from Joppa on the coast. Marduk himself seemed to catch the spirit of enterprise, and attended in person to the details of business, which he had formerly left entirely to Eliezar. Many of the traders, especially those who came from Phœnicia, and who were presumably the agents of his business, he took to his own private tent, or walked with them apart. It was rumored that he was about to open new trade routes with Egypt and the East, which would centre in Jerusalem. That Manasseh was so frequently with him gave plausibility to the report that a great mercantile combination had been agreed upon in which much Jewish wealth should be represented by the house of Ioiada, the treasury of Sanballat by his son-in-law, Manasseh, and the heaviest merchants of Tyre by Marduk, whose exhaustless genius and money-bags were the inspiration of the enterprise.

But far different movements were beneath the surface of things. The religious sentiment of Jerusalem had been shocked by the alliance of the priestly house with that of the hated Samaritan. By many Nicaso was called Jezebel, and Manasseh denounced as a traitor who aimed at playing the part of a second Ahab. The venerable scribe, Ezra, seemed broken-hearted over the defection of his favorite pupil. His lectures upon the law became lamentations.

One day the three most notable men in all Jewry were together in the hall of the high priest. There was the venerable pontiff, Eliashib, a man whose broad and bland countenance was well in keeping with his elegant attire. His whole bearing showed that he fully appreciated the secular dignity of his position, if he did not feel the religious solemnities of his sacerdotal office. He strode up and down the apartment while he talked. Ezra, presuming upon the privilege of more advanced years and feebleness, sat in his chair, scarcely raising his eyes from the floor, except as now and then they shot the light of intense conviction after some sage saying he had uttered. But the most impressive figure was that of the Tirshatha, Nehemiah. He stood rigid as the statue of some god; only turning his head to follow the movement of Eliashib, whom he seemed to regard with mingled rage and scorn. Had he drawn the short sword that hung at his side, he would not have been more the impersonation of wrathful determination. The dispute of the men had already been long, and without persuasion on either side.

"I shall submit to no such dictation in the affairs of my family," said Eliashib, throwing wide his arms, as if to stretch to the utmost his priestly robe, and the aristocratic authority that rustled in every fold of it, and thus awe his opponents. "Be content with what you have done: that I have allowed Tobiah, Prince of Ammon, to be driven from his chambers at the temple. But know, haughty governor, that I move not another step at your bidding."

• "Alas!" cried Ezra, "that I should have lived to see the law of the Lord openly broken with the countenance of the high priest, who should be its most zealous guardian!"

"The law of the Lord!" retorted Eliashib. "Ay, as the light that comes through yonder yellow curtain is the light of heaven; for so is the law of the Lord stained by the interpretation of Ezra the Scribe. Did not Moses marry the daughter of the priest of Midian, and, Boaz marry the Moabitish Ruth? Is Jehovah become a god of cruelty to drive out the helpless women and children, because their blood is not like thine?"

Then fire seemed to flash from the figure of Nehemiah. He boldly advanced, and, laying his hand upon the shoulder of the priest, glared into his face as he said:

"The time for debate is past. Know you what I have done this very day? On my way hither I came upon a band of these renegade Jews who have married themselves to the women of Ashdod, Ammon, and of Moab, whose children cannot even speak straight the language of our nation; and I cursed them, and smote certain of them, and plucked off their hair, and made them swear by

God they would put away this spiritual harlotry. And mark you, Eliashib, so will I chase from the gates the apostate Manasseh, though he be of the blood of one who has debauched the high priest's office."

Eliashib was furious, and hissed through his clenched teeth : "Not until you have first become priest and sacrificed the high priest upon the altar of your bigotry and madness. Pure blood ! Nicaso's is as pure as Nehemiah's, which has been tainted by the Persian's wine, as you were so long cup-bearer to the crowned heathen. Go back to Susa and lord it over the pages, but you shall not lord it over me. Stand guard, if you will, at the harem curtains of Artaxerxes, but you shall not stand before the curtains of, Eliashib's household."

The audacity of the high priest checked for a moment the headlong rush of the governor's passion. Or perhaps it was the training of the diplomat that led Nehemiah to reply with more deliberation :

"My decision cannot be revoked. As the Lord lives ! I will purge Jerusalem ; or, failing that, I return to Susa, and give back into the hands of the Great King the commission as Tirshatha. Then what ? O blinded priest ! Let Jerusalem perish again rather than become a harlot city !"

"The Lord prevent !" cried Ezra, rising. The high priest dropped upon a seat and sat a long time in silent musing. At length he rose, and spoke, more to himself than to the listeners :

" Alas! that the keeping of Israel is in the hands of such men as we. Our words are but wind, the hot wind of the desert, without the guidance of the spirit of the Lord. I would think and pray. Leave me, friends, before we further sin in our ignorant wrath "—and, gathering his robes about him, Eliashib left the apartment.

CHAPTER XXXVI

LATE that night the light shone in the house of Ioiada. A more stormy scene was there than even the one we have described. At first Ioiada and his son Manasseh were unyielding, but finally it was agreed that it would be discreet for Manasseh temporarily to withdraw from the city with his bride.

Though he yielded to necessity, the spirit of the young Jew was not curbed.

" I go," said he, " but I swear never to return until Nicaso and her children, if the Lord so bless our union, can come again without taunt or lessening. The Tirshatha is not God, nor the servant of God. Let him not cross my path beyond the gates, or he is a son of death!"

Great was the excitement the day following, when the triumph of the governor became known. Groups of young men gathered in the street near to Ioiada's house. Fiery speeches were made, denouncing the tyranny of Nehemiah, and deriding the senile bigotry of Ezra. Even the high priest was not spared in the oratorical bravery that swayed the crowd.

In the midst of their noisy declamation Nehemiah appeared, accompanied by a delegation from the elders of the city. The multitude turned their backs when he attempted to address them. As he retired some shouted after him:

" Put on your Persian armor and show how true a Jew you are !"

" What is the price of wine in Susa ?"

" But here comes Malachi. Let's hear what he has to say. Ezra says he will make a prophet. Why not? Balaam's ass was one."

Malachi did not stop to parley with them, but turned in at the door of Ioiada.

" If he will side with us, we will drive out the governor," said one.

" Or dip him in Hezekiah's Pool," said another.

An hour later Malachi reappeared, and with him Manasseh. The young mob went wild with enthusiasm at the prospective alliance. But Malachi parted with Manasseh at the door.

To the surprise of the crowd the latter addressed them, thanking them for their show of personal friendship, but counselling peace.

" We shall be wiser to-morrow than we are to-day. The interests of young Israel need cooler heads than ours are now. The bigotry of the governor's party cannot last. The tide is strong at the moment—too strong for us to beat back—but it will turn speedly. Then we will be strong with it. One shout for young Israel, then let's go home and wait !"

18

The shout was given with a will. "Nicaso salutes you and invites you all to the palace of Samaria," cried Manasseh, as he disappeared through the doorway.

Cheer after cheer rent the air. Just as the shouting was beginning to subside it burst out anew, for upon the parapet of the house Nicaso appeared. Her black hair and flushed cheeks made a superb contrast with her white mantle and the jewels that flashed about her brow and neck. The apparition lasted but for a moment, yet long enough to make many a swain declare that he too would leave Jerusalem if he could have so fair an attendant, and so comfortable a residence in exile as the palace of Sanballat among the hills of Samaria.

During the day the house of Ioiada was thronged with friends who came to utter within its walls such imprecations against the governor as they would not have dared to express more openly, and to pledge their personal loyalty to Manasseh during his absence. Among the visitors was the Phœnician merchant.

"Make no preparation for equipage on the morrow," said Marduk, "for I, too, am summoned northward."

"I cannot go to-morrow," replied Manasseh.

"But that is your agreement with the governor, is it not, on condition of his allowing you to retire from the city without the show of force?"

"That is my compact; yet I must seek delay, for I have a higher compact."

"'There can be no compact higher than that of a man's fairly given word," said Marduk.

"I can take no offence at your rebuke," replied the young exile, "because you will not blame me, when I tell you that I have given my word of honor to one who is of higher rank than the Tirshatha. I have pledged this person to discharge a certain obligation in Jerusalem, and I cannot discharge it before to-morrow's light."

"Who is above the governor in rank?"

Manasseh, lowering his voice, and bowing reverently, replied: "The king. The king of Tyre, and my king, if you will accept my loyalty. Has your majesty forgotten that you appointed me grand treasurer? I have so far kept fealty, and deposited the jewels beneath the very altar of God within the temple court. There they are in a little nook between the stones, full a score of cubits below the cave which I once showed you beneath the threshing-floor of Araunah. The old Jebusite never put such a precious harvest down that hole. And, for that matter, all the beasts whose blood has run through that vault since the day that Solomon slew a thousand bullocks on the altar were not worth so much as I have put there. But now see this order from the governor! I am to be unmolested, on condition of my not appearing in the streets or at the temple. The tyrant fears an insurrection against his cruelty, if I but so much as show myself. If I brave him and venture there, I will be watched. But as the Lord heard my

pledge to you, I shall not leave Jerusalem without
the treasure."

" It is serious business," replied Marduk. " Cannot some venture be made to-night to secure the
jewels? Put me on the clue, and I will go myself;
or bribe some temple-servant to fetch them."

" It is impossible. Nehemiah has seen to it
that only the most bigoted priests and servitors are
allowed in the temple precincts. The expulsion of
Tobiah was done with such a high hand that the
governor's party fear retaliation. A rumor was
started that the Ammonite's partisans might set
fire to the building and wreak their vengeance.
So they have guarded it as closely as if it were
besieged by Sanballat himself."

" Then there is nothing to be gained by your remaining," said Marduk. " Indeed, it is better that
you withdraw, and let matters settle. When suspicion is diverted, you can return. The jewels are
safe ?"

" Safe as a rock that has never been uncovered
in the earth, for no man knows their hiding-place.
As a boy in the high priest's family, I was allowed
to play among the masonry while they were repair-
ing the temple court, and I know of byways that a
mole could not find."

" Then nothing can be done until you can come
back to the city, which must be before long. This
rancor cannot last. Your grandsire will have influence for your recall. I absolve you from all obligation."

"With that assurance on your part," said Manasseh, "and a new pledge on my part that I shall not go five leagues from the city until the jewels are in some way rescued, I will join your camp to-morrow."

Immense throngs crowded the street through which, on the following day, Nicaso passed in her palanquin, attended by her husband on horseback. An unintermitted roar of applause followed them to the gates, and a gay cavalcade of young bloods escorted them to the camp of Marduk, which had been pitched some miles to the north, near to the half-built, or rather half-ruined, ancient city of Gibeah.

CHAPTER XXXVII

SEVERAL nights after the departure of Manasseh from Jerusalem, a strange thing occurred outside the temple wall. It was just beneath the towering angle of the southeast parapet that rises high above the valley of the Kidron.

The night was dark, for there was no moon, and thick clouds veiled the stars. Two men, whose clothes, could they have been seen, would have indicated that they were common laboring folk, were feeling their way among the great blocks of stone that lay beyond the temple wall—a part of the débris of the ancient city which the enterprise of the new settlers had not yet removed. As now and then a temple guard passed along the wall above them, the men stood still, and could not have been distinguished from the huge stones around. As the guard withdrew, the men moved cautiously, like foxes stealing upon their prey.

" It is here," whispered the foremost. " Lend a hand !"

Strong arms tugged at something, which did not yield.

" The club ! I have it through the ring. Now, lift !"

A slight grating sound followed, as if a heavy stone had been raised and slid upon another.

"Faugh! what a stench! No doubt about our being on the scent. Give me the rope. I've tied it under my arms. If I can't breathe, you'll have to pull me out."

* One held the rope, while the other let himself down through an opening between the great stones.

"It is all right!" came up from a vault below. "Double the rope on a stone, and slide down after me."

The second man disappeared as noiselessly as a serpent gliding into its hole.

"Breathe yourself a little until we get used to it, as a fox does when he goes to sleep with his head under his tail. * * * Now for it! It's as slippery as the side of Hermon. Mind your skull! I've just cracked mine."

"Go ahead," replied the other; "I've played the worm in worse ground than this."

The men groped their way, crouching for perhaps a hundred cubits, when the sewer—for such it was—led through the foundation of the temple wall, and enlarged into a sort of subterranean corridor. The fresher air and the echo of their shuffling feet revealed this.

"Now for a lantern! A flash of lightning in here wouldn't be seen at the opening."

A small lamp enclosed in two hemispheres of bronze was lighted from a tinder-box, and sent a gleam through a slit in one side. It revealed a passage about fifty cubits long, two or three wide, and perhaps twelve or fifteen high.

"See this! This passage must have been built in Solomon's time, yet here are the workmen's marks on the stone in red paint. You can rub it off with the finger, though it has been here for five hundred years at least. One can well believe that the Phœnician empire is to last forever, when a Phœnician stonemason's marks last so long. You would think the lizards would have rubbed them out with their bellies."

The corridor came abruptly to an end, but a small conduit opened at one side, out of which trickled a stream of blood and filth.

"How now? That is the way we are to go, if we go any farther. We will have to obey the curse the Lord put upon the devil for tempting mother Eve, and go upon our bellies, as snakes and lizards do."

"It wasn't half so bad to crawl that way among the flowers of Paradise as through such a hole as this," replied his comrade.

"Let's go in, one close after the other, so that in case one gets stuck, the other can pull him back."

The opening was wider than it appeared. Pushing the lantern ahead, the men made good progress, and at length emerged into another large chamber.

"The devil snake ate dust. I wish he could have had the mouthful I just got. He would never have risked tempting any of the children of Eve afterwards," said the foremost man, wiping the clots of filth from his face. "But let us sit and blow awhile; for, if I am not mistaken, we are a good bow-shot off our mark yet. I wish you could do what the Tyrians think you did—change yourself into a ghost and vanish through these walls."

"I wouldn't do that if I could," replied his comrade, laughing; "for I would have to leave you alone in this hole. And, by Hercules! as the Greeks say, if I hadn't pulled you a while ago, you would have been as snugly buried as King David is in his stone coffin somewhere about here."

"Not far from here, either. I think I smell something as old. Do you know the flavor of mummy skin, Marduk?"

"Right well, Manasseh! and if my eyes are as good as your nose, there lies the mummy."

A dark object wrapped in cloths was close beside them. The men moved away a few paces, and turned the light of the lantern upon it. A bat cut through the light.

"We've startled his ghost," said Marduk, with a slight tremor in his voice, for all that he attempted to be jocose.

Manasseh closely inspected the mummy, and was about to kick it with his foot.

"No, Marduk, you kick him! You are king, and perhaps he is one of the Phœnician workmen who built this vault. You have a right to abuse the bodies of your subjects when alive, and, of course, when they are dead."

"He is too small for a workman, unless he has

shrunk awfully," replied Marduk. " But it is not a body at all. See these knobs of carved wood sticking out at the ends."

Manasseh burst out laughing. " Why, it's nothing but an old copy of the Law."

Such it proved to be. It was rolled upon two cylinders, and wrapped carefully in a silken cover. Manasseh untied it and, by the light of the lantern, studied its characters.

" This is a rare document, Marduk. It has been here from before the sack of the city, in the time of Nebuchadnezzar. It looks very ancient. If I should swear it was written by Moses himself, you couldn't disprove it. For aught you and I know, it may be the identical copy good King Josiah found. It has been hidden here for safe-keeping, just as your jewels were. And they cannot be far off, either; for whoever brought this here came down from the temple. He could not have crawled up as we did; for, see! there is not on the roll so much as a stain of dirt, except that from dampness. If I establish a new worship in Samaria, as I can well do, being of the high priest's family from Jerusalem, this document will be of immense value. Ezra cannot produce a copy of the Law to compare with this in appealing to popular belief. I have seen all his copies. And now I venture a prophecy: With Sanballat's help we will have a temple on Gerizim, built expressly to hold this document, as the divinity of the place. Now for a contract with you, Marduk—I mean King Hiram. You shall

build the temple for Samaria, as your great ancestor did for Jerusalem. What say you?"

"Only what I have often said," replied Marduk.
"I shall help you in everything, as you have helped
me. But I think we shall have to get those jewels
first. Let's push on."

Manasseh hugged the copy of the Law as carefully as if it had been a child whom he had rescued
from death in the vault. A few paces brought them
against the wall. There seemed to be no outlet
from the chamber except that by which they had
entered.

"We are off the track," said Marduk. "Are
you sure that we ought not to have turned into
some other conduit?"

"How could we have mistaken it?" replied Manasseh. "We saw no other opening. Besides, we
followed up the stream of blood and filth."

"But that has disappeared. See, the floor is
dry. And so it was there where you picked up
the sacred roll. Listen!"

A dripping sound was heard. As Marduk moved
towards it, a splash of foul matter fell upon him
from above, and extinguished the lantern. It is
uncertain whether disgust or wonder predominated
in his soul at the moment.

"What's the matter now?" asked Manasseh.

"Why, the bottom has fallen out of Sheol, I
should think. Such a swash of offal as I caught
couldn't be found in Gehenna. But, worst of all,
the lantern's done for."

Manasseh broke into a low laugh. "Rub my sides, Marduk, or I shall split. Ha! ha! ha!"

The sense of the ludicrous was so largely developed in him that Marduk could not resist joining his friend in a spontaneous combustion of merriment, notwithstanding the untowardness of their surroundings.

"What now, O blind guide?" he asked, as soon as he regained self-possession.

"What now? Why, a lecture, of course, on Jewish architecture," said Manasseh. "You noticed that the temple area is flat. Well, it wasn't so originally. The Lord made a high rock, like a crown, on this hill of Moriah, the sides of which must have been very steep. And to make it level with the top of the rock men did not build solid masonry, but piers and walls, leaving great spaces beneath. These spaces were chiefly used as cisterns. In the time of Solomon they held enough water to supply Jerusalem for a month or two, in case of drought or siege by an enemy."

"But that wasn't water that struck me just now, and put out the light," said Marduk.

"No, that was blood; but it gave us more light than it put out. It must have dropped right down through a hole in the roof. That means that we have already reached the vault just under the cave of the rock into which the blood from the sacrifices first flows. Now, our jewels are in this very room. You remember I showed you the hole in the floor of the cave through which the stuff flowed?

Well, that hole is just above your head. The wall over us is very thick, and in a niche between the stones is the treasury of Tyre. I can stand on your shoulders and reach the jewels. But here is a new difficulty. I must get out of this with my jewel, this precious roll. It is worth a whole treasury to me. But I cannot crawl back with it through that narrow gutter. Its parchment would be soaked with the filth. I must go out upon the temple court."

" But we cannot get out that way," said Marduk. " The court is patrolled by watchmen. The gates are fast. And if we got into the city, we could not leave it, for the city gates are closed also. We must crawl back again. Leave your roll for a better time."

" Never !" said Manasseh. " It's as much to me as your crown will be to you, if you ever get it."

" Well, then, we will fight it through," replied Marduk.

" No, that will not do. You shall not risk your jewels. You take them, and burrow your way as you came. I'll trust the man who escaped as you did from old Tyre to get out of this place. Let me go up the shaft. I will dodge across the temple court, and drop the roll over the wall. Come, I'll climb on your shoulders, and gain the opening."

The bags were reached in this way. One by one they were passed down into Marduk's hands, who passed up the roll.

" The Lord watch between us !" whispered Manasseh, and disappeared above. He groped through the cave of Araunah and out into the air, shot across the court to the south wall, and dropped the roll over. The noise of the falling object startled a temple guard. He came cautiously near.

"Who goes there?"

"Leave me, I ask you. I am the unhappy Manasseh. Do not disturb my meditation. I have sought the quiet of the temple that I might pray."

"But how came you in? All the gates are closed."

"An angel of the Lord hath brought me hither, and bidden me go boldly to the south gate when I had ceased my prayer, promising to open it for me."

The man stood paralyzed with awe. He knew Manasseh's voice. After a long pause he asked:

"Did not the angel let you in by the south gate? for I heard a strange noise there, as of creaking of stone on stone, but saw that the gate was bolted."

"I may not answer you," replied Manasseh. "But you have disturbed my meditation, and I will withdraw."

"Pardon! pardon! O servant of the Lord," said the man, kneeling in the darkness. "But call not the angel. I myself will open the gate."

"It is the angel's prompting," said Manasseh.

The gate was unbarred. In a few moments the watchman heard a light whistle out among the stones beneath the south wall, and something that sounded like—

"Give me your hand! Up with you! And now for Gibeah!"

CHAPTER XXXVIII

TYRE was never more splendidly arrayed than
on the day set for the coronation of King Rubaal. To one approaching from the sea the island
city seemed like a mighty ring studded with gems,
so many were the bright banners that flashed in
the sunlight from its encircling walls; while the
centre of the city glowed with the golden roofs of
the Temple of Melkarth.

The day was perfect. The clear azure of the sky
reflected itself in the bending mirror of the waters,
—an omen of the favor of Heaven upon the plans
of men. Even the rough sailors from other Phœnician cities, as they turned their prows towards the
Tyrian harbor, called the slight motion of the graceful billows the nod of Baal; and when the waves
broke with pleasant murmur upon the outlying
rocks, they cried, " Behold the laughter of our
gods !"

Although more than a year had passed since the
reins of power had fallen into the hands of Rubaal,
many things had occurred to delay his formal investiture with the regal dignity. Chief among these
causes was the refusal of the Great King, Artax-

erxes, who was an unbeliever in the religion of
the Phœnicians, to grant his official recognition of
the miraculous taking-off of the late king. The
court at Susa had insisted upon better evidence
than the word of the priests for the bodily translation of Hiram to the unseen world.

Hanno, whose genius and zeal made him the
chief man in Tyre, was apparently most impatient
at the delay; and, as was commonly believed, had
spent much time at the Persian capital, laboring to
overcome the scruples of the World Monarch. He
had but lately returned, bearing, as he asserted,
the document that expressed the royal permission.
Its great seal had been seen by many, who had
also read a separate decree designating Hanno as
agent of the Persian Government, and commanding him, in the name of the Great King, to arrange
for the speedy restoration of the Tyrian throne to
its legal dignities, under the suzerainty of the empire. The Satrap of Syria had likewise been ordered to send to Tyre a detachment of several
thousand soldiers, who by their pomp should represent the glory of Artaxerxes in the ceremonial,
and by their power should defend the royal will if
it chanced to be opposed.

The Phœnician cities sent their princely delega-
tions, whose vessels fairly embroidered the coast
with their gay pennants as they came from far and
near. Inland tribes were also represented. Sanballat of Samaria sent a band of several hundred
of his braves. And Manasseh, the high priest of

the Samaritan religion, accompanied them, gorgeously arrayed in the vestments of his office. The hills of Galilee contributed a company of men, under command of Elnathan of Giscala, whose stalwart bearing compensated for their lack of martial finery.

The Great Square was transformed into a vast pavilion, beneath which tens of thousands could gather and witness the ceremonies. On one side of the pavilion was an immense dais, carpeted with the richest fabrics from the looms and dyeing-vats of Tyre. On this stood the ancient throne of bronze, with its lion-headed arms. Over it hung a canopy of purple, which was also draped behind the royal seat, and, by its contrast, made the silver dove with outspread wings seem like a veritable messenger from Astarte, flashing its white light like a celestial blessing upon the faces of the multitude. There were raised seats about the dais for the members of the Great Council, and stalls for the leaders of the various guilds of the hierarchy.

In the ancient palace of the kings of Tyre Rubaal waited impatiently for the summons to join the grand procession. Proudly he paced the chambers once occupied by King Hiram. Mirrors reflected his goodly form and attire from every side, but not so flatteringly as his attendants echoed his praise, and predicted the glory of his coming reign. His palanquin waited at the palace gate.

By it passed first the trumpeters, sounding the popular joy to the very sky with their melodious

19

clangor. Dancing-women followed, keeping step to the thumbing of their tambours. A thousand Persian horsemen clattered next. Then came high officers of state and dignitaries of foreign courts. Hanno strode at the head of the royal guard of honor, a band of his own selection from among the noblest young men of Tyre. These halted at the great portal of the palace, and gathered closely about the king's palanquin. The gate of the royal residence swung wide and closed again. Four men of gigantic stature, naked except at the loins and for the rings that shone about their ankles and arms, lifted the palanquin to their shoulders, its gorgeous curtains of silk screening the royal personage from the gaze of the people, until he should stand before them beneath the sparkle of his crown. The bands from Samaria and Galilee were honored with the next position in the cortége. A litter that seemed of beaten gold bore the noble prince Ezmunazar, son of King Tabnit of Sidon, who represented that neighboring throne. Then followed Egbalus, whose repute for sanctity and inspiration had led to his re-election to the high priest's office for a second year. Priests of all grades and divinities closed the procession.

The well-marshalled host entered the great pavilion, filing in order past the dais and throne, and allowing the dignitaries to take the places assigned them. The royal palanquin passed behind the purple hangings.

A blare of trumpets rang out. Egbalus ascended

the steps of the dais, holding in his hands a cushion
upon which lay the sceptre and ancient crown of
Tyre. Turning to the multitude, he addressed them,
rehearsing in stately speech the renown of the Tyrian monarchy through the centuries since their city
was founded by the divine Tyrus. He dwelt upon
the times of Hiram the Great, and then burst into
rhapsodic eloquence as he described the translation of that other Hiram who had been taken to
the gods.

"As surely as the beams of the sun-god shine
this day, so surely does the blessing of our King
Hiram—our divine Hiram—fall upon us. Hail
him! Praise him for the voluntary sacrifice by
which he has won forever the favor of Baal for his
people of Tyre! Think of him when the light
gleams into your homes, for Hiram is a beam of
Baal! Adore him when it flashes from the sea
where he guides your ships! Worship him in the
fire-light of your sacrifices, for the flames are the
bright rays from the crown of our invisible king!"

As Egbalus paused, the priests led the multitude
in cries of—

"Hail, Hiram the Blessed! the son of Baal!"

Egbalus resumed:

"Whither went the spirit of Hiram? O ye sons
of men! I saw the spirit of Hiram ascend into the
dome of heaven. Again I saw it descend to the
earth. It entered the form of another—of your
new-chosen king. Hail, Rubaal!"

The crowd echoed the cry, "Hail, Rubaal! Rubaal Hiram!" until the covering of the great pavilion shook and swayed as if lifted by the wind.

Then the high priest turned towards the curtain behind the throne. He prostrated himself upon the dais. Rising to his knees, and holding aloft the cushion with the sceptre and crown, he cried in his most august tones:

"Come forth, thou chosen of Baal!"

The curtain swayed aside. Egbalus stared an instant, as if stricken into stone. He dropped the cushion. Attempting to rise, his limbs became entangled in the profusion of his priestly drapery, which tripped him backward, and tumbled him shrieking with fright, together with the rattling crown and sceptre, down the steps of the dais.

The attendants did not pause to look at the high priest, for before them stood KING HIRAM, his hand upon the back of the throne. His familiar voice, sharp in its taunting sarcasm, rang through the pavilion—

"Lo! I have come forth, O priest of Baal!"

The great councillors of state climbed out of the balcony in which they were seated, and scrambled with the baser crowd to get away from the dreadful apparition. Men trod upon one another like a frightened herd. Heads, legs and arms, trumpets, banners, swords, and sandals made a confused mass of what a moment before had been as dignified an assembly as ever king or pontiff had looked upon. The prepared places of egress were not sufficient for the fleeing crowd, who tore away the canvas sides of the pavilion, and broke its cords, until the mighty canopy hung awry as if struck by a hurricane.

But the dominant passion of a crowd is curiosity. Many would risk an annihilating glance from the eyes of the god if only in return they could see what he looks like. Therefore, some, withdrawing a few paces, turned again to face the awful mystery. The soldiers from Persia, Samaria, and Galilee seemed not to have been sufficiently informed to have any fear, and, obeying a quick command which Hanno gave them through their officers, ranked deep about the dais to protect it.

A sharp hissing sound went like a flying serpent through the air, and an arrow, shot by some one in the crowd, glanced clanging from the arm of the throne. In another moment the thundering tramp of the squadron of Persian horse shook the earth as they dashed around the pavilion, sweeping priests and people into every open way, or trampling them beneath the hoofs.

The square was cleared. The priests fled towards the temple. Thither the soldiers pursued them, halting and penning them in the great court, until further orders should come.

At the same time heralds flew everywhere throughout the city, crying, " King Hiram has returned ! Down with the villainy of the priests !" Great placards were posted on the doors of the government-house and on the corners of the streets, detailing in few words the facts.

In little groups, or one by one, the more venturous or the less credulous of the people re-entered the pavilion. Hiram had taken his throne. There was no mistaking his person. He wore the conical cap with the uræus, the scarf across his bare breast, the short chiton and heavy sandals, by which his form was familiar to even the boys as well as to the great councillors of Tyre.

As Hiram gazed at the returning people an old man came tottering to the foot of the dais. He threw himself upon the lowest step. He was Ahimelek.

"Rise, Ahimelek, Councillor of Tyre!" said the king.

But he moved not. An attendant approached him. He was dead.

A commotion was made at the rear of the pavilion. Two men, the captain of the Samaritans and the captain of the men of Galilee, brought before the king the limp form of Egbalus. The miserable man turned to flee, but his captors kept his face to the throne. At length he gathered strength. That tremendous will which had so often dominated others asserted its mastery over himself. He looked Hiram squarely in the eyes.

"Thou hast conquered, O infidel king! But thou shalt not have me to grace thy triumph."

Before his guards were aware of his purpose, he had plunged his priest's knife to his heart.

"Take him away!" coolly said the king.

In the meantime men had gone to the king's

palace, where Rubaal and a few of his favorites had
awaited the summons to join the coronation procession. Wearied by the delay, they had ventured
to the door, but found it fastened. Their cries for
help were answered by the shouts which shook the
city. But now the gates were flung open. Rough
soldiers thrust Rubaal into a common palanquin,
such as was cheaply hired at the docks, and bore
him to the pavilion. There the carriage was opened.
Rubaal crouched within it like a rat in a trap.

The soldiers dragged him out. His brave apparel,
royal from purple mantle to diamond-set sandals,
was as strange a contrast with the simple garb of
the real king as the kingly look of Hiram was with
the mean and cowardly aspect of Rubaal.

"Harm him not," said the king. "There is a
drop of royal blood somewhere in his body. You
might spill that drop if you spilled more. All royalty is safe to-day. Come, cousin, sit in my chair
if you like. We have played together in the same
crib. Ah! in ill-humor again! Just so you were
as a child."

The wretched man slunk away, and sat with
averted face on the edge of the dais.

The king stepped down from his throne, and
stood a moment over the dead body of Ahimelek.

"The gods pardon him! Carry him to his house,
and prepare him for the tomb, where we will ourselves accompany him; for he was the father of
Zillah."

Reascending the dais, he turned to Hanno, who

during these scenes had stood almost motionless, watching everything, and alert lest his plan should miscarry in the least—

"Now, Hanno, for the coronation!"

A silver trumpet sounded sweetly. The curtain back of the throne moved, and through the opening Zillah came. Radiant with sparkling jewels, she was more radiant with the beauty of her queenly soul that shone through her features and dignified her every movement. Her joy in her husband's triumph, her consciousness of having shared with him his misfortunes, and of her daring to share with him the dangers that still pressed about him, gave her a royalty of appearance that even a crown could not augment.

"My Queen!" said Hiram, as he took her hand, and seated her upon the throne. He raised the crown and placed it upon her brow.

"Behold the Queen of Tyre!"

"HIRAM, King of Tyre, to Manasseh, son of Ioiada, son of Eliashib, High Priest of Jehovah in Samaria : Greeting!

"Health and the blessing of thy God be with thee! Our hearts are cheered by the tidings of thy prosperity. May thy temple rise speedily from the heights of Gerizim! Gado, the bearer of this letter, is most famed among our architects. He bears our royal commission to abide with thee so long as his skill pleases thy purpose. He carries with him a thousand minas, a contribution from our treasury to the worship of thy God. He will also present to thee a fabric of our finest workmanship, which has been wrought upon by the hands of Zillah, our Queen beloved, in which she desires that thou shalt enwrap the copy of thy Law, as thou art thyself enwrapped in our affection."

Should the reader desire to know more of the affairs of Manasseh, let him read the histories of one Josephus the Jew. And should his interest be great to learn of the subsequent career of Hiram and his beautiful queen, the faithful chronicler would refer him to the source whence he himself has derived his information. In the Museum of the Louvre is a stone coffin, in which once lay the body of Ezmunazar, King of Sidon. The sarcophagus bears this imprecation : " I adjure every royal personage that he open not this chamber, nor remove this coffin, lest the holy gods destroy that royal personage and his offspring forever." They who esteem themselves wise in such matters tell us that this prophetic curse was recently fulfilled in the misfortunes that fell upon the house of the late Emperor of the French, Napoleon III., in the reign of which "royal personage" this coffin was robbed of its contents and brought to Paris. But though the body of Ezmunazar is no longer in it, if one will listen intently at the ear-hole in the coffin, one will find it as full of historic suggestions as a conch-shell is of news from the bottom of the sea.

THE END.

THE CAPTAIN OF THE JANIZARIES.

A Tale of the Times of Scanderbeg and the Fall of Constantinople. By James M. Ludlow, D.D., Litt.D. 16mo, Cloth, $1 50.

The author writes clearly and easily; his descriptions are often of much brilliancy, while the whole setting of the story is of that rich Oriental character which fires the fancy.—*Boston Courier.*

Strong in its central historical character, abounding in incident, rapid and stirring in action, animated and often brilliant in style.—*Christian Union*, N. Y.

Something new and striking interests us in almost every chapter. The peasantry of the Balkans, the training and government of the Janizaries, the interior of Christian and Moslem camps, the horrors of raids and battles, the violence of the Sultan, the tricks of spies, the exploits of heroes, engage Mr. Ludlow's fluent pen.—*N. Y. Tribune.*

Dr. Ludlow's style is a constant reminder of Walter Scott, and the book is to retain a permanent place in literature.—*Observer*, N. Y.

An altogether admirable piece of work—picturesque, truthful, and dramatic.—*Newark Advertiser.*

A most romantic, enjoyable tale. . . . As affording views of inner life in the East as long ago as the middle of the fifteenth century, this tale ought to have a charm for many; but it is full enough of incident, wherever the theatre of its action might be found, to do this.—*Troy Press.*

The author has used his material with skill, weaving the facts of history into a story crowded with stirring incidents and unexpected situations, and a golden thread of love-making, under extreme difficulties, runs through the narrative to a happy issue.—*Examiner*, N. Y.

One of the strongest and most fascinating historical novels of the last quarter of a century.—*Boston Pilot.*

Published by HARPER & BROTHERS, New York.

☞ *The above work sent by mail, postage prepaid, to any part of the United States, Canada, or Mexico, on receipt of the price.*

www.ingramcontent.com/pod-product-compliance
Lightning Source LLC
Chambersburg PA
CBHW060556030726
47498CB00005B/1417